THE TRUTH ABOUT CELIA FROST

THE TRUTH ABOUT CELIA FROST

PAULA RAWSTHORNE

USBORNE

In memory of Paul Rawsthorne,
my wonderful Dad

First published in the UK in 2011 by Usborne Publishing Ltd., Usborne House,
83-85 Saffron Hill, London EC1N 8RT, England. www.usborne.com

A CIP catalogue record for this book is available from the British Library.

ISBN 9781409531098 JFM MJJASOND/11 00657/1

Printed in Reading, Berkshire, UK.

```
01001101 01000001 01011000 00100000
01001010 01000101 01001110 01001011
01001001 01001110 01010011 00100000
01001001 01010011 00100000 01000001
01001110 00100000 01000001 01010010
01010011 01000101 01001000 01001111
01001100 01000101
```

Celia Frost allowed her body to relax just a fraction as she lifted her coat off the peg in the bustling cloakroom. All she had to do now was get to the staffroom, where somebody would be waiting to give her a lift home. Usually she cringed at having members of staff ferry her to and from school, but today Celia couldn't wait to get into the safety of a teacher's car.

She dared to believe that she'd survived the day. Maybe he wasn't going to come after her. Maybe now he realized that she wasn't going to be one of his victims any more. Maybe, just maybe, he felt a grudging respect for what she'd done. Of course she'd been careful; getting out of the classroom quickly, making sure that she wasn't alone, doing her best to melt into the crowd. Although for Celia, being inconspicuous was never easy.

At almost fifteen, her increasingly gangling body showed no inclination to curve or protrude. She habitually walked with an apologetic stoop, and from her bowed head sprang a mass of untameable orange hair. From a distance, her sliver of a face, with its oversized features, looked like it was engulfed in a tangerine cloud.

However, it wasn't just her appearance and her gloved hands that made Celia a curiosity. She'd decided long ago that Mother Nature was nothing but a cruel old hag who'd ensured that she was in a league of her own when it came to "standing out". After all, not many pupils starting a new school get an assembly dedicated to them. And unfortunately for Celia, each "new start" was worse than the last, as she became more self-conscious and her peers less tolerant.

Six months ago Mr. Powell, her latest headmaster, had done his best, but it had still been excruciating as he'd addressed the packed hall about "Celia's special condition". She'd longed for the ground to open and swallow her up, as the eyes of every pupil turned on her. She'd slouched down in her chair, staring fixedly at the floor, as the intense heat of embarrassment rose from deep inside her and flooded her chalk-white face, turning it scarlet. The girls on either side of her had instinctively leaned away and the air filled with exclamation marks as the hall had erupted with voices.

"Oh my God, that is *sooo* terrible!"

"It makes me feel ill just thinking about it!"

"She should be in a special school, it's not right to have her with normal people!"

"What if you bump into her by accident? I'm not getting done for killing her!"

"Well I'd rather die than live like that!"

The headmaster had struggled to quieten down the assembly. He'd warned them that anyone not showing the necessary care and consideration around Celia would be severely punished, but all Celia had tuned into was the hushed chants coming from behind her, led by Max Jenkins.

"Freaky Frost! Freaky Frost! Freaky Frost!"

She was annoyed with herself for even letting it register. After all, it wasn't very original. She'd heard it before, in all the other schools that she'd passed through.

At least in the other schools she'd always managed to find a couple of girls who would let her sit with them at breaks. She was under no illusions – they'd never been her friends; they'd regarded her as a charity case and they didn't seem to be aware of how torturous it was, having to listen to them making plans to meet up after school and never being invited. Celia didn't blame them – why should anyone hang around with a liability like her? But at this latest school in Wales things were much worse. Jenkins had made sure of that.

Celia had soon discovered that Max Jenkins was more vicious, more toxic, than anyone she'd ever encountered. No one was safe from him. He fed off people's fear and operated with impunity throughout the school and, unfortunately for Celia, ever since that first assembly, he'd decided to make her his special project. He let it be known that anyone thinking of befriending her would be dealt with and for the last six months he'd revelled in watching his isolated, passive victim being ground down by his taunts and threats. Jenkins had a knack for homing in on people's weaknesses and strengths and then using both to his advantage. Therefore, as soon as he noticed all the A grades Celia was getting, he started delegating his homework to her.

It was unthinkable that Celia would ever fight back. Janice's words were ingrained in her: "You're not like other people. You must never do anything where you might get injured."

Everything Celia did, every decision she made, was dictated by this rule. In school this meant that she was excused from PE, DT, food tech and any other activity that was deemed a potential threat. At home this meant endless, lonely hours confined to the house by Janice; tormented by being able to witness the hustle and bustle of life but never being able to join in.

Celia felt like she lived her life trapped in a gloomy bubble, a gripping fear sealed in there with her. It was exhausting trying to fight off the gloom as it seeped into her mind, leaching out all the light. But she couldn't let it take hold of her; after all, how could Janice cope if Celia stopped coping?

Throughout her life this fear of injury had always overridden any other desire; until, that was, last week, when Max Jenkins had walked out of their maths class and thrown his homework book at her saying, "You'd better make it a good one."

As she'd stood there, with his book in her hands, Celia was suddenly overwhelmed by temptation.

Use binary numbers to write a coded message.

Oh yes, she'd grinned to herself. *I've got the perfect message for you, Jenkins.*

So it had been earlier that day that thirty-five pupils had sat in their maths lesson, yawning and lolling their heads on their desks, having already decoded seven dull binary messages, when they got to Max Jenkins's effort.

"Now, Mr. Jenkins, let's see what pearl you've come up with," said the uninspired maths teacher.

He wrote the digits on the board and, to chivvy them along, he made one of the boys come up and write each decoded letter in large capitals under its corresponding numbers. He chose pupils at random to work out each letter, and at first their droning voices were barely audible.

"Yes, come on, come on. Look at what we've got so far. *Max Jenkins is an...*" The teacher paused, looking concerned. "Now, Mr. Jenkins, this had better not be anything offensive. Is it offensive, Mr. Jenkins?"

By now, Jenkins was shifting in his chair, looking increasingly uncomfortable. "Course not. No one would be so stupid as to write something that would get them into *really, really* big trouble," he said, glowering at Celia. She turned her head defiantly to face him, revealing just a trace of a smile. At this, Jenkins started to panic. "I don't want mine read out," he shouted. "I haven't finished it. It's not very good... I can do better."

"Well I never, Max. It's not like you to be bashful. Now I *am* intrigued. Let's continue," said the teacher, gesturing to his scribe.

But now, instead of having to prise the answers out of the half-asleep class, it seemed that everyone was wide awake and furiously trying to be first to crack the code.

The letters came rattling out from the animated pupils faster than the teacher could stop them and before he knew it, there on the board, in large bold capitals for everyone to see, was:

01001101 01000001 01011000 00100000 01001010
M   A   X   J
01000101 01001110 01001011 01001001 01001110
E   N   K   I   N
01010011 00100000 01001001 01010011 00100000
S   I   S
01000001 01001110 00100000 01000001 01010010
A   N   A   R
01010011 01000101 01001000 01001111 01001100
S   E   H   O   L
01000101
E

A communal gasp of disbelief was immediately followed by the first nervous titter, which was followed by another, then another, until the whole classroom exploded into laughter. Hysteria overpowered their fear; tears rolled down contorted faces, bodies bent double with laughter and others, too giddy to speak, pointed from the words on the board to the silently seething boy. Even the dour maths teacher, who knew Jenkins's malicious nature only too well, could not suppress a smirk as he shouted over the uproarious class, "Mr. Jenkins! What a very peculiar thing to write about yourself!"

The whole school soon heard what had happened in the maths class and, for the first time since Celia had arrived, people weren't trying to avoid her eye, but actually acknowledged her in the corridor with approving nods and secret smiles. However, everyone knew that there would be a terrible price to pay for what she'd done. Celia knew this too, but the planning and execution of her revenge had stirred a potent mixture of excitement and dread in her that pressed dangerously against the sides of her invisible prison. It had all seemed worth it just to see Jenkins's face puce with rage, as humiliation and laughter threatened his reign of terror.

Suddenly there was a flurry of activity in the cloakroom, as pupils scattered like a shoal of fish when a great white suddenly cuts through the dark waters. Celia kept her back to the exodus and continued zipping up her bag that was on the bench. Her mind was racing, desperately trying to work out her next move.

"Hey, Frost, you freak!"

She could feel him moving in on her. The fumes from his paint-stripper aftershave clogged up the air.

Celia was aware of her body beginning to tremble. *Don't show fear. Don't show fear,* she repeated over and over in her head. She knew that any sign of distress would only excite a sadist like Jenkins. She steadied herself and turned to face him. The room was now completely empty apart from her and her tormentor.

Max Jenkins was tall and powerfully built, but once Celia straightened up her shoulders, she stood level with him. She met his stare, trying to appear unperturbed, but her owl-round eyes, framed by a thicket of lashes, always made her look slightly startled. She convinced herself that someone would have gone to get a teacher, so she decided that she just had to keep him calm and at bay until help arrived.

"You think you can do that to me?" His voice was a low rumble; a volcano on the verge of erupting. "What you did wasn't very nice, was it? You've hurt my feelings. People can't seem to appreciate this, but I'm a very sensitive person. I'm just misunderstood." He cocked his head to one side and pouted mockingly.

"Yeah. I'm sure Hitler felt the same," she blurted out, regretting the words as soon as they left her mouth. But Jenkins only gave a hollow laugh.

"Well, Freaky, aren't you full of surprises? First your little stunt in class and now an attempt at sarcasm. You obviously don't take me seriously. Perhaps I've been too kind to you – but I'm about to put that right. You see, you've given me no choice. I now have a duty to teach you a lesson. I have a reputation to maintain. People have got to be shown that anyone who takes me on will be punished. So I've been wondering what would really make an impression on you."

He paused and put his forefinger and middle finger together. He pressed them against the base of her neck, before moving them lingeringly up her face, tracing them over her sharp chin, across her thick gash of a mouth and climbing along her broad nose. They came to rest in the middle of her forehead, where Jenkins flicked up his thumb to form a gun and said, in a slow, deep whisper, "Bang! Bang!"

Celia blinked as his fingers jabbed into her forehead, her flesh crawling, but she remained composed. Her lack of response disappointed him, but he was far from finished.

"I've decided that your punishment should benefit the whole school. You must know that we've all been dying to see what would happen if your freaky body got sliced."

At these words, panic shot through her. She pushed past him. "You're going to let me go now. I'm going to walk out of here and I promise not to tell anyone what you've just said, okay?" she said firmly.

But as she quickened her pace towards the door, he grabbed her and dragged her back, pinning her against the coat rack.

"Get off me. You've had your fun," she shouted, struggling against the weight of his leaning body.

"Who said anything about fun? I'm undertaking a serious scientific experiment here, but, of course, to do that I need my implements." With this, he reached into his trouser pocket and pulled out a small, red-handled penknife. She recoiled as Jenkins prised out the shiny, silver blade and without warning sliced it across his thumb. He winced as blood immediately sprang from the short, narrow cut.

"Surprisingly, that hurt more than you'd think," he said coolly, as he sucked the blood from his thumb. Then he answered Celia's open-mouthed stare. "I wanted to demonstrate to you just how sharp my blade is," he said leeringly, "And now it's your turn!"

He gripped Celia's left wrist and yanked at the cuff of her blouse, causing the button to fly off. He pulled up the sleeve roughly, exposing Celia's long, translucent arm, her vivid veins like blue water running under a thin layer of ice.

"Don't do it, Max," she said softly, but the beads of sweat springing from her pores belied her outer calmness. "Just let me go."

He erupted, bawling in her face, the veins on his neck bulging. "Do you really think I'm going to let you go?! People were laughing at me because of you. You freak!"

"Just think about it." She fought the tremor in her voice. "Say I bleed to death? You'll spend years banged up in prison. It's not worth it, is it, Max? It's not too late. You can walk away from this right now."

But Jenkins responded by seizing her elbow and positioning the knife so it hovered over her upper arm.

"What do you think?" he taunted her. "Should I do it, should I?"

She daren't move, she daren't breathe.

Suddenly, quick, urgent footsteps could be heard coming down the corridor.

Teachers, she thought with blissful relief. *The teachers are here!*

The cloakroom door flew open. The teachers froze at the sight that faced them, with only seconds to decide what to do next. Jenkins panicked, tightening his hold on her elbow.

Oh God, he's going to do it! I've got to do something!

She jerked her arm out of his grip. There was a flash of silver, and a searing, white-hot pain as the blade sliced along her paper skin. She heard a short, high-pitched scream puncture the air – it was coming from her.

2 a & e

Jenkins shot away from her, still clutching the knife. Everyone seemed nailed to the spot, watching, sick with anticipation. Celia too was transfixed by the line of blood surfacing from the narrow wound and oozing down the contours of her quivering arm.

It was Mr. Powell who made the first move from the doorway into the room. He spoke calmly but firmly to Jenkins, all the time edging closer towards him until he'd placed himself between the boy and Celia.

"Just drop the knife, Max, and we can sort this out. Don't make things worse for yourself. Let me help Celia. You just keep back."

Jenkins looked around at the sea of anxious faces watching the scene. One of the staff was already on their mobile asking for the police and an ambulance. He unclenched his fist and let the knife fall to the ground. Immediately two of the watching teachers ran and tackled him to the ground. He didn't put up a fight but lay there, his cheek pressed against the cold, dirty tiles of the cloakroom, staring up at Celia.

"It was her fault!" Jenkins found his voice. "She moved. There's no way I was going to do it. I was only messing with her. I'm not getting done for this."

The head teacher sat the dazed girl down on the bench. The slash across her arm stung as if vinegar was being poured into it, but the pain didn't concern her. All she was concentrating on was the crimson trickles of blood.

She spoke without looking up. "When will it begin?"

"I don't know, but you're going to be okay," Mr. Powell said gently. "An ambulance is on its way."

He turned to his staff. "Get me the first-aid kit and gloves. We need to apply pressure to the wound. Phone her mother – and for God's sake get him out of my sight." He gestured towards Jenkins in disgust.

The paramedics arrived within minutes and quickly wheeled Celia down the corridor, which was lined with gawping pupils who'd flooded back into the school as news of the attack spread. Mr. Powell climbed into the back of the ambulance with Celia, but despite his efforts to distract her, she remained eerily silent, mesmerized by the blood seeping through the bandage.

The paramedic with them got off the phone to the hospital and spoke to Mr. Powell. "We could do with her GP details. The hospital computer doesn't have any records for her."

"We've got his address in the office. We've been waiting for a letter from him. There's been quite a delay, I'm afraid. We had a bit of trouble pinning the mother down, but she gave us his name eventually."

"Is the mother uncooperative?" the paramedic whispered, out of Celia's earshot.

"No, on the contrary," Mr. Powell said emphatically. "Janice Frost has been extremely helpful, providing us with all our information, keen that the school is aware of Celia's condition and knows what to do in case of an accident. It's just she's an anxious woman…comes across a little paranoid even, but that's understandable, given her daughter's disorder."

When they arrived at A & E, Celia was pushed straight through to a treatment cubicle, bypassing the hordes of people in the waiting room. Within moments, a young female doctor entered the cubicle, trying to look as alert as possible.

The paramedics had rung ahead to the department with information about a teenager with a blood clotting disorder who'd been involved in a knife attack; just what Dr. Ross needed at the end of a long, exhausting shift. The weary doctor remembered to smile at Celia and Mr. Powell as she carefully lifted the bandages from the wound.

"Hello," she began. "I'm Dr. Ross, and you must be Celia."

Celia nodded.

"And you are?" she asked the head.

"Dave Powell, Celia's headmaster," he replied.

"Well, Mr. Powell, would you mind waiting outside? I'm going to have to cut Celia's blouse off to treat the wound. Is that okay, Celia? I've got a gown you can put on."

Celia nodded again as Mr. Powell made a quick exit.

"So, Celia, you've had a nasty shock," Dr. Ross said as she disposed of the bloodied shirt. "What a terrible thing to happen."

Celia looked blank.

"I need to ask you a few questions, if that's okay. What's your date of birth?"

Celia murmured the date as if in a dreamlike state.

"Okay, so you're fourteen. Good. Now, Celia, I need to

know about your condition. You have a blood clotting disorder, right? Can you tell me more about it?"

Without lifting her eyes from her throbbing arm, Celia mechanically gave the explanation she'd heard repeated by Janice so many times before. "It's very rare. My blood won't clot like normal people's and if I bleed I might just keep bleeding. So it's very dangerous if I get cut or injured. I've got to be careful. I've always had it. I was born with it."

"Well then, it's looking like you've been lucky this time, because the blood flow seems to have stemmed nicely," the doctor said, cleaning the congealing blood from the wound.

"But how's that possible?" Celia's face clouded with confusion.

"Hard to tell without knowing more about your condition. What blood group are you?"

"O, Mum says I'm O."

"Good, it's really important we have a record of that, in case you ever need a transfusion through losing too much blood. Has that ever happened, Celia? Have you had a blood transfusion before?

Celia shook her deathly pale head. "No. I've never needed one. I've never been injured. My mum makes sure that I'm really, really careful."

"But what happens when you have your period, Celia?"

"I haven't even started yet," she said, cringing. "But Mum says everything will be normal; the disorder doesn't apply to them. She says I'm not to worry about it."

"Okay." Dr. Ross nodded her head slowly. "But what treatment do you have for the disorder? Do you have injections to help your blood clot? Maybe that would explain why the blood loss from your wound seems normal."

Celia looked up from the knife wound to the doctor, her head now throbbing in time with her arm. "I don't have treatment for it. I've looked it up myself you know, on the internet, and I asked my mum about those injections, but she said that when I was born they did all kinds of tests on me, to see how they could help, but they all agreed that it was untreatable and the only way to stop it happening was to not get injured. That's the way it's always been. I'll never be cured. I just have to live with it. It's a life sentence, my mum says."

"But Celia, you must have had a consultant. Who do you see at the hospital?"

"There's no consultant, there's no one. We've moved around a lot, you see. I think it makes it hard to find a doctor."

"Well, you *have* got a GP. Your mum has given the school his name, so at least we'll be able to get information from him." Dr. Ross inspected Celia's arm again. "Luckily the blade hasn't caused any muscle damage, so I'm just going to give you a tetanus injection and a shot to deaden the area before I put a few stitches in."

She got on with the procedures quickly and silently, both patient and doctor deep in thought. Once the area was numb, Celia was just aware of a disconcerting tugging at her skin as the needle threaded in and out.

Dr. Ross finished and snapped off her latex gloves. "If you'll excuse me, Celia, I'm just going to chase up that information from your GP and, when I get back, I'd like to take some blood to run a few tests."

No sooner had Celia heard the doctor's footsteps fade than the cubicle curtain swished open to reveal a breathless, scrawny figure.

"It's all right, love, I'm here now," Janice wheezed, looking so frail that a puff of wind could have blown her over.

Seeing Janice standing there, Celia felt a familiar guilt creep over her. She wondered how much more stress her mother could take. This shabby woman looked older than her thirty-five years. A face that had once been attractively sculptured had developed a hard gauntness and sickly grey tinge. Years of anxiety and thousands of cigarettes had left deep crow's feet splaying from her puffy eyes and fine lines fanning out from her dry lips. As much as she detested the smoking, Celia never felt that she had the right to complain. After all, wasn't it her fault that this woman was in such a state? Wouldn't the responsibility of having a child like her turn any parent into a neurotic chain-smoker? And it wasn't as if Janice indulged in anything else: she didn't drink, she didn't have a social life, she didn't even eat well, so Celia reckoned if those addictive cancer-sticks were the only calming pleasure Janice got, then she deserved them.

Up until now Celia had managed to hide the reality of her school life with Max Jenkins from Janice. But this wasn't entirely to spare her from more worry. Celia knew how paranoid Janice was about her safety. The last thing Celia wanted to do was to offer her an excuse to take away what little freedom she had. However, now, as they faced each other in the cubicle, Celia knew that there was no concealing it any longer.

Janice bent down and cupped Celia's face between her rough, red hands, kissing her cheeks tenderly. "Oh love! Are you all right? How bad is it, what are they saying?" she garbled.

"Don't panic, Mum, everything's fine. It just needed a few stitches."

"A few stitches! Oh my poor baby," Janice whimpered. "And what about the boy who attacked you? How's he?"

"How's he?! It's very charitable of you to inquire," Celia said sarcastically. "He's fine, thank you, apart from being a violent headcase. But what about me? I stood there waiting to bleed to death or something and it didn't happen. The doctor said everything looks normal. How can that be?"

"You've been lucky, that's all," Janice said dismissively. "Now where is this doctor?"

"She's gone to speak to my GP; you never even told me that I had a GP! She's going to do a blood test, find out what's going on."

Janice suddenly looked panic-stricken. "Come on, love, we're going," she said hurriedly.

"What do you mean? The doctor hasn't discharged me yet. We've got to wait for her."

"Look, we haven't got time. You just told me she said you were fine, so let's keep that wound covered up and get home. You'll feel better once you're out of here."

"I'm not going anywhere," Celia said defiantly. "If this doctor can tell me more about my disorder then I'm staying to hear it. Maybe I'm cured! Maybe, by some miracle, my body has sorted itself out."

Janice's tone changed to a hushed hiss. "Don't talk rubbish. You'll always have it, it will never go. Now get up or I swear I'll drag you out of here."

But it was too late. Dr. Ross appeared through the curtain, not quite sure what to make of the scene that greeted her.

"Is everything all right here, Celia?" she asked, concerned.

Janice backed away from Celia and straightened herself up.

"Yes, everything's fine," Celia replied, flashing a frustrated look at Janice. "It's just my mum here; she isn't too fond of hospitals. They make her nervous."

"Oh, so you're Mrs. Frost." The doctor smiled, extending her hand.

"No, it's Miss. I'm Miss Frost." Janice kept her hands at her side.

"Sorry," replied the doctor, surprised by the woman's prickliness. "Well anyway, I'm just relieved that you're here. As you can see, your daughter is fine, though understandably shaken after such an incident. Luckily the wound isn't too deep and the bleeding wasn't heavy. Which we're obviously relieved about, but also a bit baffled by, given the information we have from the school and Celia herself."

"Well," said Janice brusquely, "I don't know what they've told you but it's bound to be a bit muddled. It's hard to get your facts straight when you've just been attacked by some knife-wielding thug."

"Absolutely, Miss Frost, and that's why I am hoping you can clear things up for me. You see, I've just got off the phone with the GP you told the school Celia was registered with, but he has no record of Celia or you."

"Well," Janice said, flustered, starting to search her pockets, "it's probably me getting the name wrong. I've a terrible memory for names."

"Sorry, but you can't smoke in here," Dr. Ross said firmly at the sight of the packet of cigarettes emerging from Janice's pocket.

"Of course...I wasn't thinking." Janice ran her nicotine-stained fingers down her jaded face.

"Anyway, while I certainly can't claim that haemophilia conditions are a speciality of mine," Dr. Ross went on, "I've never read of any case, no matter how severe, where it couldn't be managed by injections of the missing clotting factor."

"Well maybe you need to read more cases then," Janice snapped back.

"Maybe you're right," Dr. Ross responded, undeterred. "But I think that your daughter's condition needs further investigation."

"Why? I know all there is to know about it. We've coped with it just fine up till now. I don't want Celia being poked and probed by you lot."

"We have no intention of doing that," Dr. Ross said calmly. "But what if there's a treatment that could change Celia's life?"

"I've been into all that. Her condition isn't treatable!" Janice's voice was rising.

"Just let me do a blood test and we could start to get some facts. Wouldn't that be great? Isn't that the best thing for Celia?"

Celia jumped up. "Yes, yes," she pleaded. "Do the blood test, do it right now. I want to know." She stretched out her uninjured arm towards Dr. Ross, but Janice pulled it away sharply.

"I absolutely *don't* give you permission to take blood or anything else from my daughter. I appreciate your concern but there really is nothing for you to be worried about. We've managed for fourteen years without you people interfering and, as you can see, my Celia is fine. So if you'll excuse us, we have to go."

Janice took tight hold of Celia's hand and marched her past the flabbergasted doctor.

The boredom of the patients in the waiting room was momentarily lifted as the gown-clad girl was dragged past them, protesting loudly.

"Mum, let me go! I want that blood test!"

"Shut up, Celia. I know what's best for you."

As they stepped out through the sliding doors of the department they were greeted by Mr. Powell, who'd been waiting anxiously.

"Miss Frost," Mr. Powell began earnestly, "I can't apologize enough for what's happened to Celia. We're all appalled and let me reassure you that the boy in question is being dealt with by the police and I am recommending his permanent exclusion."

"We have to go, Mr. Powell," Janice said without stopping.

"Yes, of course. Have they discharged her? That's just great. Please, Miss Frost, I'll phone you, we'll have a meeting. You need to be reassured that our school is a safe place for Celia and it would be good to clarify a few things about her medical condition."

"Celia won't be back for a while."

"Quite right! She should take a few days off to recover. I'll see you soon, Celia," he called after them as Janice ordered Celia into the nearest taxi.

On reaching their house, Janice immediately marched to her bedroom and pulled out an array of holdall bags from under the bed.

"What are you doing?" Celia asked in alarm.

"I'm packing up."

"Packing up what?"

"As much as we can carry. We can't stay around here."

"What are you talking about? I'm not moving! Not again. Please, Mum, not again!" Celia begged.

"You'll do as you're told, young lady! This place isn't safe for you. No way can we stay here with violent thugs attacking you at school."

"But it was a one-off. It's not like it'll happen again," Celia protested.

"You don't know that! That boy might come after you. We can't afford to take any chances."

Tears of resignation welled up in Celia's eyes as she headed for the door. "I'm going to say goodbye to Mary then."

"Mary? The old woman across the road?" Janice said, puzzled.

"Yeah. She's always been really nice to me. I can't just go without telling her."

"You'll have to. We haven't got time for goodbyes. Now, get your stuff!"

3 *frankie byrne investigations*

Being a policeman had not worked out for Frankie. He had soon discovered that he and the criminals often shared the same set of morals. His habit of supplementing his income with bribes from suspects had led to him resigning from the force before he was investigated.

Anyway, he never felt bad about his sideline. He did his job, he helped put his fair share of people behind bars – regardless of whether they were guilty or not – and he was always useful to have in the interview room. Sometimes all it took was one look at PC Byrne to loosen a suspect's tongue; sometimes it required a more "hands on" approach. In his prime, Frankie had the build of a heavyweight boxer

– his big bullet head and stubby neck sat atop shoulders so broad they looked like a stretch of motorway. His tree-trunk legs and bulging arms made the seams of his uniform strain, and his meat-cleaver hands could be very persuasive, especially when clenched in a fist.

Frankie remained philosophical about the way his career had turned out. If he hadn't been made to resign from the force he would never have thought of becoming a private investigator, and therefore would never have found his niche.

Over the last ten years, Frankie Byrne Investigations, with its eye-catching acronym, had built up a reputation for taking on cases that other, more reputable, private investigators wouldn't dream of touching. Word spread amongst his target clientele that he wasn't one to ask too many awkward questions and was prepared to do whatever it took to get results, regardless of its legality.

Of course, Frankie knew that the more "unorthodox" the case, the more generous the clients were willing to be. So he made a good living tracking down bad debtors to feed to loan sharks and rooting out squealers who should have known better than to inform on the kind of client that Frankie attracted. Occasionally, during dry patches, he'd dabble in "exposing cheating partners". While these infidelity cases dented his faith in romance, they didn't stop him from lamenting the fact that he hadn't found himself a wife – someone to share his life with, someone who could sort out his paperwork, and who would keep their mouth shut about his irregular working practices.

His office was a room above a bakery, a location which he blamed for his ever-expanding waistline. Every day the delicious smell of baking pastries rose up through the floorboards, and every morning he couldn't resist popping downstairs to get a supply of artery-clogging delights. However, on this particular morning Frankie decided to open his mail first, as a fat brown envelope bearing a London postmark had caught his eye. *This could be it*, he thought, with a frisson of excitement that the prospect of money always induced in him.

A week earlier he'd received a short, unsigned, typed letter inquiring whether he would be willing to take on a case which involved locating two people. It emphasized that the case required absolute confidentiality and discretion, and that his reputation had brought him to the client's attention. The letter promised that, should he take on the work and be successful, he would be paid very generously indeed.

Frankie knew that any client coming to him because of his reputation wasn't going to be some little old lady looking for her cat. He didn't even have to think twice about it. He'd written back immediately to the PO Box number provided, informing the correspondent that he was willing and able to take on the case but would appreciate an advance as a sign of goodwill.

He pulled out the contents of the envelope: a couple of sheets of paper, a photograph, and a thick bundle of twenty-pound notes tied with an elastic band.

"Wowee!" he said, counting the wad. "This one means business."

Next he turned his attention to the letter.

PO Box 87
London
SW8

Dear Mr. Byrne,

Thank you for accepting the case. I now enclose the necessary information. The names of the two people in question are Celia Frost and Janice Frost. The report should provide you with enough information to locate them.

The photograph enclosed may possibly be of Janice Frost. It was taken some years ago. If you find them it is imperative that you supply me with a DNA sample from Celia Frost, taken without her knowledge. You must not identify yourself or give these people any reason to think that they are being sought. This case will be terminated unless the DNA you supply confirms the girl's identity so, once obtained, you must send it immediately to the above PO Box address and await my instructions.

I cannot emphasize strongly enough that this case requires absolute confidentiality. There is to be no involvement from the police or from any other official agencies. As you can see from the enclosed advance, I am willing to pay well for your services and discretion.

NEMO

Frankie quickly Googled the word *Nemo* and nodded approvingly on seeing the result. He'd dealt with people before who wanted to remain anonymous, but signing off as "Nobody" showed more style than his usual clients.

He picked up the grainy photo enclosed. It was of a young woman with dark, windswept hair.

Early twenties, Frankie mused, studying the angular face, *definitely not unattractive. Heavily pregnant by the size of that bump*, he thought, noting the bulge beneath her long winter coat. It was a strange shot. Frankie could tell it was a still from a CCTV camera. From the brightness of the foreground he assumed that she was in the glare of a security light, but the background was as black as a bottomless pit. Her startled almond eyes were looking straight into the lens, but this troubled-looking woman wasn't posing for the camera, she'd been captured by it.

Next he opened the other sheet of paper. It was a photocopy of a report dated two weeks ago from a hospital A & E department in Wales.

The patient's name was Celia Frost – a fourteen-year-old, white British female. Next of kin was recorded as *Janice Frost (Mother)*. There was a home address and a mobile number. The short report read that Celia Frost, who had a reported blood clotting disorder, was brought in by ambulance with a lateral knife wound to her upper left arm, which required suturing and a tetanus injection. The patient couldn't recall ever receiving treatment for her clotting disorder and yet the blood flow stemmed normally with no sign of problems. The mother arrived in the department and presented as nervous and uncooperative. She had supplied the name of a GP but, when checked, both mother and daughter were unknown to that surgery. The mother removed the patient from the department, refusing any further investigation into her daughter's condition and without waiting to sign a self-discharge disclaimer.

The report was signed by a Dr. Ross.

Questions buzzed around Frankie's head. What kind of client was willing to fork out such a big advance, and able to procure confidential hospital reports? And what was all this stuff about the mother dragging her kid out of the

A & E department? If this was a missing persons case, then he knew from experience that often the "missing" didn't want to be found and it became more like a game of hide-and-seek.

He fingered the wad of cash to help him refocus his thoughts. The bottom line for Frankie was that he wasn't there to question the client about their motives. If his investigation ended up finding people who didn't want to be found, and reuniting people who didn't want to be reunited, so what? The consequences were none of his business. He collected his fee, hoped for a bonus and closed the case. A smug smile crept over his face as he reread the A & E report. *Look at all these lovely personal details*, he thought. *Finding this pair will be the easiest money I've ever earned.*

4   *a place to call home*

"We're not going to spend another day walking around this city are we? I'm sick of looking at one grotty house after another," Celia protested.

"No, we're not actually," Janice replied cheerfully. "We're going to go to the park. We need some fresh air." She noticed Celia's pale, soft hands. "Why haven't you got your gloves on? Come on now, we're not leaving this room until they're on."

"I don't want to wear them. It's sunny; they just make me look odd."

"Better to look a little odd than risk getting a cut." Janice smiled sagely.

Celia scrutinized her smiling face before reluctantly pulling on the black leather gloves. Then they made their way down the stairs, through the dark, strange-smelling hallway, and out of the front door.

"Those women are there every day," Celia whispered as they squeezed past the display of cleavages and painted faces loitering on the front steps of their guest house. "No one dresses like that at ten in the morning. I think we're staying in a brothel."

"Don't be so silly," Janice replied, hurrying her away down the street. "They wouldn't do a full English breakfast in a brothel!"

"Full English breakfast!" Celia scoffed. "You could bounce those fried eggs off the walls. If we don't get food poisoning from this place, we'll catch something off the bed sheets. Have you seen the stains on them? I bet they've never been washed."

"Our room is all right – nothing that a bit of air freshener and a good scrub couldn't fix. Anyway, we may not be here for much longer. I'm expecting a call from a landlord. Today could be our lucky day."

"Why? What's going on?"

"I'm not telling you yet. Don't want to get your hopes up. Let's just say that I've been doing my research."

"I still don't understand why we had to leave our last place. Even if you were worried about me going back to that school, there were plenty of others I could have gone to."

"Give it a rest, Celia. You sound like a broken record."

"I'll stop asking when you give me a decent answer."

"I've told you, I couldn't have us living anywhere near that thug Jenkins. That place wasn't right for us anyway. We needed a fresh start."

"I've had enough of fresh starts. I want to settle somewhere."

"Of course you do, love. That's what I want too, but you know that we've always got to be so careful with your disorder. I'm just trying to find a place where you'll be safe."

They walked in silence towards the park, Celia deep in thought. She'd always accepted Janice's paranoid behaviour as a consequence of looking after a child like her, but now, since the knife attack, previously unthinkable questions had been plaguing her, making her feel physically sick.

What if Mum's got it wrong all these years? What if she really is just paranoid?

They entered the park and walked past the playground, already busy with pre-schoolers falling off climbing frames and burying each other in the sandpit.

"What's up, love?" Janice asked. "You're awful quiet."

Celia looked at her uneasily "I...I..." The censored words refused to form.

"Out with it," Janice laughed. "You know there's nothing you can't discuss with your old mum."

Celia braced herself, forcing the words out before she changed her mind. "I want to talk about my disorder."

"Oh," Janice said coldly. "What's there to talk about?"

"It's just weird, don't you think? You've always told me that getting cut could make me bleed to death. But I didn't, did I? And your only explanation is that I was lucky!"

"Well? You *were* lucky this time," Janice said, exasperated. "Just be thankful and don't go fretting about it."

"But what about that doctor, what she said? She seemed to think I could have those injections to help my blood clot. She seemed to think it was all a bit odd."

"What the hell does she know?" Janice snapped. "She's no specialist. I'm your mother. I'm the one who's looked after you all these years."

"But why haven't I been seeing a consultant, a doctor, anyone who could help me?" Celia persisted.

"Listen to me. That stupid woman has just stirred you all up. You know that they did all the tests when you were born and there's no way of treating it. I just have to keep you safe. Keep you from getting injured."

"But—" Celia continued.

"'But' nothing, young lady! To be honest with you, Celia, I'm finding all this questioning a bit offensive."

Tears appeared in Janice's eyes. "It's making me feel like you don't trust me or something. I've spent the last fourteen years looking after you and have I ever once complained? Have I ever once said anything to make you feel bad about all the stress your disorder puts me under?"

Celia's head dropped in shame. Suddenly she felt more freakish than ever before. "Sorry, Mum," she mumbled.

On seeing Celia chastened, Janice brightened. "Don't worry about it, baby," she said, pulling Celia to her and stroking her mop of hair. "We've both been feeling the strain. We won't mention it again. Look, the duck pond's over there." She rummaged around in her plastic bag. "I took some bread from breakfast."

Celia picked out the brick-like bread. "We're meant to feed them, not knock them out."

"That's more like my girl," Janice laughed. Her mobile started to ring. "This'll be him!"

Celia attempted to break the bread into pieces as she listened to Janice affecting a businesslike tone to her caller.

By the end of the short conversation, Janice was bubbling over with excitement. "It's all sorted. I've found us the perfect place to live."

"Where?" Celia asked.

"One of those commuter-type places, well away from the city. So you won't have to put up with all the traffic and pollution that you hate so much. You've always said you'd like to live somewhere more rural. Well, this place sounds right up your street."

"If it's so good, how can we afford it?"

"He's doing us a fantastic deal on the rent. Says he'd rather see homes lived in by families than standing empty." Janice grinned.

"Okay then." Celia nodded. "So what's this wonderful place called?"

"The Bluebell Estate!" Janice announced proudly. "Sounds pretty, doesn't it?"

5 *frankie goes to wales*

Frankie set off early the next morning. He'd lovingly packed all the tools of his trade into the boot of his car. With his surveillance equipment, tracking devices, false IDs and case full of outfits, he felt ready for action; especially as, hidden behind a false back in the glove compartment, he'd placed his most comforting possession. He'd acquired the handgun from a raid in his police days. They'd stormed a gang's meeting place and in the ensuing chaos it had been easy to slip one of their confiscated guns inside his uniform. He always knew that it would come in handy in his line of work and, over the last ten years, that weapon had got him out of a few sticky situations.

It was a long, hot journey to south Wales and, as soon as Frankie drove up to the row of terraces, his heart sank. A *To Let* sign hung outside the house he'd hoped to find them in. He parked further down the street and changed into a uniform of tan trousers and matching jacket with a courier company emblem on the breast pocket. This was his favourite part of the job. Frankie's acting ambitions had been thwarted at school as, year after year, he was banned from participating in the Christmas play. Even now the injustice of it still rankled; just because he'd cut a clump out of a whinging girl's hair or set the fire alarm off at parents' evening. But now, pretending to be someone else to procure information was an essential part of his job and it meant he got to act to his heart's content.

He got out of the car, carrying a big, brown parcel bearing Janice Frost's name and address. He strode purposefully up to the house and casually looked through the front window. The room was sparsely furnished with no personal belongings in sight that would suggest someone was living there.

Frankie made a big show of knocking on the door and ringing the bell. As he expected, there was no answer. He went through the alleyway a few doors down. From here he could gain access to the back of the house, safe in the knowledge that he wouldn't arouse suspicion in his uniform. The yard gate was no obstacle, as it was already hanging off its hinges. Approaching the house, he peered into the back room and then the tiny kitchen. Again, they were poorly furnished and showed no signs of life. A wheelie bin, with the number of the house daubed on it, stood in the yard. He looked around to check he wasn't being watched and then opened the lid, preparing to sift through the contents. Even though it was a dirty job, it often produced great results. He knew that every day people threw out bills, letters, bank statements, expired membership cards – all kinds of things that were a goldmine of personal information and could let someone like him into their lives in a second. However, today he wasn't in luck. The bin had recently been emptied and all that remained was the lingering stench of rotting rubbish.

He returned to the car and phoned the number printed on the *To Let* sign.

"Hello," a man answered.

"Oh hi," Frankie said. "Are you dealing with the property to let on Central Street?"

"Yeah, I'm the landlord."

"Good," Frankie said. "I'm interested in renting the house. Is it still available?"

"Yeah, absolutely," the landlord replied eagerly. "It's a great little house; very homely. It's only been vacant a couple of weeks. It'll probably get snapped up."

"Why did the last tenants leave then? Not problems

with the neighbours was it? Because I've been through that before," Frankie said, injecting his voice with anxiety.

The landlord snorted. "No! Nothing like that. Must have been money troubles. They did a flit out of the blue – still owe me a month's rent."

"Oh, bad luck mate." Frankie feigned sympathy. "Could I see round the house then? Say at…five o'clock today?"

"Sure, no problem. I'll meet you there, Mr…?"

"Mr. Hughes. Paul Hughes. I'll see you later then."

In light of these developments, Frankie's next step was to call the mobile number that was on the hospital report. If Janice Frost answered, then he was ready with his usual patter about how she'd won a big cash prize in a draw that she may not even remember entering and how he just needed to confirm her details before sending the cheque out to her. Frankie always found that the thought of winning money caught even the most cautious people off guard and before they'd had time to think it through, they'd already told him all he needed to know. However, when he rang the number, the line was dead.

"This case is going to be more legwork than is good for me," he sighed, rubbing his round belly.

He pulled himself and the parcel out of the car again

and went knocking at the houses on either side of the empty property. There was no reply from the house on the left but, on the other side, a woman answered.

"Sorry to disturb you, madam, but I've got a parcel for Janice Frost at the address next door. You don't know how I can get hold of her, do you?"

"I haven't got a clue. One morning they were here, next minute they were gone." The woman began to shut the door.

"Is there anyone on the street who might know how to contact her?" Frankie asked hurriedly.

"Shouldn't think so. The woman wasn't a mixer. Very quiet, although the kid used to play her music too loud sometimes, but I never complained. I felt sorry for her. The mother never let her go out. I thought it was cruel." And with that the door was closed on him.

Frankie was beginning to think that the neighbour had been right. He'd knocked on ten houses up and down the street and gained no information, apart from the odd comment about how the Frosts had only been on the street a few months and how the mother might have said hello but never wanted to chat.

Frankie decided to try just one more. He'd spotted an old lady in the house directly opposite, looking out from her front room. To his surprise, as he approached her door, she beckoned him in.

"Just give it a push, dear. I always leave it on the latch; saves me having to get up," she called out cheerily.

Frankie pushed the door which opened straight into the room.

"Come and sit down. Have a rest. I've been watching you going up and down the street. You must be exhausted in this heat. Do you want a glass of water?"

Frankie sat down and patted his glistening face with his hanky.

"That's very kind but no thanks," he said, trying to make his gravelly voice as unthreatening as possible. "I'm not having much luck. I'm trying to deliver this parcel to a Janice Frost, but the address is empty."

"Well, yes, it will be, dear. I saw them. They were in such a hurry. Laden down with bags. Poor Celia looked very upset. A taxi arrived and off they went."

"Do you remember what taxi firm it was?" Frankie asked, thinking quickly.

"Of course. It was A2B Cabs. I use them myself. Their office is only on Mount Road."

"And when was this exactly?"

"Oh, a couple of weeks ago now. It was a Friday. I remember as it's the day I get my hair done and I wasn't too pleased because Doreen – that's my hairdresser – well

I don't know what she was thinking of, she made me look like a dog's dinner. I keep washing it but I still think it looks a mess," she said, patting her lavender hair.

"No, it looks lovely. Really suits you," Frankie said with a sickly smile.

"Oh, that's very kind of you, young man." The old lady giggled like a schoolgirl.

"Did you know the Frosts then?"

"Only Celia. Such a lovely girl! I don't know what could have happened to make them run off like that."

"Have you got any idea where they might have gone? Do they have friends or relatives around here?" Frankie asked. "Because I'd really like to get this parcel to them."

"No. I don't know much about them. Celia never used to talk about herself really. She'd pop over after school sometimes, do a bit of shopping for me at the corner store before her mum got back from work. Her mum didn't like her going out, you see. She was meant to stay in the house until Janice came home. I'd often see her looking out the window at the other kids playing in the street; I tell you, it used to break my heart. She didn't seem to have any friends who called round. She's a striking-looking girl – so tall and pale, with all this orange hair – but you know how cruel other kids can be. And then, of course, she had this illness."

"What kind of illness?" Frankie asked.

"I'm not sure," the old woman replied. "She didn't talk about it, but when I told her that she should be getting out like other teenagers, she just said she couldn't, that she had this disorder and her mum was worried about her hurting herself."

"Where did her mum work? Maybe they could give me her new address," Frankie asked.

"Well…I don't know. She had cleaning jobs all over town. The poor woman always looked worn out. It must be hard for these single mums."

"Any boyfriends who'd know?"

"Not that Celia ever mentioned. I never saw anyone go over their doorstep. It was always just the two of them."

Frankie pulled the photo out of his pocket. "Is this Janice Frost?" he asked tentatively.

The old woman peered closely at the grainy image. "Oh, well. I can't be absolutely sure. This photo isn't very clear and the girl here looks a lot younger than Celia's mum, but it could be her… Yes," she said after some consideration. "Put a good few years on her, make her face thinner, more lined, and it could well be her."

On hearing this, Frankie's adrenalin started pumping.

"But why have *you* got a photo of her?" the old lady asked curiously.

"The person sending the parcel gave it to us," he answered without hesitation. "They were anxious that it got delivered to the right person. I think it's something very precious. Family mementoes or something."

"Oh, what a shame she won't get it."

"I'm not giving up yet. Could I leave my mobile number? Then if Celia ever gets in touch with you, perhaps you could let me know and I could get this parcel to her mum." Frankie wrote his first name and number on a card.

"Yes, of course. What a good idea. I must say, it's lovely to meet someone who's so dedicated to their job."

"I like to do my best, Mrs…?" Frankie said.

"It's Mary. Call me Mary."

"Well, Mary, you've been so helpful," Frankie said, getting up to leave, "but if you don't mind me saying, in future you shouldn't leave your door on the latch. There are some very unsavoury people out there who could take advantage of a nice lady like you."

A buoyant Frankie returned to the street at five o'clock. He'd kept his courier uniform on in case Mary was looking out of her window. He didn't want her to get suspicious, and hopefully, if she saw him going into the house, she'd think he was still on his quest to deliver the parcel. The landlord arrived promptly and looked Frankie up and down.

"I've just knocked off work," Frankie told him.

They entered the front room, which was chilly despite the heat of the day. A depressing aroma of damp and bleach permeated the shabby place. The landlord took him through, confidently describing the abode as if it were luxury accommodation. But Frankie was happy for him to prattle on as he scanned every room for clues.

"You can look as hard as you like," the landlord said proudly. "You won't find any dirt here. The previous tenants may have done a runner but they always kept the place spotless."

But Frankie had spotted something as they entered the second bedroom. Under the bed was a hairbrush and entwined around the bristles were springy strands of orange hair. He needed to distract the landlord.

"Is that the doorbell?" Frankie frowned.

"I didn't hear anything," the landlord replied.

"No…listen. It's just gone again."

"Really? Well, I best go down and check then."

As soon as the landlord had left the room Frankie quickly pulled his gloves on and got a specimen bag out of his pocket. He carefully picked up the brush and placed it in the bag, sealed it and hid it in his jacket. The landlord came up the stairs, puffing.

"There was no one there," he said. "Do you want to see the bathroom? It's fully carpeted!"

Frankie walked straight past him. "I don't think I'll bother. This house just isn't doing it for me," he said, heading for the front door.

Back at his car, Frankie changed his jacket, inputted the taxi firm's details into his satnav and drove to A2B. Once there, he slipped the radio operator forty pounds to put the question out to all the drivers.

"Who did a pick-up from 14 Central Street on Friday the 23rd? It was a woman and a ginger girl. They had lots of bags with them," the operator asked. The radio waves were silent.

"Tell them that there's forty quid in it for the driver. That should help jog their memories," Frankie said. Within seconds of hearing this additional information, a driver responded.

"Yeah, it was me. It was an odd pick-up. The girl seemed really upset. I took them to the coach station in town."

Frankie felt like he was on a roll and went straight to the coach station, where he knocked on the door of the drivers' staffroom. Armed with the photo of Janice, he began his story of how he'd come home one evening to find that his wife had left with their daughter.

"My Celia was distraught. She didn't want to go. I even

found a note she left, pleading with me to come and find her. She's a girl you'd remember; fourteen, tall with orange hair. It was the evening of Friday the 23rd. All I know is that they came here, and I really need to know where they were heading. She won't let Celia get in touch with me; she's using her to get at me. I need to find them. Doesn't my daughter have the right to decide for herself who she wants to be with?" Frankie said, in angst-ridden mode.

He was greeted by a lot of sympathetic noises from the room full of male coach drivers. Some of them knew what it was like to have their kids taken from them by estranged wives, and the sight of this bruiser of a man, obviously ripped apart by it, moved them.

"Listen, don't worry, mate," one driver said, slapping Frankie on the back. "You leave that photo with me. There's loads more drivers out on the road who might have taken them. Leave us your number and I'll ask around."

"You're a real gent," Frankie said, managing a brave smile.

6 bluebell towers

Celia stood on the balcony of the latest shell that she had to call home. A smiling Janice came out to join her. Janice loved the vertigo-inducing balcony of their twentieth-floor flat. She'd sit at the rickety table, drinking tea and humming some Rat Pack tune, as her cigarette smoke rose into the blue, cloudless sky. From her crow's nest she could observe hundreds of other balconies. Many were cluttered with bikes, prams, clothes horses and pot plants. A few even housed colourful, exotic birds, who twittered manically in their tiny gilded cages. Janice enjoyed these secret snapshots into people's lives, as they flittered in and out of view, hanging out washing, calming crying babies, having blazing rows. But for Celia, being able to see these people and knowing that they were all strangers only made her feel more alone. However, the balcony was her only escape from the stifling temperature of their flat, whose radiators, despite being turned off, belched out heat day and night. When Janice had complained to the Bluebell Tower Two caretaker, he'd just shrugged and said that all the flats had the same problem.

"Think of it as a built-in sauna," he'd replied facetiously. "You'd pay a lot of money for one of those in some penthouse apartment."

Celia's heart sank as she surveyed the four monstrous high-rises. They rose out of the landscape like a fortress, casting permanent shadows over the warren of houses spread out at their feet. This was the Bluebell Estate, but if there had ever been any bluebells growing, then they had long ago been buried under thousands of tonnes of dirty grey concrete.

Her eyes followed the long, winding road which cut through flat, parched fields and bypassed a sprawling wood before continuing its journey into the distant city. How she wished they'd stayed there, instead of coming here, to this godforsaken place in the middle of nowhere.

Far from being a commuter-belt haven, the Estate had been built in the late 1960s to accommodate all the inner-city residents whose slum houses were being demolished.

At first people had been happy to relocate, seduced by the thought of modern homes and amenities. Unfortunately, once they arrived, the new residents discovered that their promised land offered them nothing but cells in the sky, and the only way for them to go was down.

Celia turned to Janice. Her smug face wound Celia up.

"I don't know what you're so cheerful about," she griped.

"This place, of course. It's perfect for us."

"Are you even on the same planet as me?" Celia threw her arms out at the view in disgust.

"I like it up in the clouds. No one's going to bother us here," Janice answered.

"Yeah, it's the kind of place you could be lying dead in your flat for weeks and people would only notice because of the stench of your decaying body."

"Exactly, just the kind of place I like," Janice cackled. "People leave you alone."

"It's okay for you. You're out at work all day. What about me? You've been saying that you're going to sort out a new school since we got here. I'm going out of my head with boredom stuck in here."

Janice took a deep drag on her cigarette, avoiding Celia's gaze. "Well, there's only a couple more weeks until the summer holidays. It's not worth starting a new school now, is it?"

"It'd be better than doing nothing in this place all day. Anyway, you need to contact them now to get me a place for September."

"Actually, love," Janice mumbled. "I know I said I'd look into it, but I've come to a decision about your education."

"Oh yeah." Celia was instantly worried.

"Yes." Janice summoned up her voice of authority. "I've decided that I can't trust *any* school to take care of you properly. I think we've seen that, haven't we? I'm not happy putting my little girl in danger every day. I don't want to send you to a place where some thug might attack you."

Celia's head jolted back in shock. Janice took another puff on her cigarette.

"You're having me on, aren't you?"

Janice exhaled, forming a smokescreen between them. "I wouldn't joke about something like this. I can't send you to school. I'm not prepared to take the risk any more."

"But…but…you can't do this! I've got to go to school."

"No you don't," Janice said triumphantly. "They can't make you. Not if I'm going to teach you at home."

"Teach me at home? You can't teach me at home!" Celia screeched.

"Yes I can. I should have done it years ago. Other people do it. At home, I can guarantee you'll be safe."

"No way! You're not doing this to me."

"I'll do whatever I like; I'm your mother. What's wrong with you anyway? Any kid would be jumping for joy at not having to go to school."

"Yeah, but I'm not any kid, am I?" Celia said bitterly. "Other kids have a life, friends, things to do… You don't let me go anywhere, do anything. I may get treated like a leper at school, but at least I'm with other human beings apart from you!"

"We have a nice time together, don't we?" Janice said desperately. "What about our takeaway and DVD nights? You enjoy them. And it's not like we don't have a giggle together, reading those trashy mags and watching those makeover shows."

Celia sighed. "I know you try to do your best for me, but it's not exactly normal for a teenager to hang around with their mum all the time, is it?"

"I understand," Janice said sympathetically. "I know it's hard for you, Celia, but this way I can keep you safe."

"No!" Celia snapped. "This way you're wrecking my chance of passing any exams, and I want to do something with my life, not like—" Celia stopped herself, but it was too late.

"Don't worry. I know what you mean." Janice smarted. "Not like me; you don't want to end up like me, cleaning up other people's dirt for a living."

"But think about it, Mum," Celia said, straining to be gentle. "How are you going to teach me? You left school with no qualifications, nothing."

"I'll get books out. I'll find out what you're meant to be learning."

"You can't spend your time doing that. Who's going to earn the money? Who's going to pay the rent on this dump? You need to work, Mum, and I need to go to school."

Janice took Celia's hands. "You're a bright kid, Celia; you don't take after me. We can make this work."

Celia pulled away, knowing that Janice wasn't going to back down.

"You're more like my jailer than my mother. You can't keep me a prisoner in this flat!"

"Don't be such a drama queen. You're not a prisoner. There are plenty of things we can do together. It'll be fun," Janice said unconvincingly.

Celia stormed inside, looking around in disgust at the place that was to be her cage. Just like everywhere else they'd lived, the flat came furnished with sagging sofas, paper-thin curtains and threadbare carpets. They didn't seem to own anything – always on the move, always having to fit their possessions in a few bags.

Janice had tried to personalize the living room by sticking photos on the walls. But today, the sight of them only made Celia feel more upset. Her whole life seemed to be charted by the gallery of curling pictures. One showed a wide-eyed toddler being cuddled by a youthful-looking Janice, the ravages of worry yet to carve themselves into the woman's features. Others captured happy days of picnics in the park, story time in the library and endless games involving teddies and tea parties that Janice would patiently play along with. These were the days when she'd be taken to work; sitting with colouring books and a bag of sweets as Janice cleaned office after office, singing and dancing around with her duster to make Celia laugh. These were the days before she grew up and Janice let her fear overshadow their lives as she could no longer control every minute of Celia's time.

Celia looked at the row of portraits from the many different schools. They were a painful reminder of the toll she was paying, as her maturing face stared out from them; with each passing year her smile seemed weaker, her eyes duller and her head held lower. She no longer felt like the special little girl that Janice always told her she was – she just felt like a freak.

She walked into her bedroom and slammed the flimsy door. She smoothed the creases out of her precious posters, which came with her wherever they moved. The Clash, Blondie and The Sex Pistols looked down at her from the wall, with their "two fingers up to the world" snarls. She'd tried to like the music that other kids were into. She wanted to be able to join in their conversations about handsome boy bands and warbling divas. She'd listened to rappers, but their macho rants had left her cold. Pop was too forgettable and none of the guitar bands seemed to be the real deal. Music had never meant anything to Celia, until a couple of years ago when she'd tuned in to a late-night radio show and had been blown away by the noise that flooded her senses and shook her insides.

Punk may have had no meaning to her classmates, and did nothing for Janice – who preferred Frank Sinatra to The Sex Pistols – but to Celia those three-minute songs were short, sharp shocks of pure joy: the thrashing guitars, the thumping drums, the singing that was more like shouting but always sounded like they meant every word. Celia loved everything about punk: the anarchy of it, not caring what anyone else thought of you, the feeling that anything was possible. She loved the outrageous way the girl punks had dressed; safety pins through noses, pink hair stuck up with soap, Dr. Martens boots and ripped fishnets, pulling themselves into skintight PVC dresses no matter what shape or size they were. As far as she could see, punk had welcomed anyone who ever felt like they didn't fit in. She imagined that in another life, one where she didn't have this stupid disorder, there'd have been no stopping her – she'd have been Queen of the Punks, without boundaries, without rules, without fear. Everything she wasn't.

There was a knock on the door.

"Celia, love, don't go shutting yourself in your room. We need to talk about this."

Celia responded by putting her Clash CD on ear-bleedingly loud. The noise tore through the walls. "Leave me alone!" she shouted.

"I'll go out then. Give you a bit of space."

"Good – and don't bother coming back!"

As soon as she heard the front door shut she threw her bedroom door open and began to jump around the living room like someone possessed, all her anger and frustration channelled into the raw energy roaring out of the speakers. She bounced on the sofa, singing along at the top of her voice, as The Clash yelled about breaking rocks and fighting the law.

She was pogoing so high that she could touch the ceiling. She stomped up and down their narrow kitchen in time to the thrashing guitar, punching the air. There was nothing else in the universe except this wild music surging through her like an electric shock…

Then the banging on the wall started.

"What are you doing in there? Turn that bloody music down or I'll come round and turn it down for you," raged an angry voice.

Celia ran out onto the balcony, pumped up and ready to take on the world.

"Up yours!" she bellowed to the whole estate, before remembering herself and rushing inside to turn off the music. Flopping down on the bed, her heart pounding, her face glowing, she laughed giddily, and for a few short minutes her gloomy bubble was flooded with glorious sunshine.

7   *the bus journey*

Celia woke after another fitful night, but it wasn't just the heat that kept her awake; she couldn't shake off the questions that tormented her.

Janice had already left for work. No matter where they moved, she'd pick up employment within days. But Celia reckoned that years of constant cleaning jobs had only added to her mother's neuroses, leading her to fill their homes with bottles of disinfectants and boxes of disposable gloves.

Janice's latest employer was the chicken processing factory on the outskirts of the estate. Here she spent the day clearing the floors, which became awash with the gruesome remains of the birds. She'd return from work at six p.m., stinking of ammonia and chilled flesh. Despite already having phoned several times during the day, Janice wouldn't relax until she'd seen for herself that Celia had come to no harm. Only then would she settle down for another suffocating evening together. But all her attempts to engage Celia in conversation were futile as, since coming to the Bluebell Estate, Celia had nothing to report but mind-numbing boredom.

Celia was washed, dressed and eating her cereal when she found Janice's note on the kitchen worktop.

Stay in and I promise we'll do something nice when I get home. Remember to use my new number when you phone. Have a good day. Love you, Mum xxx.

She crumpled up the note in disgust. *Trying to pretend everything's all right. Well, if she thinks she can keep me a prisoner in here, she's got another think coming!*

She looked out at the sky; the sun was rapidly burning up the clouds. It was going to be another scorching day. Slinging her bag over her shoulder, she approached the front door. With its thin wood and cheap lock, it was hardly a great obstacle, but for Celia, at that moment, it was as if a thousand volts ran through it. She wasn't used to defying Janice. And what if something happened to her and there was no one around to help? She braced herself, taking a deep breath, and quickly opened the door with her gloved hand. She stepped into the corridor, only exhaling once she'd shut the door behind her. Bypassing the two lifts, she headed for the stairs. For most people, using a lift was just a convenient method of getting up and down a tall building, but to Celia it was like entering a metal coffin. Just looking at one gave her palpitations – the thought of the doors sliding shut, being sealed inside the windowless box, encased on all sides by solid brick as it travelled between floors; the thought of it breaking down, being trapped as the air ran out and the walls closed in. No – choosing to walk down from the top floor of a high-rise seemed the saner option for someone like Celia, who'd feared enclosed spaces for as long as she could remember.

On leaving the foyer of Tower Two, she crossed the square that sat in the middle of the four towers. No one ever lingered here; instead people scurried across, as if it were a no-man's-land in a battlefield. She reached the shopping precinct which lay behind Tower One. It consisted of two rows of shabby-looking shops, which sat facing each other. The ugly, flat-roofed Bluebell Pub was sandwiched between a cut-price minimart and a betting shop. Two young men, built like bulldozers, were opening it up. Old ladies with shopping trolleys sat chatting on the central benches. A kid on a moped came screeching past, nearly frightening them to death, and everywhere the whirring of CCTV cameras could be heard as they swivelled to monitor people's every move.

Celia headed for the post office, cutting through the listless queue waiting to collect their benefits. With relief, she dropped her letter to Mary into the postbox. What must her old neighbour have thought? Mary had always been so kind to her and then they'd just disappeared, without even saying goodbye. At least now the old lady would know it wasn't Celia's fault.

She continued through the precinct and found herself in a maze of boxy houses with slits for windows. These had been built later than the Towers, when the council realized the estate's potential as a dumping ground for problem families, undesirables and unwitting immigrants who'd come in search of a better life. Each time she tried to find her way out through one of the covered passageways, she only ended up in the centre of yet another barricade of houses. Celia approached a man who was attempting to assemble a motorbike which lay in a hundred pieces in his front yard.

"Excuse me. How do I get out of here?" she asked.

"We'd all like to know the answer to that one," the man laughed bitterly. "Just keep going right. You'll hit the main road eventually."

* * *

Ten minutes later Celia was heading towards yet another passageway, more disorientated than before. It wasn't until she entered that she saw the group, clustered against the left wall of the passage, with their backs to her. She glanced at them out of the corner of her eye, her pulse quickening. They all looked the same, shrouded in hooded black tops and oversized jeans, which hung precariously from their bony hips. Chunky sovereign rings glimmered on their fingers, while the soles of their brilliant white trainers, thick as moon boots, made them look unnaturally tall. In the middle stood a male who could have been sixteen or sixty, so pinched and granite-like was his face. He was holding the lead of an enormous hulk of a Rottweiler, but the animal's ribs were clearly visible through its battle-scarred coat, and on the tip of its mauled left ear was a weeping wound. Spotting her, the dog gave a volley of barks, making the whole gang turn around. She caught glimpses of pasty, pimply faces as they glared at her through puffy eyes.

"What's with the gloves?" the granite-faced youth demanded.

Celia put her head down and kept walking.

"Hey girl, don't walk away from me. I asked you a question," he shouted.

Celia stopped. "My hands are sore," she mumbled into the ground.

"Are you sure you got hands, cos you sure look like a *dog* to me."

This set the others off, whooping and barking at her.

Celia's cheeks burned as she started to walk on.

"That's right, darlin', keep walking or you'll be next."

Next? Celia looked back to see what they'd been surrounding. For a second, there on the ground, all she registered was a heap of filthy clothes topped by a mass of matted hair. But suddenly the hair rose up, revealing traces of a crumpled, ruddy face. The figure lifted a beer can to his mouth but, before he could take a sip, one of the gang kicked it clean out of his hand. The passageway echoed with sickening laughter.

"Feck off!" the man grunted, hitting out at the air. "Leave me the feck alone!"

"You need a wash, man, you stink. Should we give him a wash?" the granite boy asked, as if he were in a pantomime.

"Yeah, Razor, give him a wash," they chorused.

He picked up the half-full beer can and poured its contents over the cowering man. Celia gasped.

"You still here?" Razor snarled, letting out the dog's chain. "Mind your own business, girl, or Rocky will take a chunk out of you."

The dog was only centimetres away, straining at the leash and snarling. Celia backed slowly out of the passageway, her heart beating madly. As soon as she was out of sight, she grabbed the phone from her bag and pressed the numbers with shaking fingers.

"Police… There's a guy, a homeless guy…there's a gang…he's in trouble. They might hurt him. You've got to stop them… Where am I? On the Bluebell Estate… No, not at the flats, I'm at the houses… I don't know, they all look the same. It's in one of the passageways… Yeah, I'll look, hang on." Celia tried to calm down, gather her wits. She looked around frantically at the walls of the surrounding houses until she found a sign. "It's Spring Court," she said with relief. "They're in the passageway off Spring Court… I don't know who they are. There's six of them, white boys, black hoodies, they're all wearing these big sovereigns. Razor, they called the one with the dog Razor… No, I don't want to give my name. I just want the police here, now!" She cut the operator off.

As the minutes passed, the noise from the passageway got louder, more aggressive. Celia moved closer, desperate to see if the man was okay. Razor was hectoring his victim.

"See that?" He pointed to the wall. It was daubed with a gold chain, a sovereign hanging from it like a noose. "That means this is part of The Sovereign Crew's turf – our turf – and you've gone and parked your stinking body on it. So how about we just take all your clothes as rent."

The gang's heckling came to an abrupt halt as the man growled.

"Turf? Turf? It's not a football pitch, you feckin' eejit."

"That deserves a good kicking," Razor spat.

Celia looked around, panicking. Still no sign of the police. She had to do something.

She walked into sight. "Stop it!" she screamed into the passageway. "I've called the police. They're coming now, right now."

"You stupid bitch!" One of the gang lunged at her as the sound of sirens cut through them.

"Leave her, Shane. She'll be easy enough to find." Razor winked at Celia. "I'll catch up with you soon, darlin'." He yanked at the dog's lead and the mob secreted themselves deep into the estate.

Celia bent down to the huddled man. "The police will be here in a second. Are you going to be okay?"

"Piss off, the lot of yeh," he grunted, waving her away. She was happy to oblige. It was best if she wasn't around when the police arrived. She didn't want to be dragged into giving a statement. She didn't want them contacting her mother. Janice would go mad if she found out that Celia had put herself in danger.

With leaden legs she followed the sound of the sirens, looking the other way as three flak-jacketed policemen ran past her. She needed to sit down. She needed to calm the sick feeling in her stomach. But more than anything, she needed to get out of this place. The sirens led her to the main road. Opposite was the police station. With its razor-wired walls, surveillance cameras and iron-barred windows, Celia realized that they were more under siege than in control of the estate.

She spotted her mode of escape. The approaching bus was heading for the city. She made her legs run to the stop, waving her arm dementedly to flag it down. But her relief on entering the bus was short-lived, as she squeezed past the passengers who were packed in like battery hens. Celia stood for five kilometres, her face pressed up against a window. She felt like an insect pinned under some grubby boy's magnifying glass, waiting until the sunrays made her catch fire. Her jeans and long sleeved blouse clung to her wilting body. Her gloved hands itched to be released. She tried to distract herself by focusing on the uninspiring landscape outside. As the bus bounced and jolted along the road, the muscle-bound man next to her, who was wearing a sleeveless T-shirt, stretched out his arm to stop himself falling. Celia felt his wet, hairy armpit brush her face, sending her stomach into spasms. The bus jolted again and she was crushed against the window. Bile rose up into her throat; she gagged.

Celia attempted to shout over the noise of the engine and the chatter of the passengers who appeared immune to the trials of the journey. "Let me off, please. I need to get off!"

The driver didn't hear her but the people around her did and they stared in alarm.

"Are you all right, love?" a woman asked. "You've gone green."

"Please…I just need to get off," Celia spoke slowly, concentrating on not throwing up.

The woman saw Celia's watery eyes as she gagged again, instantly creating a space around herself.

"Driver, stop the bus now," bellowed the woman.

"This is not a designated stop," the driver shouted back.

The people around Celia started to protest.

"Let the girl off! She's not well."

"Do you want her throwing up on your bus?"

At this, the driver slammed the brakes on and moments later, as the bus juddered away, Celia was left crouching on the roadside, vomiting into a ditch.

8 *into the woods*

The last retch heaved from Celia's body and she sat up, patting her clammy face with her sleeve and wishing that she'd brought some water to get rid of the vile taste in her mouth. Behind her lay fields of wizened, forgotten crops in the hard earth. In the distance, a few isolated houses were dotted along the road as it stretched onwards towards the city. Looking back towards the estate, the four towers were still visible, their brooding presence mocking her attempt to escape them. But on the other side of the road, set right back, lay the sprawling woods that she could see from their balcony. She realized that the trees offered the only shelter from the sun, which beat so fiercely now that she could already feel the top of her head beginning to burn.

Celia crossed the road and tramped through the barren fields. Walking in among the trees, she immediately felt the coolness provided by their canopy. Soft, mossy ground sprang beneath her feet. Dappled sunlight shone through the leaves, throwing patterns on the woodland floor.

As she ventured deeper into the woods, a rabbit bounded unwittingly towards her, stopping abruptly as it saw the unexpected visitor. Celia and the rabbit stared at each other for a moment before the creature bolted. Celia smiled. She'd never had much to do with nature. Janice had always dragged them from one overcrowded city to the next, where nature was an endangered species. As she stopped to investigate a fox hole, a gleam caught her eye. Sunlight was reflecting off something further into the woods. Walking towards it, she discovered that it was a wire fence, which seemed to form a sudden perimeter. It stood at least three metres high, topped off with barbed wire.

"What's that about?" Celia said out loud.

She peered through the mesh. All she could see was more trees, although the vegetation beyond the fence looked different to that where she stood. She chose a direction and followed the fencing around. It seemed to be endless, without a single gap. Every so often, buckled, rusting signs had been tied to it. *DANGER! KEEP OUT,* some warned. Others read: *BEWARE. DOGS ON PATROL,* and *TRESPASSERS WILL BE PROSECUTED.*

At last she spotted a shallow tunnel that went under the wire and through to the forbidden side. Curiosity gnawed away at her better instincts as she sized it up.

Could I fit through there? Celia wondered excitedly.

All her life she'd been conditioned to avoid risk. Even walking through the woods as she'd just done should have been a painstaking journey, watching out for every tree root, every twig or thorn. But now, even though her doubt felt like a betrayal, it was proving more powerful than years of conditioning.

She paused a moment; she had to think it through. Of course she'd just been lucky to survive the cut Jenkins gave her – what other explanation was there?

Trespassing would be a totally irresponsible and reckless thing to do. She smiled to herself as she passed her bag through the gap to the other side and then proceeded to lie on her front. But as she slid her long, skinny body through, her cloud of hair got caught in the spiky wire and jerked her head back painfully.

"Oww!" she yelped. Bending her arms behind, she felt the tangled mess. She tried to work the hair out of the wire but only made it worse. Her arms and neck were starting to ache and she realized that the only way to get free was to rip the hair loose, even if it meant leaving a clump attached to the wire. But Celia was overzealous and yanked it with such force that her head shot forward and smacked into the earth, her mouth hitting a stone jutting out of the soil.

Immediately blood flooded her mouth. She pushed herself completely through to the other side and spat out the crimson liquid. No sooner had she done this than it filled up again. She felt inside her mouth. At least all her teeth were secure; she'd never been to a dentist and she didn't want to start now. But she could feel the soft sliding skin of her gums where they had split, and the smarting of her right cheek, which had also felt the impact of the ground. Her lip was already ballooning. Celia spat again. From her bag she fished out the first-aid kit that Janice insisted she never went anywhere without.

Useless! she thought, rifling through bandages, plasters and disposable gloves.

She patted her cheek with an antiseptic wipe. There was only dirt; at least the knock hadn't broken the skin. But as her mouth filled with blood yet again, Celia became jittery.

It isn't stopping, not like the knife wound. It isn't stopping.

Stupid, stupid, stupid! I shouldn't have doubted her. As if she'd lie about this. Think, Celia, think... Phone! Phone an ambulance.

Celia looked in horror at her mobile.

No signal! No signal!! Right…run back to the road. Flag down a car… Would anyone stop? How much blood could I lose before someone stopped?

But amid her growing panic, her senses couldn't help registering the metallic taste in her mouth. She suddenly fell still, eyes glazed, as her mind transported her back to a scruffy yard… She was no more than five years old. Janice had on bright yellow washing-up gloves and was carefully pulling a dangling baby tooth from Celia's mouth. She'd experienced that same taste then, as the tooth came away from the gum. She'd squealed even though it didn't hurt. Janice kept giving her sips of water, telling her to swill it around her mouth and swallow it. They'd sat in the yard together until the bleeding had stopped. Then she'd been taken inside, given an ice pop, a blue ice pop, and everything had been fine.

Yes! Everything had been fine! The bleeding had stopped, just like it must have done for all my other baby teeth – that must have happened. So, if it stopped then, there's no reason why it wouldn't stop now.

Celia pressed the wipes onto her damaged gum. She concentrated on blocking out the voice that was telling her to run and get help. She had to know the truth once and for all. She breathed deeply, changing the stained wipes, each time checking the amount of blood. She held her nerve until eventually it slowed down to a few specks.

Celia removed the final wipe. It was clear.

"She lied," she whimpered like a wounded animal. But rage and relief quickly gathered force.

"The lying cow!" she howled into the air. "The crazy, lying cow!"

9 *making an entrance*

She lost all sense of time as she sat, confused and enraged, tears rolling down her dirty face.

How could she do this to me? Why would she do this to me? She stared at the dense woodland in front of her. *Get up. Get up, Celia, and stop feeling sorry for yourself. Don't waste your energy on her; she'll keep. You've just been given your freedom after fourteen years. What are you going to do with it?*

She stood up, wiped her running nose across her sleeve and dusted off the dirt from her clothes. "Whatever's through those trees, bring it on!" she proclaimed, striding into the thickening undergrowth.

The atmosphere was distinctly different beyond the fence; less like a wood and more like a forest. Here the air was more balmy and sweet-smelling, infused with the scent of flowers that blossomed from lush bushes. Ivy entwined around towering trunks and giant ferns sprouted from the fertile soil. And the noise! The deeper she ventured, the more intense the birdsong was, which mingled with the sound of crickets as if in some eccentric orchestra.

There was no pathway; no evidence that another human being had ever set foot in here. The vegetation was so dense now that it was impossible to see any distance ahead. But Celia kept pushing forward, drawn by the mesmerizing birdsong. She started to feel a sense of urgency rising in her. She had to know what lay ahead. Quickening her pace, she strode across the forest floor, weaving in and out of the trees, jumping over roots. She was almost running now, focusing on the birdsong, light on her feet, giddy with anticipation. A cluster of ferns lay ahead, like enormous fans blocking her path. She flew at them, brushing them aside with both hands without missing a step, emerging into dazzling sunlight. She didn't even have time to realize that the ground was no longer beneath her feet as she plummeted over the edge of the cliff.

It all happened in an instant. She heard flapping birds scattering in fright and saw a flash of green sticking out from the rock face as she hurtled towards it. She instinctively grabbed for it and the next moment her descent was halted. Winded and dazed, Celia found herself clinging to a thick, sprawling bush that was growing out of the cracks in the rock. Gripping the mass of spindly branches, she looked down and saw, some six metres below, her terrified dangling image reflected in sparkling, blue water. Turning her head very slowly, she looked around. A lake stretched out below, strewn with lily pads, humming with hovering dragonflies. It was encircled by formidable cliffs. The only possible place to gain access to it was opposite, where enormous slabs of blue-grey slate ran down the side of the cliff face, forming a staircase to the water's edge.

Celia looked up. The smooth rock face loomed above her and she immediately knew that there was no way she could climb back to the top. Her dangling feet desperately felt around for any kind of support. She shrieked as her movement unsettled her refuge and fragments of rock started to fall away from around the bush and hit the water with echoing plops.

Her arms were aching. The newly healed wound from Jenkins's knife throbbed and strained. She couldn't hold on much longer. The deep, blue water beckoned her.

Celia cursed Janice. *I'm going to die because of her!*

Janice had never allowed Celia to learn how to swim. It seemed ironic, now, that swimming was on Janice's endless list of activities that she'd considered too risky for her child.

Celia shrieked as the bush sagged lower under the weight of her body.

"Help, please, someone, help me!" Her voice rang out into the isolation.

Suddenly she heard an almighty splash as something entered the water. Celia craned her neck to see, as her hands started to slip down the branches. The head and shoulders of a boy bobbed up from under the water. It was difficult to make out his age. His boyish, smooth brown face and skinny arms gave nothing away.

"Jump," he shouted up at her. "Push yourself away from the rock and just jump in."

"I can't jump. I can't swim!"

Alarm flashed across the boy's face. "But there's no other way. Get rid of your bag and chuck yourself down."

"I'll drown!"

"You're going to fall any second anyway. You've got no choice. You jump and I'll get you out of here."

"Can you? Can you really?" she shouted with relief and disbelief.

"Of course I can," the boy replied, looking terrified.

Celia threw her bag into the lake and then, closing her eyes tightly, she filled her lungs with air and let go, pushing away from the cliff face with her feet.

The lake swallowed her on impact. Down, down, down she sank. Her eyes and mouth remained clamped shut, her hair splaying out around her like a flaming halo. Every second of the descent felt like an eternity.

I need to go up, when am I going to go up?

She started to flap her arms against the pressure of the water, trying to fly up through the depths, but the effort only put more strain on her lungs, which felt like they were about to burst. Her eyes opened to the watery kingdom. Sparkling shafts of sunlight penetrated the clear blue water, fish darted past her falling body, and all around her she could see the sheer cliff faces continuing down into the seemingly bottomless lake.

Her lungs were burning. Her brain was desperately trying to override her reflexes that were ordering her to open her mouth. Suddenly she felt something – like the pull of a yo-yo string – and she began to rise. Looking up, she saw the boy through a riot of champagne bubbles, his hand around her arm, his legs kicking frantically. She held on as they broke through the lake's shimmering surface. With an enormous gasp, Celia filled her lungs with sweet air, but no sooner had she done this than the depths tugged at her once more. She grabbed at her rescuer, pushing him under as she tried to keep her head above the water. He wrestled himself out of her grip and swam out of reach. She thrashed around, gulping in water, more terrified than ever.

"Don't panic," he gasped. "I'll get you out, but don't grab me. You'll drown us both. Keep still and I'll do the rest."

He approached her cautiously, cupping the palm of his hand under her chin, tilting it out of the water. As he pulled her head into his shoulder she fought the urge to cling to him. His limbs strained and his breath laboured as he propelled them to the giant stone slabs on the opposite side of the lake. Celia clung to the lowest slab, shaking.

"It's okay. You can reach the bottom now. It's shallow just here," he panted.

But she just clung even tighter, too petrified to believe him. He clambered onto the side and took her arms, dragging her out onto the smooth slab. They both collapsed, exhausted.

It was minutes before either of them could speak.

"I can't believe you saved me," Celia spluttered, water running out of her nose.

"To be honest," he wheezed back, "neither can I."

They shot a look at each other and burst into relief-riddled laughter.

Celia took a surreptitious peek at her rescuer. She reckoned he was a bit younger than her, a little more skinny than lean. His cherubic face sported a brilliant smile that was impossible not to return, but she noticed that his eyes were flitting to and fro – as if he was trying not to look at her.

She looked down at her gloved hands and it suddenly struck her. "Oh yeah, these things. I know they look odd but the thing is, I don't even need to wear them," she said, delighting in peeling them off and throwing them on the ground.

The boy shrugged. "I hadn't even noticed the gloves."

Celia looked down again, puzzled, until she noticed her blouse, now completely transparent and clinging to every detail of her torso. Mortified, she folded her arms across her chest, blushing deeply.

"Look, I've got a towel," he said, trying to cover her embarrassment, "and I've got food if you want it, but I don't suppose you could face food right now."

"No, both would be great. I'm Celia, by the way. Celia Frost. Thank you."

"No worries. I'm Solomon Giran, but people call me Sol."

Sol picked up a rucksack from the slab and pulled out a towel, along with sandwiches, packets of sweets and cans of drink.

"You're organized," she said, wrapping the towel round her.

"This is nothing. I keep all sorts of stuff here: frying pan for cooking, hacksaw for cutting up wood, rope for making swings."

"What are you, SAS?"

"Is it that obvious?" he said, raising an eyebrow.

They sat, silently devouring the food. Celia moved into the shade, protecting her face from the fierce sun and soaking up the scene before her. The azure waters of the lake seemed to plunge into a bottomless crater, the towering cliffs and surrounding forest guarding it from the outside world. Everywhere there were bursts of colour against the lush green of the trees as wild flowers flourished along the cliff tops and tumbled down the rock. She'd never seen anywhere so beautiful.

"What is this place?" she asked in wonder.

"It's an old slate quarry. They flooded it years ago. No one comes here. No one seems to know about it. I think all the people who would remember it have died of old age, and they don't exactly advertise it. They don't want people like you, coming here and drowning."

"How come *you* know about it then?"

"I found it by accident, about two years ago. I go out on my bike a lot. I need to get away from the Bluebell Estate, it does my head in." Celia nodded knowingly. "Anyway," Sol continued, "one day I was passing these woods and thought I'd give them a closer look and this is what I found. I come here loads now."

"I can see why," she whispered in awe.

Suddenly a flash, like a flying jewel, shot across the lake.

"What's that?" She pointed excitedly at a tiny, brightly coloured bird.

"A kingfisher. Fantastic hunters," replied Sol as the bird darted down into the water and emerged with a small fish flapping in its beak. Sol handed her a pair of binoculars from his rucksack. "Now watch where he goes."

Celia trained the binoculars on the flitting bird and watched as it disappeared into a tiny hole in the grass bank above the cliff.

"Why's it gone in there?"

"It's made a tunnel. They have a chamber at the end where they build their nest. I watch them. They started using that chamber about…" He hesitated while he rooted in his bag and pulled out a notebook. He flicked through it. "It was about six weeks ago. Here, look."

Celia studied the page. It displayed a detailed drawing of the bird, accompanied by notes about sightings, nesting and feeding habits. Celia leafed through the rest of the book. It contained page after page of coloured illustrations – herons, song thrushes, woodpeckers, owls, willow warblers, dippers, and one labelled *mandarin duck* that was unlike any duck she'd ever seen.

"Did you draw all these?"

Sol squirmed. He obviously regretted showing her them. He'd got carried away.

"Yeah," he said defensively. "I suppose you think I'm a complete nerd."

"No! They're great. I've never even seen most of these birds," Celia said.

"Yeah, well," Sol said, putting the book away. "I spend a lot of time here on my own. I just kind of got into it."

"I bet a bird like that kingfisher sounds beautiful," Celia mused.

"No. You'd think so, but the kingfisher doesn't have a great song. You see, it's mainly male birds that sing, to attract mates, and so the good-looking ones don't have to try. But the unattractive ones, well, most of them have amazing songs."

"How's your singing then?" Celia asked mischievously.

"Terrible," he replied, poker faced.

She smiled, taking another handful of sweets. "How come you're here anyway? Shouldn't you be at school?"

"I could say the same to you," Sol answered.

"Yeah, well, my mum wants me at home."

"Lucky you! My mum would kill me if she knew I was bunking off. It's a good job the holidays are coming up; I've been getting up extra-early for weeks, just to make sure I get hold of any letters from school before her – I'm knackered!"

"Haven't they sent anyone round to check up on you?"

"Nah, there's more kids skiving than turn up for my

school. Anyway, I've only been doing it seriously for a couple of months. Before that I'd only miss odd days here and there."

"Is the school that bad?"

"Yeah! Half the teachers are off with stress and the other half just do crowd control. Anyway…there's some kids there…started using me for target practice." Sol began skimming stones across the lake. "I don't exactly fit in. I'm rubbish at football, I'm fifteen but I look about twelve, and I'm not interested in joining any gang. I could have told my brothers – they would have threatened to break their legs – but I didn't want to go there."

"Maybe I'm better off staying at home. I've just moved to the Estate. Tower Two, top floor."

"We're in one of those crappy houses. It's a right dump, isn't it?"

"Tell me about it. This morning I was threatened by some scumbag gang. They were going to beat up this homeless guy so I phoned the police."

"Who were they?"

"A bunch of ugly white boys who wore all these rings – called themselves The Sovereign Crew," she said, rolling her eyes.

Sol took a sharp intake of breath. "I've heard of them."

"Oh God! They're going to get me, aren't they?" Celia winced.

"Nah," he said, looking at his feet. "Just keep your head down. There's loads of gangs on the estate, so they're all too busy fighting each other. Anyway, at least you've only just moved there; I've had to live there nearly all my life."

"Where were you before then?"

"In Ethiopia."

"So why did you leave?" Celia asked.

"We had to. My dad was arrested."

"Arrested!"

"He's not a criminal or anything. All he'd done was write stuff about how corrupt the government was. He sent a message from the prison to my mum; said that they were coming to arrest her too, so we had to get out, quick."

"But what happened to your dad?"

"We had to leave him," Sol said gravely. "My mum made the decision. She says it was what Dad wanted; that she was no use to him or us if she was locked up as well. She's spent the last ten years campaigning to get him released but we've heard nothing from him. The government denies that they were ever holding him. They sent letters to her saying that they couldn't help her find her husband. They tried to make out that he'd had an affair or something and abandoned us."

"God, that's terrible!"

"I know, but my mum's having none of it. She refuses to give up. She's *big* into praying; believes that God will help her," he said, not looking convinced. "She writes loads of letters to anyone she thinks can do something. My brothers tell her that it's time to move on. They say that she's kidding herself if she thinks we're going to find him after all this time. But she goes mad at them, shouting 'Shame on you! Just wait until your father returns. Wait until he hears that you gave up on him.'" Sol wagged his finger, impersonating his irate mother. "I just keep my head down. I'm meant to be her *good* son."

Celia didn't know what to say.

"Anyway, enough of my depressing stuff," he said, breaking the silence. "I want to know what you were doing throwing yourself off a cliff."

"I couldn't see where I was going. I just ran off the end," Celia said, embarrassed at how stupid that sounded.

"Well, you haven't done yourself any damage, although your face looks sore." He looked concerned.

"I know." She felt her ballooned lip and bruised cheek. "But that's not from the fall. I did it when I was crawling under the fence to get in here."

"You're not having a very good day, are you?"

"Weirdly," she answered, wide-eyed, "I'm having a *great* day."

"Why?" Sol was confused.

"Well…I think I've just burst my bubble," Celia said enigmatically.

"And is that a good thing?"

"Oh yeah!" Celia said, with a smile so wide that her swollen lip hurt.

Sol felt none the wiser. "So, bubble-bursting girl, I've told you my life story. What about you? What about your family?"

"Oh, it's just me and my mum."

"Where's your dad?"

"I haven't got one," Celia replied matter-of-factly.

"Everyone has a dad."

"Yeah, but I never knew mine."

"How come?"

"Well…" Celia replied sheepishly, "this is going to make my mum sound terrible because she's not like this at all, but I'm the proud product of a one-night stand. She didn't even know the guy's name."

"Ah. Couldn't she have made up a nicer story for you?"

"No." Celia's tone darkened. She started to examine her pale hands with agitated eyes. "I'd rather know the truth. It looks like it's the only thing that she hasn't lied about."

"What do you mean?"

"It doesn't matter. You wouldn't believe me if I told you."

"Try me." He shrugged.

Celia stared at him; she didn't know what it was about

this boy. Maybe it was the fact that he'd just saved her life. Whatever the reason, she felt she wanted to tell him everything.

As she let it all pour out, Sol listened, open-mouthed.

10 *mad or bad?*

Celia finished her tale. "So what do you reckon? Why would she lie about this disorder – to me, to everyone! What is she, an evil cow or a serious nutcase?" Celia said in disgust.

Sol hesitated. "Do you really want my opinion?"

"I'm asking, aren't I?"

"Listen, I do have a theory, but I'm not saying it's right. It's just something that came into my head when you were talking."

"Go on," Celia said apprehensively.

"Well, there's this condition – I saw a psychiatrist on the TV talking about it. Loads of people rang in with their stories. It's a mental thing, really heavy stuff. I remember it because it was *so* weird. He was talking about this case where a mother had pretended that her kid was sick for years. Telling her kid that he was really ill, getting loads of sympathy off people and all the time there was nothing wrong with him. The psychiatrist said that the mother was doing it for all the attention everyone gave her and for the control and power she had over her kid. Every time people started to suspect something didn't add up, this woman would do a runner with the kid and start it all over again where people didn't know them. It took years for anyone to realize what she was up to, but when they did, the kid was taken off her and the mother was sectioned; locked up in some mental hospital."

Celia seemed stunned.

"Oh my God! That's it," she whispered. "That's what's wrong with her."

"It's only one theory," said Sol, alarmed. "Really, what do I know? It's just something I saw on daytime TV."

"NO! I think you're right. It makes sense. It all fits in. She wouldn't do this to me on purpose – she loves me. I know she loves me, but she's not well, it's not her fault. She's totally screwed up… Do you know that I'm named after a cook from a children's home she lived in? Mum says that cook was the only person who ever cared about her. It's no wonder she's turned out mad."

"Listen, isn't it best for you to talk to her first? Hear what she has to say?"

"Yeah. I need to get back." Celia stood up urgently. "She's got to face this. She's not ruining my life any more with her craziness."

Celia looked around for her bag, then suddenly remembered. "My bag! It had my mobile, my keys, my bus money in. They're all at the bottom of the lake."

"Well, at least it isn't you down there. Look, don't worry. My bike's on the other side of the fence. I'll give you a scater, drop you off on the edge of the estate. We don't want people seeing us together and asking questions, do we?"

"I've never been on a bike before."

"It sounds like you've got a lot of catching up to do."

"I know, pathetic, isn't it?" Celia mumbled.

"No. It just means you've got loads to look forward to." His kindness made Celia smile. "You're not going to tell anyone about the quarry, are you?" he asked.

"Course not. I promise. It's your place. You wouldn't want anyone else here, ruining it."

Sol suddenly looked bashful. "Actually, I'll probably be here tomorrow...about eleven. If you're not doing anything, maybe you'd want to come along? You could tell me how it went with your mum."

"Okay," Celia said, trying to sound nonchalant. "Why not?"

"Okay then, it's a date!" Realizing what he'd said, Sol started to stammer with embarrassment. "No...no...not a DATE, date. You know what I mean, don't you?"

"Yeah, don't worry – I know what you mean," Celia said reassuringly.

11   *proof*

Celia didn't even get a chance to knock at the door of their flat before it was flung open by Janice.

"Where have you been?" she bristled. "I couldn't get through to you on your mobile. What have I told you? Always keep it on! I've been worried sick. I left work early to try to find you." Then Janice noticed her face. Celia's lip was thick and her cheek was now covered with an angry-looking bruise.

"Oh my God! What have you done?" Janice screeched.

"It's none of your business," Celia replied coldly.

"What do you mean, it's none of my business? I'm your mother."

"You don't deserve to be a mother," Celia said venomously. "Mothers are meant to protect their kids. Kids are meant to be able to trust their mothers, but you…!" She stabbed her finger towards Janice's stricken face.

"What are you talking about?"

"You *know* what I'm talking about," hissed Celia. "Look at my face, my mouth. Do I look like I bled to death? Do I look like I've lost pints of blood?"

"Was anyone with you? Did anyone help you?"

"No," Celia said without a flicker.

"Well, you've obviously got more lives than a cat."

"Don't you dare!" Celia's voice was full of fury. "Do you honestly think I'm going to believe you this time?"

"Of course you should. Your disorder is rare, so rare that there's bound to be things they don't know about it. It must be unpredictable."

"I want to see proof about my 'disorder'," Celia said, forming inverted commas in the air. "Anything will do – a doctor's report, a medical certificate. It's not a difficult request. You must have something official about such a life-threatening illness."

"You know me…" Janice tried to withstand Celia's stare. "I'm not one for keeping paperwork. I threw all that stuff out years ago."

"Not to worry. I'll just make a doctor's appointment,

have a blood test. We'll soon know the truth," Celia said with a menacing breeziness.

"NO! Don't do that."

"Why not? If you're telling the truth, what have you got to be worried about?"

"Celia, you don't understand. They'd take you away from me."

"Exactly!" Celia shouted triumphantly. "I'd be taken away because we'd all find out that you've been lying! There is no blood disorder, is there? You've made it all up!"

"Why would I do that to my little girl? Why would I put you through that? Why would I tell every school about your condition?"

"Because you're sick, mum, sick in the head!"

Janice gave a forced laugh. "Oh, so you think I'm a nutter now, do you?"

"Yeah – a big-time nutter! I don't think that you've been lying to me on purpose, to hurt me – it's just you can't control yourself, can you? There's this psychiatric illness and I think you've got it. You need professional help. There's probably some kind of medication you should have been on all these years."

"Oh yeah and who's put all this into your head? Who have you been talking to?"

"Who I talk to is none of your business. You've done your best to make sure that I never had anyone to talk to.

Everywhere we've ever been you made people think that I was untouchable. The girl with the freaky illness, the girl no one wants to hang out with in case I bleed to death on them! You've never let me stay anywhere. Always dragging me from one place to the next. But now I know why: it's when people start to get suspicious, isn't it? It's when they start to think you might be lying."

"Celia, love, you've got to believe me. Everything I do is for you," Janice implored.

"Shut up! Just shut up! The lies have got to stop right now. Either you show me proof or I'm going to the police."

"I can't give you proof but I'm begging you to trust me. If you bleed it could be disastrous – it's dangerous."

"Dangerous!" Celia shouted. "The only danger I'm in is from you."

"I'd never do anything to hurt you!"

"I think the evidence contradicts that, don't you?"

"I wouldn't put you through all this for no reason."

"I know, but there is a reason and it's that you're a total nutcase who's used me and an imaginary illness to get attention from people; to make yourself feel important, because you're nothing, you're no one. Isn't that right?" Celia bawled at her.

"No, Celia. I've just been trying to keep you safe. Even if I can't explain it, I need you to trust me."

"No way! I've trusted you for fourteen years because

you're my mother so I believed what you told me, like any kid would. But not any more."

"Celia, I love you. Don't do this to us," Janice pleaded.

"Shut up. Just looking at you makes me feel sick."

Janice's voice hardened. "You need to stop and think about this. What will happen if they take you away from me? Do you really want to end up in care like I did? People being paid to look after you. Paid to pretend to like you. Surrounded by kids who've been so screwed up that they'll do anything to drag you down with them."

"I'll get fostered. Some lovely, *normal* family will take me in," Celia answered.

"Don't kid yourself," Janice laughed bitterly. "No one wants to foster teenagers. You'd be dumped, left to rot in some kids' home until they chucked you out at sixteen with nothing and no one. You know there's no one else to look after you. It's always been just you and me."

Celia knew she was right. Janice never spoke of her parents. She'd only ever say that she didn't know or care where they were. There had never been any mention of grandparents or aunties and uncles. Janice was all Celia had.

"I love you so much, Celia," Janice began to crumble. Tears welled up in her eyes as she buckled at Celia's feet. "You're all I live for. I would die for you."

"Stop! Just stop with all the acting. Emotional blackmail is one of your specialities, isn't it? You've always been able to make me do what you say because I felt so guilty, so frightened; thinking I was causing you a life of pure stress with my 'disorder'; thinking I could bleed to death. How could you do that to me?"

Janice sobbed. "You mustn't do anything stupid. We've got to stick together. I'm the only one who can look after you."

At that moment Celia wanted to feel such hatred for Janice, but she found she couldn't: it would go against everything that she'd ever felt for this woman – this sickly-looking wretch who had devoted her life to Celia, lavished love on her, worked to provide for her until her hands were raw and her frail body ached.

"You keep out of my way," Celia hissed. "No more telling people that I'm ill. No more telling me what I can and can't do. You don't ask me where I'm going or what I'm doing. These are my conditions. You stick to them, otherwise I swear that I'll go to the police and social services and have you sectioned! Do you understand?"

"Yes. I understand. Anything, Celia, anything you want. Just stay with me." Janice clung to her legs, a quivering, sobbing bag of bones. Celia looked down on the pathetic sight and knew that Janice wouldn't survive without her. She felt overwhelmed by a mixture of pity and disgust, for this, the only person in the world who loved her.

12 *nemo calls*

Frankie's Oscar-winning performance at the coach station paid off. He'd been back in his office for a couple of hours when he'd received a call from one of the drivers telling him that he'd picked up the woman in the photograph and an orange-haired girl on that Friday. He remembered them among the coachload of passengers because the girl had been crying.

"I knew it," Frankie said to him. "She didn't want to go with her mother. She wanted to stay here with me. So where did they get off?"

Frankie was hoping it would be a town small enough to have a chance of tracking them down, but when the driver replied that they'd disembarked in one of the biggest cities in England, his heart sank.

"Did anyone meet them off the coach?" Frankie asked.

"No one that I saw. I handed them their luggage and they disappeared into the crowd. I really hope you find them, mate."

"So do I," Frankie replied with genuine feeling.

Frankie had immediately posted a report and the hair-enmeshed brush to his client. He'd tried to get on with his other cases while he awaited instructions. However, as each day passed he knew that the Frost trail would be getting colder and his job harder. He decided to contact Julian, who was less than pleased to hear from him.

Julian had been Frankie's best investment. They'd met back in Frankie's police days, when he'd dealt with allegations that the nineteen-year-old IT student had been hacking into his own bank account and changing his overdraft to a healthy credit. Frankie had made the allegations go away in return for Julian's help "now and then". It had sounded like a good deal at the time, but now Julian was thirty and held a senior position in one of the biggest telecommunications firms on the planet, and the crooked ex-cop was still demanding information that only a skilled hacker like him could provide.

"Just a little favour, Julian," Frankie had said to the

protesting man. "Here's a couple of names. See what you can find out."

A few days later Frankie's mobile rang.

"Hello," Frankie said. He never answered his phone by announcing his name. He always waited to hear who the caller would ask for as, in the course of his numerous investigations, Frankie used several pseudonyms to protect his identity. He, of all people, knew what powerful information it was to know someone's real name.

"Hello," a cultured female voice replied. "Is that Mr. Byrne?"

"Who's calling, please?" he asked in his most polite voice.

"This is Nemo."

Frankie was taken aback. "Yes, this is Frankie Byrne. Did you get my package?"

"Yes and I'm very satisfied with your progress, Mr. Byrne. I now have the results from the hair you provided and its DNA proves beyond doubt that this is the girl I am looking for. This, together with the fact that people recognized the photograph as Janice Frost, means that I am confident that we have positive identifications for these two people."

"Yeah, and I've got more information for you." Frankie was pleased with himself. "I got a contact of mine to fish around on a few databases and he found out that this

Janice Frost was brought up in care. There's no mention of any contact with relatives; she doesn't seem to have any roots. Also, she spent a few months in a young offender institution in her late teens for persistent shoplifting. After that, there's nothing on her. From the data on her National Insurance contributions it would be fair to say that she must work for cash in hand, never claims benefits and doesn't use credit cards. She's obviously a lady who isn't keen on people having information on her."

"I hope this information wasn't obtained using any official channels. You have understood that there must be no police involvement in this case whatsoever, no matter what happens," Nemo said curtly.

"Of course – that goes without saying." Frankie's pride was hurt. "I am used to dealing with cases of a 'delicate' nature. Anyway, I've found out more from the searches, something really odd."

"Go on."

"Well, it looks like Celia Frost's birth was never registered, not using that name anyway. Janice Frost has never registered any child's birth or claimed child benefit or anything else for her."

"Mr. Byrne." The client's tone was stern. "I appreciate that as part of your investigation you may well unearth certain information that is, perhaps, perplexing, but you must remember that, for now, your only concern is to locate these people. Whatever else you find out can be passed on to me and then any evidence of it destroyed and forgotten about. You must not get involved in areas which do not concern you. Do I make myself clear?"

"Crystal," Frankie answered.

"I came to you because you have a certain reputation. I hope that you're not going to disappoint me."

"No, madam, you won't be disappointed."

"From now on you can contact me on this mobile number. I need you to put all your efforts into finding these people. I need regular updates. They mustn't know that they are being looked for. We can't afford for them to run away again."

"Yes, madam, but you've got to appreciate that it may take some time. Even though we know what city they travelled to, that was three weeks ago and we have very little else to go on. All I've got is an old photo of Janice Frost and no photo of Celia – nothing to show around."

"I know that this will be time consuming, but the quicker you find them the more I'm prepared to pay," Nemo said.

"But I have other ongoing cases. I have other clients depending on me too."

"I need you to work exclusively on my case. Put the other cases on hold and I guarantee that I will compensate you."

"You must want to find these people pretty badly," said Frankie.

"Mr. Byrne, I've been looking for them for a long, long time. If I was only at liberty to explain to you how important it is to find them, I guarantee that you wouldn't eat or sleep until you did."

13 *the flooded quarry*

Sol looked at his watch again: quarter past twelve. She wasn't coming. Why did he feel so lousy? She was only some stupid girl, who'd nearly got herself killed by running off a cliff. It's not like he needed her here, invading his space. And all that stuff about her mum and the blood disorder – it was all too weird; he was best off out of it. He started to pack up his rucksack; he'd suddenly gone off the idea of spending the day here. Just then, Celia emerged from the trees and stood next to him on the top slab. She was breathless and flustered.

"I didn't think you were coming," Sol said, unaware that a beaming smile had spread across his face.

"I'm sorry. I've had a nightmare getting here. The closest bus stop is nowhere near and then it's taken me ages to find the way back to the lake. I lost track of where the hole under the fence is," Celia said, plopping herself down on the warm, smooth stone and feeling immediately calmed by the scene that surrounded her.

"Are you sure that you've got enough suncream on?" asked Sol as he looked at the white goo smeared on every inch of Celia's exposed skin.

"Factor 50. It's impossible to rub in, but I thought it was best to be on the safe side. This skin isn't used to sunshine," she said, waving her squelching arms and legs about. "Mum's always made me wear long sleeves and trousers in case I fell over," she sneered. "But not any more. I'm going to wear what I like from now on."

"How did it go with your mum?"

"Well, you were right. She's definitely got that mental thing – she's a complete and utter nutter," Celia answered, trying to sound matter-of-fact.

"What?! So she *really* has been lying about the blood clotting thing!"

"Yep, I gave her the chance to prove it but she couldn't. She just kept spouting a pack of lies about needing to keep me safe," Celia snorted in disgust. "She even admitted that if social services investigated, I'd be taken off her."

"So what are you going to do?" Sol asked anxiously.

"Nothing! If I grass on her, I'd only end up in care…and it's not like she's a bad person or anything, just crazy. Anyway, she knows the score now. She can't tell me what to do any more; she can't keep telling all those lies."

"Are you sure you've thought this through?"

"Yeah…I can handle it," Celia said, her voice finally faltering, tears pricking her eyes.

Sol stood there awkwardly, debating whether a pat on the back was appropriate. He opted for supportive words. "Of course you can handle it."

"Anyway, I don't want to talk about it. I don't want to talk about *her*. She's wasted enough of my life already. I've got fourteen years of boredom to make up for." She dabbed her eyes, putting a veneer of a smile on her face. "So come on, do something exciting for me!"

Sol was happy to move on, thinking for a second before announcing, "Okay then. How about some magic?"

"What, are you going to pull a rabbit out of one of the holes?" Celia gestured into the forest.

"No, much more impressive than that. But you must promise me that whatever happens, you won't panic," he said mysteriously.

"What do you think I am, some hysterical little girl?" Celia answered indignantly.

"Okay then, but don't say I didn't warn you." With this he started to get undressed.

"What are you doing?" Celia screeched.

"You're not panicking already, are you?" Sol laughed as he got down to his trunks. He walked to the edge of the top slab, glancing down at the sheer drop below, before elegantly diving from the great height into the lake.

Celia waited for him to surface. What was he up to? She shielded her eyes from the glare of the sparkling water, and surveyed the lake intently. He hadn't come up, there was no sign of him, and already it felt like too long.

How many minutes can someone hold their breath? Celia racked her brain. *Maybe he's like one of those pearl divers that they make documentaries about. Maybe he has an amazing lung capacity and can stay underwater for ages.*

Minutes ticked by and she paced up and down the slab steps, peering into the fathomless lake. She couldn't see any air bubbles.

He said not to panic, she scolded herself. *Think of a logical explanation.* But Celia couldn't. There was no way he had managed to sneak out onto the slabs without her noticing, and the rest of the lake was completely surrounded on all other sides by the towering cliffs. Just then, a heron flapped out of the bed of reeds on the far side of the lake. *Of course! That's where he's hiding.* She climbed back up to the top slab so that she could look down into the reeds. They were densely clustered together, but nothing was concealed among them. Celia was undeterred.

I bet he's just below the surface, using one of the reeds as an air pipe.

"Very clever," Celia shouted across the lake. "A real action man, aren't you? You can come out now; you've managed to impress me."

But there was no movement. "Come out, Sol. You're boring me now."

Still the reeds remained undisturbed.

"Come on, Sol, enough is enough," she said, exasperated. But there was nothing and her eyes ran over the sparkling lake again, her brain racing, trying to work out other explanations. Another minute passed.

God, say he's trapped down there! Maybe his trick's gone wrong? It's been over ten minutes. He could have cracked his head on a rock and sunk to the bottom. He might have got tangled in weeds, struggling to free himself, and I've been stood here, just waiting.

"Sol," she shouted desperately. "Please, Sol, if this is part of the trick, it just isn't funny. Come out now. I'm worried. Don't do this to me."

Another minute passed and still the eerily calm water stared back at her. Despite the heat, goose bumps had erupted on her skin. *What can I do? I'm useless – useless!! I can't jump in and look for him and there's no one else for miles.*

"Sol…please, Sol…stop it now!"

"BOO!"

She shrieked as the voice boomed behind her. Swinging round, she was greeted by a dripping, smug-faced Sol.

"You weren't panicking, were you?" he asked, feigning innocence.

"No," she answered haughtily, "of course not."

"Well that's strange, because I could have sworn that I heard someone who sounded just like you, someone who sounded in a real panic," he said, bursting into laughter.

"Well, what the hell do you expect?" She shoved him. "I thought you'd drowned!"

"It's nice to see you care. And what did you call me? I believe it was Action Man!" He chuckled.

"Captain Underpants, more like." She shoved him again.

"Come on, don't be mad at me. I did warn you not to panic and you have to admit it's a great bit of magic," he said proudly.

"Yes, very impressive," Celia said drolly. "But I didn't take my eyes off that lake, so how the hell did you get out without me noticing?

"Come with me and I'll show you," he said excitedly. She followed him into the forest, skirting around the lake. He stopped. They were at the top of one of the cliffs, but the lake was hidden by a row of thick trees.

"Look," he said to her.

"What am I looking at?"

"Look down at your feet."

Inspecting the ground closely, she saw that thick layers of bracken and twigs were camouflaging planks of wood that had been roped together to form a makeshift cover.

"It looks like a trapdoor. Did you make this?" Celia asked.

"Yes, I needed to make it safe. When I first found it, it was just covered with overgrown moss and plants. You could easily have just fallen into it," he said.

"So what's down there?"

"Come and see," Sol said, lifting the cover to reveal a gaping hole that plummeted down into darkness.

"How do you get down?" Celia asked dubiously.

"It's easy. There's loads of rock sticking out that you can grab onto. Watch me. I'll go first." And with that he disappeared down the mouth of the shaft. A couple of minutes later he shouted up to her. "Come on, Celia."

"I'm not good with enclosed spaces," Celia called down anxiously.

"What's enclosed about it? It's nice and wide. Just focus on the daylight and feel your way down. Come on, don't be a baby."

She gingerly clambered down the shaft, her feet and fingers picking their way, finding the footholds, her eyes flicking back and forth to the wide, bright opening to keep herself calm. She reached the bottom, proud of herself.

"You see, that wasn't so bad was it?" Sol said.

The temperature had dropped dramatically. Her teeth starting to chatter, her eyes strained to adjust to the dim light.

"I keep a torch down here," Sol told her. "Just wait a sec." The next moment, the place was illuminated, revealing the glistening walls of a cave.

"What am I looking for – prehistoric cave drawings, dinosaur fossils?"

"There's nothing like that," answered Sol. "It's just another chamber that was blasted years ago when they were looking for more slate."

"Sol, I like secret caves as much as the next girl" – she shivered – "but basically you've just brought me down a very cold, very big hole underground and I still don't understand how you got out of the lake."

Sol turned his torch off. "Look towards the light over there."

Celia could now clearly see light coming through a deep letterbox-like slit in the far wall of the cave.

"Is that daylight?" she asked.

"Yeah. There's more than one way to get in and out of here. All you need to do is get through there," he said pointing to the slit.

"No one could get through there, it's too narrow."

"Trust me – it's okay once you know how, although it may be even more of a squeeze for you. I reckon it's about five metres long, but you have to keep as flat as you can and watch that you don't hit your head on the rock. I lie on my front and push myself along using my hands and feet. Once you're in, there's no space to turn around. Just make sure that you stop before you fall out the other end."

"Why, where does it lead to?"

"The lake of course. I don't reckon they found any slate in this chamber because they didn't bother blasting it right through to the main quarry, but they did leave this tunnel. It comes out just above the water level, behind all those reeds."

"But I was looking right down at those reeds and didn't see any opening in the rock."

"I know, it's magic, isn't it?" Sol said. "You can't tell it's there; the reeds provide cover for it and the opening has moss hanging over it, so it's completely camouflaged. Once you reach the end of the tunnel, you can just push yourself out and into the water. Why don't you just see if you can fit in?"

"I wouldn't put myself in there if my life depended on it," she said, bristling at the very thought of it. "I can't even go in lifts without having a panic attack."

Sol sighed. "I thought you wanted some excitement in your life."

"Yeah, excitement, not terror," she answered.

"Okay then. How about a race? I'll go through the slit and you go up and around. We'll see who makes it back to the slabs first."

"You're on!" Celia shouted, heading for the bottom of the shaft. She looked behind and saw the soles of Sol's feet disappearing into the wafer-thin tunnel. She climbed as fast as she could, quickly gaining in confidence and surprising herself with her nimbleness. She heaved herself out of the hole and sprinted through the cliff-top forest. She caught glimpses of Sol through the trees, cutting through the water with an elegant stroke. She skidded down the slope and towards the slabs just in time to see Sol pulling himself out of the water, breathless but victorious.

"I seriously need to get fit," Celia panted, the gloopy suncream sliding down her face.

"You look like you're melting," Sol laughed. "Why don't you get in the water and cool down. You can stand up in this bit." He slid back into the lake and stood, head and shoulders above the surface. "See, you'll be fine, it's fairly shallow here."

Celia wiped the dripping cream away from her eyes, looking apprehensively at the water.

"My first dip in this lake wasn't exactly fun," she said.

"You'll just have to be careful; stick around this part. After a few metres the ground suddenly disappears – it shelves right down, so deep you can't even see the bottom."

"Thanks, that's reassuring," she said sarcastically.

"Oh, come on. It's great once you're in. You're not going to go out of your depth."

Celia took off her trainers and socks and inched herself in. She felt like a red-hot horseshoe being plunged into a blacksmith's icy water, but once she felt the solid ground beneath her feet and the coolness of the water sucking the uncomfortable heat from her body, she started to relax.

"See, I knew you'd like it – but you still need cooling down," Sol said, using both hands to push a wall of water up at Celia.

She screamed as the cold water hit her full in the face. Grabbing hold of the slab sides, she declared, "This means war!" Her long legs kicked with such ferocity that a tidal wave enveloped Sol.

The surface erupted as they both pummelled the water. Celia suddenly shouted above the roar of their splashes. "Sol, do you think you could teach me how to swim?"

Sol stopped his attack. "*Me*, teach *you*?"

"Yeah – I want to be able to swim in this lake. I don't want to be stuck in the shallow bit like a little kid."

"Well," he pondered. "If you're serious about learning, it'll take a lot of work. We'd have to spend a lot of time here."

"That's okay with me if it's okay with you," she said apprehensively.

"Sure. Why not?" He smiled shyly.

"Great!"

"But of course," he said with a glint in his eyes, "if you want me to teach you then you've got to surrender now and declare me the winner."

"In your dreams!" Celia blasted water at him as the flooded quarry echoed with the cries of their battle.

14 *needle in a haystack*

Meanwhile Frankie Byrne wasn't having such a good day. On arriving in the city he'd booked into a cheap hotel, with dozens of small dark rooms and breakfast served in a damp converted cellar that had the air of a crypt. He reckoned that if his work here was going to take some time, then he might as well maximize his income. It was an old trick of his: stay somewhere cheap and charge the client for a more expensive hotel – that way he pocketed the substantial difference. He never had any trouble finding some underpaid, unappreciated receptionist at a swish hotel who would oblige him with a fake bill in return for fifty quid or so.

Frankie had already been on to Julian, demanding that he access the local education authority's register to see if Celia was attending any of the schools.

"Frankie, this just isn't fair. I've more than fulfilled any obligation I had to you. Have some decency, find someone else to do your dirty work," said the frazzled man.

"Unfortunately for you, Julian, decency is one of the many things I lack. Don't get bitter. We're a great team, so don't do anything stupid. If I get put away there's no one to miss me, but you, Julian…well, your kids don't want to be visiting their daddy in jail, do they?"

Frankie knew that he had Julian over a barrel, but he didn't want to push him too far and make him do anything irrational. So he decided against asking him to hack into the database for the city housing. He was confident that he could get the information he needed without his help.

He started his inquiries at the main coach station but, after hours of effort, he came away with nothing. He'd shown the picture of Janice around and given them the story of his wife running off with his daughter, but no one could remember seeing them. When he asked all the taxi drivers waiting for business outside the station, he got the same response. "You must be joking. Thousands of people pass through here every day and you're asking about a couple from over three weeks ago."

He headed to the main housing office in the centre of the city. Positioning himself in the busy waiting area gave him a good view of all the workers behind their desks, who were dealing with a constant stream of people. He watched and listened, soon picking up who were the more senior housing officers and who were the junior, inexperienced ones. The senior staff dealt with the clients quickly and efficiently; they steered people away from spilling out their terrible life stories and kept it strictly to getting facts and dealing with the housing issue. On the other hand, he observed that one of the younger workers was unable to control the interviews with his clients. He fumbled around with his papers while Frankie kept hearing him say, "Actually I'm not too sure about our policy on that, but I'll look into it for you." At one point a colleague came and whispered in his ear. The younger man coloured up, saying, "I'm going as fast as I can."

Frankie knew that this was his man: inexperienced, kind and harassed – just the type to give out confidential information on trust. He walked up to his desk, politely interrupting his current conversation, and motioned towards the pile of business cards there. "Yes, take one," said the worker, "it's got my direct line on." Frankie smiled his thanks and left.

He went across the road into the Tourist Information Centre, found a quiet corner and phoned the number.

"Mike Channell, housing officer, how may I help?" came a harassed-sounding voice.

"Hello, this is Paul Hughes from Newport District Housing. I was wondering if we could help each other. You see, we believe that a woman and her daughter have recently moved to your area and have probably been housed by you. We just wanted to let you know that the woman left us owing substantial rent arrears and was classified as a nuisance tenant."

"Oh," said the housing officer, "we could do without that. You'd better give me their name and I'll check on our system."

"Janice Frost and her daughter, Celia Frost. They would have arrived about three weeks ago. If you do have their address we'd appreciate having it so we can begin proceedings to recoup the rent arrears," Frankie said, crossing his fingers for luck rather than because he was spouting a load of lies.

There was a long pause and Frankie could hear the tapping of a keyboard down the line.

"Do you know what, Paul? I'm going to have to call you back. I've got a big queue of people waiting and I'm having no luck finding them," said Mike, sounding even more hassled.

Frankie knew that he couldn't let this happen. He couldn't give a mobile number when he was meant to be sat in an office in Wales – he would be rumbled straight away.

He thought quickly. "Please, Mike, could you keep looking? I'm actually meant to be on leave but the boss has insisted I come in to sort this out. I can't go home until I do."

"You shouldn't be coming in on your day off," said Mike sympathetically.

"You know how it is with our job, Mike. We're slaves to it, aren't we? Always giving 110 per cent and even then they want more."

"You're telling me. Hold on for a minute while I keep looking."

"Thanks, you're a real pal," replied a relieved Frankie.

The news came a couple of minutes later. "Sorry, Paul, but they aren't on our system. She's not come to us to be housed and it looks like she's not claiming housing benefit either."

Frankie couldn't disguise his disappointment. "Where else could I look?"

"They could be anywhere in the city, and then there are all the suburbs and outlying towns. They've all got tons of low rent, low quality private housing. It'll be like looking for a needle in a haystack."

"Thanks anyway, Mike," Frankie sighed.

He was just contemplating going to find a bakery to

cheer himself up, when his phone rang and his day got even worse.

"She's not on an admission list for any school in the area. Now leave me alone," Julian said, switching his phone off before Frankie could even get a word out.

Frankie couldn't believe it; he'd been relying on at least one lead. He walked over to the tourist enquiry desk.

"How many people live in this city?" he asked the smiling woman behind the counter.

"Just over a million, sir."

Frankie stood, silently brooding.

"Is there anything else I can help you with?" prompted the woman, feeling slightly uncomfortable.

"Only if you can find a needle in a haystack," he grunted.

15 *just the one*

"Maybe we should just forget it. I can't get the hang of it," a frustrated Celia said, attempting to climb out of the lake.

"No you don't," replied Sol from the slabs. "Stay in there. You're no mermaid, but you just need to keep practising. Go back and try again."

"It's all right for you, sitting there like Robinson Crusoe, with your fire and your sausages."

"Yeah well, maybe if I see you putting some effort into your swimming, I'll cook you one," he said, teasingly lifting the spitting sausage from the frying pan and taking a big bite.

Celia reluctantly waded back out into the water, making sure her feet could feel the solid ground.

"Okay. Now remember, I want to see clean strokes and strong kicks," he ordered, demonstrating with his arms from the comfort of the slab.

Celia launched herself forward and started kicking frantically, while trying to scoop the water with her hands. Sol couldn't stop himself laughing as she immediately headed under the water like a submarine, only to emerge seconds later, spluttering, with a curtain of hair plastered over her face.

"Stop laughing at me," she said, peeling her T-shirt away from her skin. She was glad that she'd invested in the baggiest, darkest T-shirt she could find. "If I'm so bad then it's your fault. You should be in here with me, not shouting orders from there," she said.

"Okay then," he replied, slipping into the lake. "If you get on your front, I'll sort your arms and legs out."

Celia felt Sol's hand on her stomach, supporting her prostrate body. She fixed her eyes straight ahead, far too conscious of his touch.

"It's all right if I hold you up, isn't it?" he asked, feeling her body tense.

"Yeah, why wouldn't it be?"

"Right then. Now kick your legs. No...don't bend them right up. Keep them straighter, closer together." He pressed gently down on her legs with his free hand, trying to keep them under control.

"Now do your arms like this," he said, guiding her limb with his hand. "Don't take them too far out of the water. It should be a smooth action – pull the water back with your hands like this." He put his hand over hers and dragged it through the water.

Her eyes strayed. She couldn't help looking at him. She wasn't used to being close to anyone and now here she was, half naked and practically entwined with a boy in a lake. It was all too overwhelming; Celia stopped kicking and put her feet on the ground.

"What's up?" Sol said, surprised. "Was I holding you too tightly? Sorry, I just didn't want you to sink."

"No, no, it's fine, honest. I was getting tired," she lied, flustered.

"No worries. We can get out and cook the rest of those sausages." He smiled reassuringly.

Celia's mobile rang out from her bag on the slabs.

"I'll get it for you," Sol said.

"No, don't bother," she said. "It'll only be my mum."

"Celia, why don't you just answer your phone? Do you think I'm stupid? I know you're ignoring my calls. Be a good girl, phone me. I'm just in the precinct, on my way home. Let me know when you'll be home – please, Celia!"

Suddenly, Janice heard a noise. Looking down the precinct, she could see a group of young lads sprinting towards her. Seconds later, another gang appeared, flying after them, a large, shabby Rottweiler pounding by their side. The smattering of shoppers in the precinct deftly moved aside to avoid being knocked out of the way. Janice quickly followed suit. The first gang rocketed past her; fear and exhilaration oozing out of them – and then, closing in, their pursuers came roaring past, their faces twisted with vicious intent.

The gangs vanished from view as quickly as they'd appeared and people in the precinct wordlessly resumed their business. Janice groaned as she went and sat down on a nearby bench. She felt so weary, so completely knackered. But it wasn't just because of this estate, overrun by gangs. It wasn't even because she'd hardly eaten recently, or because she'd just finished another long shift at the stinking chicken factory; Janice could cope with all of that. But what she couldn't cope with was Celia running around God knew where, with God knew who. Not letting her know if she was okay. Coming home late, barely speaking, full of secrets; her eyes brimming with contempt every time Janice asked her a question. Janice was aware that she was pushing Celia further and further away as her anxiety became uncontainable. But she couldn't help it. The more powerless she felt to keep Celia under control, the more desperate she was becoming. She could feel her body and mind being eaten away by the stress. She didn't know how long she could go on like this.

"Steady as you go, mate. See you tonight when you've sobered up." A booming voice shook Janice from her morbid musings. She looked across the precinct to see a mountain of a young man gently guiding a customer out of the Bluebell Inn. He gradually unhanded the intoxicated old gent, who wobbled away like a baby taking its first steps.

"Thanks, Abs. You're a good lad," the drunk called back with a wave and a lopsided smile.

Abs saw Janice watching the scene. "Another satisfied customer," he laughed, walking back into the pub.

Yeah, he looked like he didn't have a care in the world, Janice thought jealously. And then it dawned on her. *That could be me. Not sloshed or anything. I could just have the one. Something to take the edge off. What harm can it do?*

Janice marched into the dingy pub before she changed her mind. She ordered a gin at the bar, sat down and braced herself. She'd gone through a phase of cider drinking when she was a teenager – she'd found it deadened the loneliness for a while – but no alcohol had passed her lips since Celia was a baby. With Celia, she'd always felt that she couldn't afford to relax, but now, with the state she was in, she couldn't afford not to.

She took a sip of the clear liquid. Her face screwed up as she spluttered out a dragon-breath gasp.

I've just wasted my money on something that did nothing but burn my throat and tasted like firewater, she thought bitterly. But she persevered and after a few more sips she started to notice subtle changes. Her shoulders had dropped from around her ears, the knots in her back seemed to be loosening, and the constant gnawing in her head began to dull. Janice relaxed into the beer-stained chair and nodded to herself approvingly.

Well, once you get used to the vile taste I can see why it's so popular. I suppose if it feels like this after one, it must only get better after two.

She was right; the second gin slid down without a fight and the gnawing disappeared. She was seeing everything with new, bright, optimistic eyes.

Abs came to wipe her table. "I haven't seen you in here before," he said.

"No. First time. I'm not a drinker."

"That's what they all say," Abs replied with a conspiratorial wink.

Janice burst out laughing as if this was the funniest thing she'd ever heard. She couldn't stop herself and the unfamiliar sound of her own laughter delighted her.

Suddenly it didn't seem to matter that everything was out of her control. So what? Everything was going to be okay. Janice hadn't felt this relaxed in years and all it had taken was a couple of glasses of this innocuous-looking drink.

She suddenly felt a bit queasy. Her empty stomach was protesting at her liquid lunch. Janice knew it was time to leave.

Blinking in the bright sunlight, she left the pub and popped into the minimart next door. She picked up a loaf and a can of beans, smiling bounteously at the other customers, who gave her a wide berth. On her way to the checkout she passed the heaving shelves of the Bargain Booze aisle, noting the bottle of "Supersaver Gin" that cost barely more than her drinks in the pub.

"What a temptation for the weak," she tutted, walking on defiantly.

16 *the news*

Celia breezed into the flat, late again. She'd done the same for the past three weeks, ever since she'd met Sol, and she didn't care. She wanted Janice to suffer. She was humming something that had lodged itself in her head: one of the R & B tunes on Sol's iPod – catchy but nowhere near as good as her stuff.

I must introduce that boy to some decent music, she thought.

Janice rushed in from the balcony, a cigarette in hand. Her eyes flitted over Celia's body, searching for any cuts or bruises.

"Don't inspect me every time I walk through the door," Celia snapped.

"I'm not, love, honest. I was just thinking how well you look."

This wasn't a complete lie. Over the last few weeks, Janice had noticed a transformation in Celia. She still possessed her inevitable gawkiness, courtesy of her long, gangly limbs, but instead of walking around with her head bowed and shoulders bent, she now held herself up to her full, impressive height. The sparkle of her pale blue eyes was visible now they were no longer clouded by anxiety. Her skin had erupted in freckles from the exposure to the sun, giving it a warm, healthy sheen. Everything about her seemed stronger, more confident, as if at last she was free from fear and comfortable in her skin. Janice noted all of this and felt her stomach knot.

"I got us fish and chips," Janice said with a desperate cheeriness. "I waited so we could have it together. I'll heat it up. I didn't think you'd be back so late."

"I keep telling you not to wait for me. I can sort myself out," Celia said flinging her bag down and heading for the bathroom.

"Will you be long?" Janice asked, biting her lip.

"I'm having a shower. Do I have to ask your permission?" Celia shut the door on her.

Janice waited until the shower had been running for a few minutes before picking up Celia's bag and rifling through it. She pulled out suncream, an empty Coke can, a purse, keys, and the new mobile that Celia refused to answer whenever Janice rang. Janice tried the phone and groaned with disappointment. Celia had locked it, her texts and address book safe from intruder's eyes. Next, Janice pulled out a damp towel. Wrapped inside it were wet shorts and a T-shirt.

What's going on? She couldn't have been swimming. She can't swim and there isn't even a pool around here.

Janice felt at the bottom of the bag and pulled out a hardback notebook.

"Bingo," she whispered triumphantly. She'd been regularly searching Celia's bedroom for a diary and now she thought she held it in her hands. She opened it hurriedly, hearing the squeak of the shower control being turned and the water stopping. But inside, instead of all of Celia's exploits and innermost thoughts, she found delicate sketches of dozens of birds, with sightings dated next to them and details of nests and hatched eggs. Janice was confused; some of the dates went back over two years.

These couldn't have been drawn by Celia.

She flicked through the book and there, on the last pages, two portraits stared back at her. The first was unmistakably of Celia. But it wasn't the face that she allowed Janice to see. These days, when Janice looked at Celia, all she saw disdain and contempt. But this portrait captured a luminous quality in her; carefree and happy, so happy. Janice had almost forgotten what an incredible mile-wide smile Celia possessed. The second portrait wasn't as skilful as the first, but it drew the observer in with the boy's cheeky grin and mischievous eyes.

Janice was so engrossed in these pictures that she didn't hear the bathroom door open.

"What are you doing with my stuff?" roared Celia, charging towards her in a dressing gown, a towel wrapped around her head.

Janice immediately went on the attack. "Who's this boy?" she demanded, holding the notebook aloft as Celia tried to grab it.

"No one. None of your business," she hissed.

"What's all this about? Why have you got wet clothes in here? Where do you go?"

Celia ignored her questions and, snatching the book and her phone, she stormed into her bedroom, shouting through the door, "I'm not telling you anything and if you *ever* go through my stuff again you'll never see me *again*. Do you understand?"

"Don't do this, Celia," Janice pleaded, "you're torturing me. Staying out all day, coming in late. I can't stand not knowing where you go, if you're safe. It's cruel of you!"

There was a stony silence from the other side of the door and Janice knew it was going to be a long, tense night. She made a beeline for the kitchen cupboard, breaking the seal on the bottle of gin by unscrewing the top. She'd decided to buy it for emergencies only; for those times when she desperately needed to stay calm and relax. Now, definitely felt like one of those times.

Celia sat crossed-legged on her bed with her phone. She was seething as she deleted the messages between her and Sol and then began to delete the photos that captured their days at the flooded quarry. It pained her to do it, but she would rather die than have Janice find them.

Celia had spent all those years trapped in the gloomy bubble Janice had made for her, gripped by fear, feeling like a freak, but now she had so many great things to tell: like how, for the first time in her life, she couldn't wait for each new day to begin; like how it felt to have a friend, the most amazing friend, a big, soft kid who made her laugh, who taught her how to climb trees and build campfires, who timed her as she threw herself around their woodland assault course, every day getting faster and faster. A friend who spent hours trying to teach her how to swim and who, every evening, took her back to the estate, pedalling like a maniac, as she clung onto the back of his bike with white-knuckled hands and a racing heart. Just thinking about him made her forget how life was before. But she knew that she could never tell Janice any of this. Sol and the flooded quarry were hers, *all hers,* and Janice must never be allowed to ruin them with her madness and paranoia.

Janice paced the floor of their tatty living room. *What if he's her boyfriend?* she fretted. *She can't, she wouldn't.* She leaned without thinking on the hot radiator and cursed as it branded a red welt onto her hand. *This bloody place,* she grumbled. *Maybe it's time to move on. Get her away from whatever she's up to. Yes, I shouldn't push it though. I'll bide my time, plan a proper move.*

Janice waited half an hour before gingerly knocking on Celia's door.

"Come on, love. You must be starving. Your dinner's here," she said coaxingly, peering around the door.

Celia's stomach rumbled as the smell of fish and chips wafted in. "You haven't even apologized," she grunted.

"I'm sorry, really sorry. I shouldn't have gone through your things. I won't do it again. I know you're a good girl. I know that you won't be up to anything stupid. Now come out and eat. You can have it in front of the telly; there's a new makeover show on."

Janice sat next to her on the sofa and tucked into the food. The atmosphere between them was beginning to thaw. Celia found it too exhausting to stay angry in this oppressive heat.

"This is nice isn't it?" Janice said, patting her on the knee. "You and me watching the telly together – 'chilling out'."

Celia rolled her eyes.

Half an hour later, the woman on the makeover programme had been reduced to tears by the ridiculing presenters and then sliced open by a smarmy surgeon, who sucked bits out of her before stuffing other bits into her and botoxing her face into an expressionless mask. The finale was unveiling her new look to her husband, who was suitably stunned and declared that she looked nothing like the woman he married and he was delighted. As the programme finished, Janice hoisted herself up from the saggy sofa.

"Can I get you anything while I'm up?" she asked.

"No thanks," Celia muttered.

Janice went into the kitchen. Celia switched channels to the news.

"Results published today of preliminary clinical trials on cancer patients point to a potential breakthrough in the fight against the disease. Many in the medical profession are hoping that we could be on the brink of a cure. A British scientist, fifty-four year old Professor Melanie Hudson, has devoted years into engineering a so-called 'smart virus' that, when injected into cancer sufferers, will selectively attack cancerous cells, destroying them, while leaving healthy cells untouched. The virus, which has been named The Saviour Virus, has been shown to successfully eliminate cancerous cells in many forms of cancer. The report shows that most patients involved in the trial have, so far, remained cancer free. Earlier today our reporter, Nick Devaney, spoke to Professor Hudson at her London home."

The image cut to a beautifully furnished sitting room, where a poised, attractive woman sat opposite the reporter. Celia was struck by the impressive figure. Maybe she'd been expecting some eccentric scientist who didn't have the time or head space to even brush her hair, but the woman on the screen oozed elegance. Flawless make-up gave her a dewy complexion and enhanced her fine features. Subtle blonde highlights made her look younger than her years. Her deep brown eyes were framed by dark, arched eyebrows, and her smooth hands, with their manicured nails, rested on her silk skirt. Immediately Celia's thoughts turned to Janice and her corroded, dry hands and bitten nails, her worn face and shrunken body.

"Professor Hudson – do you believe that you may be on the brink of one of the biggest breakthroughs in the history of the fight against cancer?" the reporter began.

"Well, we must remain very cautious – these are only preliminary trials – but the results have been encouraging." She smiled modestly.

"You've devoted your entire career to researching a cure for cancer. Was there ever a time when you felt like giving up?"

"Of course there was. Many a time, when I came to yet another dead end, I felt like I couldn't go on, but then I'd remind myself that the stakes were too high to give up."

"And why do you think you have made this breakthrough with your genetically modified virus, when so many other scientists have failed?" he asked.

"I have the utmost respect for my colleagues and their research but I guess that I just had that luck you need with any research. Once I became convinced that I could engineer a virus that had the potential to eradicate cancerous cells, I persevered, spending years developing and refining it."

"And what about your children? They must be very proud of you." The camera zoomed in on a framed photo on the mantelpiece of two handsome identical boys, who looked about ten years old.

"Oh yes." She beamed at the photo. "And I'm proud of them too. Being an older mother makes you appreciate your children so much more, but it's been difficult for them when their mother always seems to be working. We've all made great sacrifices to get to the stage we are at today. But I believe, that if we can make this work, those sacrifices will have been worth it."

"I'm sure the world would agree," replied the awestruck reporter.

From behind, Celia heard the clink of ice as Janice prepared another drink. Celia couldn't stop herself comparing the two women. This amazing mother of twins on the TV had achieved so much...and then there was *her* mother: what had her crazy mother ever achieved? What had Janice ever done, apart from clean up dirt and fill her lungs with smoke?

"Mum, you should watch this," Celia called, determined that Janice took an interest. "This scientist might actually have discovered a cure for cancer."

"That's good," Janice said, coming to look. "But when are they going to discover a cure for wrinkles?"

Janice's chuckle suddenly became a pained gasp, as if someone had punched her in the stomach. Celia turned around to see Janice's mouth slack, her drink suspended centimetres from her lips. Her hand began to shake uncontrollably, the contents of the glass sloshing over the rim. Celia took hold of Janice's jittering hand and prised the glass out of her grip.

"What's wrong?" she asked anxiously.

Janice steadied herself, taking holding of the back of the sofa. It took a few seconds before she seemed to come round, tearing her eyes away from the TV. She turned her ashen face towards Celia, her mouth now forced into a thin smile.

"It's…it's nothing… My drink…it went down the wrong way. I'm fine," she stammered.

Celia took a cautious sip of the clear liquid. "Yack! What is this?! Gin? Vodka? Since when did you start drinking? No wonder you looked like you were having a mini-fit. You can't go knocking this stuff back. You're not used to it, Mum."

Janice's eyes darted back to the TV screen. The newsreader was now talking about the heatwave.

"Not since 1976 have we experienced such sustained high temperatures, and around the country it seems most people are enjoying this long hot summer…"

"Mum, are you even listening to me?" Celia scolded as if she was telling off a child.

"I just needed a little something to calm my nerves," Janice answered meekly.

"You need tranquillizers to calm *your* nerves," Celia retorted.

Janice turned her agitated eyes on Celia. "Well, maybe if you'd stop running wild I wouldn't be such a mess, would I? We need to get back to how things were – just you and me. Safe and sound."

"Is that what this is all about? You can't cope seeing me happy; you can't cope not being able to control me and screw me up," Celia seethed.

"No! No! But say you hurt yourself, say you bleed?"

"Don't you dare start that again!"

"Celia, please…if you want to help me get better then promise me you'll keep safe – always remember what I've told you to do if you hurt yourself."

"How could I forget? You've been saying it all my life." She mimicked Janice's neurotic tone. "Make sure you cover any injury to try to slow down the bleeding, Celia. Don't let people help you without gloves on, Celia. Always use your first-aid kit, Celia." She paused, anguish swamping her face. "Mum, playing along with your madness isn't going to make you get better. When are you going to get the message? You need professional help."

Janice's head drooped, her body seemed to shrink. "Not now, Celia. I can't handle a lecture now," she whimpered. "I'm not feeling well. I need to go to bed." She shuffled to her room as if she'd aged a hundred years.

17 *close encounter*

"I could do with a drink," said Sol, as they picked their way through the hordes of shoppers filling the city centre streets. The sweltering heat meant that there were acres of flesh on display, in all shapes and sizes. Half the people they passed seemed to be cursing global warming, while the other half were lapping it up.

"Next cafe we see then," answered Celia, swinging her shopping bags.

She'd taken some convincing to make the journey to the city. She hadn't known if she could face the overcrowded bus and couldn't see the point of going anywhere else when they had the flooded quarry. However, Sol had persuaded her that she'd enjoy it and he'd been right. Being here, amongst the buzz of the city, reminded Celia that not everyone had to live in the atmosphere that hung over the Bluebell Estate like a toxic cloud.

"This place looks good," said Celia, walking into a busy, shiny, American-style diner. They ordered two deluxe chocolate milkshakes topped with chocolate-chip ice cream, sprinkles and sauce, and then searched around for seats. They found the only vacant booth in the whole diner and plonked themselves down on the red leather seats. At the table behind them was a gaggle of girls poring excitedly over their purchases, and in the booth in front was a man who was so thickset that he appeared to have no neck. He was sat with his back to them, his head bent over his phone, chomping through a plate of doughnuts and slurping his coffee. Sol and Celia pulled faces at each other, trying to suppress their laughter at the noise of his slurps, but the sound of the chattering cafe soon drowned him out.

Frankie clicked on the last advert on his iPhone. As he rang the number, he prepared himself for the same conversation he'd already had twenty times before.

"Hello, Spotless Cleaning, how may I help?" came a voice.

"Hello," Frankie said, "I'm enquiring about your services."

"Yes sir. Is it a domestic or business property you require cleaning?"

"Domestic. I've used your firm before and was particularly impressed with one of your cleaners. Her name is Janice Frost. Would it be possible to have her again?" he said.

"I'm sorry, sir, we don't have anyone of that name working for us. In fact, I can't remember a Janice Frost ever being on our books. However, we do have some wonderful cleaners and I can guarantee that you'll be happy with their work," the woman replied.

Frankie unceremoniously cut her off.

Running his fingers through his short spiky hair, he let out a groan. That was the last local cleaning firm listed and he hadn't got anywhere. He was tired and fed up. He'd been searching this city for four weeks and yet every avenue he'd tried had led to a dead end. He'd spoken to every housing agency in the city, every housing association, even the homeless hostels, but no one had dealt with the Frosts. He'd walked around dozens of estates, knocking on doors, asking if anyone new had moved into the area recently. He'd handed out too much money for information that had led nowhere.

For the first couple of weeks, in desperation, he'd taken

to waiting in his car outside various secondary schools in case Celia was attending under a different name. He reckoned that if there was a slim chance he might spot Janice coming to collect her then it was worth trying before the schools broke up for the summer. However, this line of investigation had come to an abrupt end when a posse of mothers had rapped on his window and asked who he was waiting for. Frankie quickly made up a name but the women weren't convinced.

"And whose form is he in?" they'd asked.

Frankie said he wasn't sure.

"Listen," they snarled at him, "we've seen you here a few times, watching all the kids coming out, and we're warning you, if we see you here again we'll get the police on you. Do you understand?"

He drove off at speed. He felt he'd hit rock bottom now that people thought he was a pervert.

In other circumstances he would have put a notice in the local paper, with his number and some tale about how he was trying to track them down to inform them of a death in the family. On other cases this strategy had proved fruitful, as sympathetic people rang him with useful information about the whereabouts of the people he was seeking. However, in a case such as this, Frankie couldn't take the chance that the targets might also read the notice and flee the city, leaving him in a worse position than before.

His phone rang. He groaned again. It was Nemo. She'd been phoning daily to check on his progress, each time sounding more frustrated.

"Hello," he said, bracing himself.

"Have you any news for me?" She spoke with forced civility.

"Well, the good news is that I've been able to eliminate numerous lines of inquiry," he said, trying to put a positive spin on things.

"That's the good news?" she said in disgust.

"But I'm making progress each day, getting closer to them. It shouldn't take long now."

"Mr. Byrne, to say that I'm disappointed would be an understatement. Unless you find them soon you can forget about any bonus," she said curtly, putting the phone down.

Frankie slouched in his seat, grumbling to himself. *What does she think I've been doing here – having spa treatments?! I'm working my backside off. Look at the state of me.* He rubbed his expanding belly. *I've aged ten years since I arrived here. She hasn't got a clue how difficult it is to find these two.*

Frankie was fed up. He turned the phone off and rested his aching head on the back of the cushioned seat. His ears immediately picked up the melodic chatter of the couple behind him.

* * *

"Maybe I should get my nose pierced," Celia was saying.

"I wouldn't if I was you. It'll make it hard to pick," Sol replied.

Celia ignored him. "I should do *something* now there's nothing stopping me embracing my inner punk."

"Well, you can't sing and you can't play an instrument, so you're probably ready to form a band."

"Ha, ha, funny boy. Why don't you show me what you've been buying?" she said, nodding at the bulging plastic bag.

"Prepare to be impressed," he announced. "I've purchased some serious weaponry."

"What are you on about?" she sighed.

"Only these beauties," he said, emptying the bag with a clatter. "Pump-action jet water pistols. Reach of six metres. Closest thing you can legally get to a riot squad's water cannons. These things can knock you off your feet."

"And you think you can take me on?" Celia narrowed her eyes.

"I don't *think*, I *know*."

She passed him a small bag. "Well, I've got you a little present."

"Really?" Sol said, surprised. "You shouldn't be buying me presents!"

"I wanted to. I owe you – you've done loads for me."

"I haven't done anything," Sol mumbled.

"Yeah, I suppose you're right; you've only saved my life, tried to teach me how to swim, and let me hang out with you at the best place on earth," Celia said, counting them on her fingers.

"Oh yeah, I have done loads, haven't I?" Sol grinned.

"I'm not joking. If I hadn't met you, I don't know what I would have done." Celia's voice started to crack.

In the booth in front, Frankie found himself unintentionally engaged by their conversation. He shook his head. *Typical female, totally OTT.* Frankie had never been able to understand women. They were a bigger mystery to him than most of his cases. He seemed to make them nervous. He never knew what to say to them. In fact, the only times he felt at ease with women was when he was pretending to be someone else.

"Well, don't get upset about it. I find it just about bearable having you around." Sol's words teased her but, for a fleeting moment, the look in his eyes made Celia forget to breathe. "Anyway," he continued, back to the Sol she knew, "let's see what you've got me."

"Okay." Celia sounded flustered, still trying to work out what had just happened.

Sol pulled out a CD. "*The Best of Punk*," he read, looking dubious.

"You're going to love it. It's loads better than the stuff you listen to."

"I happen to have great taste in music. Punk is just a load of shouting," he replied.

"Please give it a try; I bet you'll be blown away."

"If it'll make you happy, I'll put it on my iPod and give it a listen. Hey…how about I get you an iPod, off my brothers?"

"Your brothers are like Father Christmas – they're always giving you stuff. But why should they give me anything?" Celia asked.

"Because I'll tell them to. It's called blackmail. They'll do whatever I say. A few months ago, I followed them to their lock-up and saw that it was full of nicked gear."

"What! They steal things?" Celia said, outraged.

"No, they only fence it for some regulars in the pub they work at."

"Which pub?"

"The one in the precinct."

"You've never told me they work there!"

"You never asked."

"But I've seen them," said Celia excitedly. "You don't take after them at all. They're massive blokes, aren't they?"

"They may be massive but they're still scared of my mum; that's why they give me things, so that I keep my mouth shut."

Frankie couldn't help chuckling to himself, remembering how terrified he'd always been of his mum finding out he was up to no good. She may have been half his size, but she had a clout on her that felt like being hit with a shovel.

"Oh," Celia said with an air of disapproval. An uneasy silence was only broken by the noise of them sucking up the last drops of their milkshakes.

"You don't approve do you?" Sol said.

"Well, it's not exactly the right thing to do, is it? Accepting bribes of stolen goods to keep your mouth shut," she said haughtily.

"Okay then, Miss Self Righteous. What about you? Where are you getting all your money from?"

"It's pocket money from my mum."

"You seem to be getting a lot of pocket money lately."

"What are you talking about? It's only a few tenners."

"It's a lot out of your mum's wages."

"So?" Celia shrugged.

"So, you're fleecing her. You know that she'll give you whatever you want because she's terrified she's going to lose you."

"Yeah. So what? She owes me big time."

"You're exploiting her."

"She exploited me all my life. Are you expecting me to feel bad about taking her guilt money?"

"You know your mum's got problems."

"She deserves to suffer," Celia said half-heartedly.

"Maybe she's suffered enough. She sounds like she's losing it."

"She lost it years ago, but yeah...you're right, she's not getting any better and her bottle of gin isn't helping. She's not eating properly and she doesn't sleep – I can hear her tossing and turning all night. She keeps getting to work late. She's already had a written warning from her boss."

"Then you need to cut her some slack before it's too late. Stop her worrying so much; at least phone her during the day to let her know that you're okay."

Celia hesitated. She wanted to punish Janice so much for all she'd put her through, but even though she'd tried to harden her heart, she was finding it increasingly painful to watch Janice falling apart.

"Okay. I'll phone her, but only once a day. I don't care how mental she is, I'm not letting her control me again."

Sol stood up. "Come on. If we go back now I'll have time to annihilate you in the battle of the Super Soakers and we could probably fit in a swim."

"You can hardly call my doggy-paddle 'swimming'," Celia said despondently.

"You're doing fine. In fact you're probably ready to go out of your depth," Sol said.

"No way," Celia protested. "I'm nowhere near ready."

"Tell you what – if you swim out of your depth, I'll let you have my share of the marshmallows."

"You'll have to do better than that," she said, heading for the door.

Frankie glanced up from his coffee as the teenagers passed. He was curious to see this pair, kidding themselves that they could be just friends. He felt like putting them straight – with all those raging hormones, it was bound to end in tears.

He'd expected the boy to look older, but his bright eyes seemed more like those of an excitable kid than a cynical adolescent, and apart from his voice having broken, his skinny frame and baby-smooth face showed no signs of being in the usual teenage turmoil. And the girl… Frankie's mind raced as his eyes registered her appearance.

Short, thick, orange plaits stuck out from under her black baseball cap. He noted her almond slice of a face, swamped by saucer eyes, broad nose and wide mouth; her long, skinny legs and telescopic arms gave her the air of a baby giraffe.

Striking, that's how the old woman in Wales had described her. *Tall with orange hair and very striking*, he mused.

Celia opened the diner door. "I'll only swim out of my depth if you give me the extra marshmallows *and* admit that my music is loads better than yours."

"No way, Celia Frost! I don't want to see you drown that much," he replied, following her out.

The mug of coffee fell from Frankie's hand as he shot up from his seat, the contents of his stomach audibly sloshing around with the sudden movement. "The boy just called her Celia Frost, didn't he?" he said out loud to the bemused customers. "I heard him say Celia Frost!"

In his haste to extract himself from the table, he upset everything on it, causing more of a stir amongst the customers. As he reached the door, he found himself facing a barrage of middle-aged women laden down with bags and in need of a sit down. They marched into the diner in an unbroken line, like a Roman legion.

"Is there a bloody coach party of you?" snarled Frankie.

"Manners don't cost anything," snapped back a woman, deliberately stopping in the doorway to block him.

"You're going to cost me my job if you don't get out of my way." He pushed her out of the doorway, ignoring the tirade of protests as he waded through the women and into the steaming pedestrianized street. He stood on his tiptoes, looking left and then right over the sea of shoppers' heads. He spotted them. Celia's black cap and orange plaits were unmistakable, bobbing up and down through the crowd. He locked his sights on his target and began his pursuit. When he was a comfortable distance behind them he slowed his step and discreetly kept pace with them. He could see them chatting and laughing as they strolled along, oblivious to his presence. They took a sharp turn down a narrow cobbled lane lined with shops. The crowds were less dense here and Frankie had a clear view of them. However, halfway down the lane, Celia suddenly turned around and began to walk back towards him.

How did she know? He hurriedly went through his repertoire of responses for when he was challenged. Celia was now only two metres away from him but she didn't say anything – she didn't even look at him. With relief, he realized that she'd turned around to look in one of the shops.

"I really need a costume," she called to Sol. "I can't keep swimming in my shorts and T-shirt."

They both headed into the shop as Frankie put his head down and crossed to the other side of the lane. He turned his back to them and stared in the shop window opposite. In it he could see the reflection of the sports shop and observe everyone coming in and out. Then Frankie noticed that the window he had to pretend to be so fascinated by was a women's lingerie boutique. As the minutes ticked slowly by he could see the lingerie assistants glowering at him from behind the window display of knickers and bras.

At long last he saw Celia and Sol's reflection leaving the sports shop and continuing up the lane. At the end of the lane was one of the city's busiest junctions. Celia and Sol darted across it, dodging the lanes of fume-belching traffic as if they were invincible. This left Frankie still on the other side of the road and rapidly losing sight of them. Every time he went to put his foot off the pavement another car roared by and he had to retreat. A pedestrian crossing lay a hundred metres or so ahead, but by the time he'd used that they'd be gone. In desperation he launched himself onto the road, both hands held out towards the oncoming traffic, causing cars to screech to a halt. Furious drivers pounded their horns and hurled abuse at him.

Once on the other side, he ran in the direction that they'd taken, but he had no idea whether or not they'd turned down one of the many side streets he was passing. Now, even on tiptoe, it was impossible to see over the burgeoning crowds. He needed to be higher, he needed something to stand on. That's when he spied the council workers fixing a street lamp further along the pavement; their yellow elevator ladder was just perfect. He ran up to them and flashed an ID card.

"Listen, I'm in pursuit of a suspect; mugged an old lady. I've lost sight of him. I really need to use your ladder," Frankie said, with such urgency and authority that the workers immediately responded by putting him in the caged platform and raising it as high as it could go. From six metres up, Frankie had a bird's-eye view and spotted

Celia and Sol just about to turn towards the main city square.

"Okay, I've seen him. Get this thing down now," he barked at the workers. He climbed out of the cage and sprinted through the crowd, pushing out of the way anyone who slowed him down. His shirt was clinging to his sweating body as he panted his way to the city square, just in time to see them disappear into a mass of people. He pursued them, barging through the crowd, but came to an abrupt standstill when he found himself in the middle of a huge circle of spectators.

"G'day to you, mate," said a bronzed young Australian man, slapping Frankie on the back. "Ladies and gentlemen, boys and girls, please give this brave man a big clap for volunteering."

The encircling crowd clapped encouragingly. Frankie looked around, bemused. There were four young men in the circle with him, but he was the only one not wearing a shiny skintight jumpsuit.

"What's your name, mate?" said the Aussie loudly.

"Sorry, I've got to go," said Frankie, trying to move, but the young man held his arm.

"Come on. Don't be shy. Tell us your name," he insisted.

Frankie looked around the audience and spotted Celia and Sol looking back at him. A couple of metres from them stood a police officer, giving Frankie an encouraging smile.

Maybe I should play along, he thought. *At least I can keep an eye on the girl from here.*

"Paul," Frankie mumbled.

"Well, Paul, put your stuff down. We just need you to stand in the centre here, legs together, arms by your side, but stay very, very still," said the Aussie cheerfully.

Frankie reluctantly complied.

"I think that we should hot things up a bit. Would you like that?" the Aussie shouted to the audience.

"Yes!" they all chorused back.

"Okay, then," he said and the four performers pulled out two batons each from a bucket full of liquid and proceeded to set light to them. Frankie couldn't believe his eyes.

"No way are you going to use them near me," he said tensely.

"There's nothing to it, mate. We've done it a hundred times and only ninety volunteers ended up in hospital."

The audience were laughing but Frankie wasn't.

"Come on. A big strong bloke like you can't wimp out. You'll be fine just as long as you don't move a muscle; we wouldn't want to toast you," the Aussie guy said.

The ever-growing audience was getting excited and shouted at Frankie, "Come on. You can do it."

Frankie's macho pride was at stake, so he remained in position as the four performers formed a crossroads around him and started the crowd clapping to their beat before counting, "One, two, three…" On the next beat, four flaming batons came hurtling through the air towards him. Two whizzed past either side of his face, flames licking at his ears, while from the other directions, one skimmed past his belly, and another seared the seat of his trousers. The audience gasped and Frankie held his breath and stomach in as a barrage of flying fire kept rocketing past him in time to the claps of the crowd. He got a whiff of singed hair as one baton veered far too close to his head. He refused to close his eyes but instead fixed his stare ahead, where Celia and Sol stood in the crowd, clapping in awe as the jugglers skilfully caught the handle of each burning baton while simultaneously tossing the next one a whisker past Frankie's statue-like body to their partner. But Frankie was horrified to see Sol tap his watch and gesture to Celia to go.

"If we don't go now we'll miss our bus," Sol said.

Frankie was stuck, unable to move a muscle unless he wanted to be barbecued. He could only watch helplessly as they made their way out of the crowd and out of sight. Meanwhile, the audience were *ooh*ing and *aah*ing as the flames continued to pass dangerously close to Frankie, who looked like he might spontaneously combust with fury.

At last the batons stopped whizzing past and the performers ran and put their arms around their volunteer, whose bulky body quivered with a mixture of anger and the effort of staying so still.

"Let's hear it for Paul. What a good sport!" There was a roar of appreciation from the crowd, which conveniently covered Frankie's words as he hissed to the jubilant jugglers, "If I ever see any of you again, I'll put those flaming batons of yours where the sun don't shine, do you understand?"

The jugglers quickly pulled out of the group hug, looking less cheerful. Frankie pushed his way through the back-slapping crowd and out into the middle of the city square, where he stood, futilely scouring the area, as hundreds of sunburned shoppers swarmed past him like an army of red ants.

18 *celia meets the family*

It was sunset when Sol suggested that they ought to be getting home. Celia was reluctant to leave. She was happy just lying on the sun-warmed slabs. This was her favourite time of the day to be at the quarry; it was at its most magical as the sun turned orange and the scent of the forest reeled from the day's heat, sending the birds into a frenzy of song.

"We've still got some marshmallows to toast," she said, poking the fire.

"Well, you shouldn't have them. You didn't even swim out of your depth."

"I tried my best," she protested. "I did it for a second."

"Yeah, a nanosecond."

"It's not my fault. It's just that as soon as I can't feel the bottom I start to sink," she said, pouring water on the fire.

"It's just about confidence, Celia. No one does a better doggy-paddle than you," he laughed.

"You may be better than me at swimming, but who's the best at climbing trees?" she retorted, crossing her arms.

"I admit, you are pretty good, but that's only because you learned from the master," he said, with a martial arts-style bow.

Celia rolled her eyes, giving him a shove. "Come on, Jackie Chan. Let's get going."

They made their way through the trees to where Sol kept his bike. Minutes later, they were tearing down the road at breakneck speed, Celia clinging onto the bike seat. Suddenly Sol swerved to avoid a pothole. Celia grabbed for his waist as she felt the bike leaning, dangerously off-centre. He managed to right the bike without stopping.

"Sorry about that," he shouted back to her. She let go of him and put her hands back on the seat.

Sol looked over his shoulder, smiling. "You can keep holding on to me if you like."

She returned her hands to his waist, her face plastered with a wind-set smile.

As he pedalled along the main road into the estate, Sol spotted a group of hooded lads in the distance. They were all leaning against a wall, swigging from lager cans, glazed-eyed with boredom. Sprawled at their feet lay a Rottweiler, panting with thirst, its dry, pink tongue lolling out of its cavernous mouth. The gang were too far away for Sol to identify them, but he'd lived on the Bluebell Estate long enough to know that it wasn't worth taking any risks. Like a Venus flytrap, it might only take an unwitting victim to cross their path to spark them into action. Sol took a sharp turn through the nearest passageway.

When they were around the corner from Sol's house they dismounted and were about to part company when Sol suddenly became flustered.

"Get down!" he said.

"Why?" asked Celia.

"I've just seen my brothers. I don't think they saw us."

"Hey, Sol," a deep voice boomed from behind. "Sol, wait up!"

Seconds later, hands squeezed his shoulders and two mountainous young men bounded in front of them.

"Hey, little brother, aren't you going to introduce us?" One of them grinned, holding his hand out to Celia.

"Celia, this is Abs and that one's Yacob," Sol mumbled, pointing at them dismissively.

"Sol never told us he had a girlfriend," Yacob said with a schoolboy smirk.

"We're just friends!" Sol and Celia protested in unison.

"Oh, yeah! Sure!" Abs said teasingly. "Well, what have you two 'friends' been up to?"

"Just hanging around." Sol shrugged.

"Where are you going now?"

"What is this – an interrogation?" Sol glared at them.

"I'm on my way home," Celia answered, amused by the childish pair despite her embarrassment.

"Well we can't have that," Yacob said. "Why don't you come to ours? Mum would love to meet you. Wouldn't she, Abs?"

"Oh yeah," Abs enthused. "It'd make her day."

"Get lost," Sol grunted. "She has to get home. Don't you, Celia?"

"Well…I suppose I could come round for a bit," Celia replied, curious to meet Sol's family.

"Brilliant! Let us escort you, mademoiselle," Abs said with a flourish, as he and Yacob linked arms with her and Sol groaned with embarrassment.

From the exterior, the Girans' house looked like any other on the soulless estate, but once across the threshold, the bleakness of the outside immediately melted away. Celia's eyes were soothed by the rich hues of the terracotta walls. Thick woven rugs felt luxurious underfoot and tapestries adorned the walls, depicting scenes from a faraway land. Colourful baskets nestled around the large television and the windowsill was adorned with a cross of green, yellow and red. On a shelf, in pride of place, incense candles flanked a framed photo of a slight, youthful-looking man, sporting a moustache. He had the same bright eyes as Sol. She inhaled the candles' heady cocktail of cloves and cinnamon, but as Sol's brothers opened the kitchen door, more mouth-watering aromas wafted teasingly into the room. Abs and Yacob sauntered into the kitchen and stuck their fingers into a pan of spicy stew, bubbling on the stove.

"Hey! Get your dirty fingers out of my cooking." A tall, broad woman appeared, clothed in a long, heavy white dress bordered with bright stitching and ornate crosses. Her hair was swathed in a high white headscarf, which added to her stature, and Celia immediately got the impression that this woman was more than a match for her overgrown sons.

She puffed out her already round cheeks. "I hope you two have been good today," she said to the huge men as if they were little boys. "Every day I pray that my boys are keeping out of trouble."

"How could you doubt us, Emama? You know what

172

angels we are." Abs and Yacob planted kisses on her cheeks.

"Emama, we've brought someone to meet you," Yacob said, beckoning Celia out of the doorway, where she'd been shielded from the mother's view.

"Hello," Celia said shyly.

"Hello, darling. I'm Mrs. Giran." The woman's whole face smiled. "How do you know these terrible boys?"

"Oh no, Emama. This is Celia, Sol's girlfriend," said Abs mischievously.

Sol ran to defend himself. "They're kidding, Mum. We're just friends. Aren't we, Celia?"

"Yeah, of course. We just hang out together," she said, not knowing where to look.

Mrs. Giran rolled her exasperated eyes at her big sons and addressed Celia.

"Please ignore my silly boys. I'm still waiting for them to grow up," she said. "It's so lovely to meet one of Sol's friends at last. He's never brought any of them home. I was beginning to think he was ashamed of his old Emama."

"I love your house, Mrs. Giran," Celia said quickly, to cover Sol's embarrassment.

"Thank you, Celia. I've tried my best with it. It's good that the boys are surrounded by memories of our homeland. As the years slip by, I worry that they will forget."

"No chance of that. Not with you going on about it all the time," Yacob sighed.

"How can I not, with your father still there?" she replied, hurt by the remark.

"Sol told me about his dad. I'm really sorry," Celia said.

"Don't be, Celia. I'm going to find him one day and we'll all be together again," she said, brightening again. "What about your family?"

"Not much to say really," Celia censored herself. "It's just me and my mum. We live in Tower Two. We haven't been there long."

"And you and Sol – how did you meet? Are you in the same class at school?"

"Same year," Celia said, trying to avoid lying.

"And how's he getting on at school? He never tells me anything," Mrs. Giran asked.

Sol shot a look of panic at Celia. "Mum," he jumped in, "Celia has to get home now. She's starving."

"Why didn't you say?" his mother exclaimed. "Celia, you must stay for dinner. It's all ready and I'd love to chat. Why don't you phone your mother and check if it's okay?"

Celia ignored Sol's face, which was imploring her to go. She didn't have to be asked twice. "Thanks. I'd love to," she answered. "But I really don't need to phone my mum. She won't mind."

19   *the call*

Frankie began to wonder how he was going to get back to his hotel. He was having trouble even remembering the name of it. He contemplated ordering another whiskey but saw the barman eyeing him up with a look that said, *Don't even think about it.*

He laid his head down on the beer-soaked bar. That felt better. The room wasn't spinning so much now.

"I hate this case," he muttered to himself. "Seeing her like that was like being handed the winning lottery ticket, then losing it."

What more could he do? He'd already gone back to the American diner to ask whether they knew anything about the kids, but they'd never seen them before today. He'd even gone and enquired in the sports shop, but they were a dozy lot who couldn't even remember her coming in.

His head was throbbing from going over and over the conversation he'd heard; trying to remember every word, hoping that there'd be some clue. But what had he learned? That the girl liked punk, that her mum was drinking too much, that the boy had dodgy brothers who worked in a pub. So what! There were hundreds of pubs in the city and he didn't even know the boy's name. Then there was that bit about the boy saving her life and showing her the best place on earth. Well, you had to take that with a pinch of salt. Frankie knew how girls exaggerated. He reckoned that the "best place on earth" could be any old dump she had some romantic idea about. And then they were going to swim, but so what? What should he do – hang around in all the local leisure centres and get accused of being a pervert again? No! It was ridiculous. He could waste months chasing up one dead end lead after another.

His mobile rang and he fumbled around in his pockets for it. Nemo flashed up on the screen.

No way am I answering that, Frankie thought to himself. *What am I going to tell her?* "Well, madam," Frankie rehearsed, "I've got some good news and some bad news. I've seen the girl, but I lost her and haven't got a clue where she's gone." *Yes that was bound to go down well.*

He waited until the phone stopped ringing and tried to negotiate climbing off the bar stool. It had been a lot easier getting on it, but now the floor kept moving. He'd had enough of this case. It was affecting his health. For weeks now he'd been living off substandard cakes and fast food. He missed the delicious pastries from the bakery below his office; he missed his favourite takeaways that he lived off when he was home. He was sick of the dingy hotel room with its lumpy mattress. He longed for his own bed in his bachelor pad. No one could ever describe Frankie's flat as homely, and it lacked a certain level of cleanliness, but it had all the necessities of life: his forty-inch plasma screen TV, his surround sound home cinema system, his state-of-the-art music system, and enough computer games to keep him company for years. Thinking about home made Frankie even more melancholy and he came to a decision.

"I'm going to pack this case in," he declared to himself while lurching to a nearby table. "That's it. I'm going home. I don't need this hassle. I'll pick up other cases, spy on a few cheating husbands; they always pay pretty well and aren't half the work of this. So what if the client doesn't like it? That's her problem. She can pay me what she owes and find some other sucker."

The phone rang out from his pocket. He ignored it. *It'll be her hassling me again. I'll tell her my decision in the morning. I just need to lie down now.* But seconds later the phone went yet again. *She's not going to stop until I answer.* Frankie growled in irritation.

"What do you want?" he said grumpily, but the voice that replied was not the one he'd expected.

"Oh...hello," came a frail, lilting voice. "Is that Frankie?"

Frankie hesitated. "Who wants to know?" he replied.

"It's me, Mary," said the voice.

Frankie's mind was a blank. "Listen, love," he slurred, "I don't know how you got my number but I don't know any Marys."

"Well, you do sound different to how I remember. Do you deliver parcels by any chance?"

Frankie's head hurt. What was this senile old woman going on about? "Parcels? You want me to deliver a parcel?"

"No. *You* wanted to deliver a parcel...to Janice Frost; does that ring any bells?"

Frankie shook his head, trying to clear the fog. "Did you just say Janice Frost?" he asked tentatively.

"Yes dear, it's me, Mary, their old neighbour. I'm sorry to call so late, but I've been searching and searching for the piece of paper you left your number on and I've just found it. You'll never guess where I'd put it."

Mary paused to give him time to have a guess, but Frankie didn't answer as he was frantically rifling through his befuddled brain, trying to recall the details of his encounter with the woman. It was an occupational hazard trying to remember which lies he'd told to which people.

"Oh, can't you guess?" Mary said, sounding a little disappointed. "Well, I'll tell you then. I'd put it in the pocket of my dressing gown, but then I got a new one the other week – it was an absolute bargain, I would have been a fool not to buy it. So anyway, I put my old dressing gown away in the wardrobe and of course completely forgot that I'd put your piece of paper in there. Aren't I a twit?" she ended cheerfully.

Mary's waffling had given Frankie time to get his act together. "You're no twit, Mary. Sorry I was a bit abrupt. I think I'm coming down with the flu," he said, his voice as rough as sandpaper.

"Oh, you poor dear. You sound dreadful. Well hopefully I can cheer you up," Mary said.

"How can you do that?" Frankie said, dreading the thought that she might have just rung for a chat to fill her lonely evening.

"Have you delivered that precious parcel to Janice yet?" she asked.

"No. I'm still trying to find her," he answered.

"Well then, you might want to write this down, because I've got her new address here," Mary said proudly.

Frankie convinced himself that he must be in the

middle of a cruel drunken dream. "Mary," he whispered into the phone, "are you really there?"

Peals of laughter greeted his question. "Oh, you silly boy, of course I'm here."

"But how have you got their address?" he said, still bewildered.

"Celia wrote to me. She was so upset at leaving like that and not getting a chance to say goodbye. I told you she was a lovely girl, didn't I? Anyway, they're living somewhere called the Bluebell Estate; sounds nice, doesn't it? Now, if you're ready, I'll give you their address."

Frankie couldn't control himself. He started to shake with laughter, tears streaming down his face.

"Frankie, what's the matter? Are you laughing or crying?" Mary asked in alarm.

"Mary, I think I love you," Frankie howled.

"Oh! That's nice, dear," replied a rather startled Mary. "Now just you make sure that you get that parcel to Janice. Won't she get a lovely surprise?"

20 *under surveillance*

Early the next morning, despite a splitting hangover, Frankie Byrne woke in a triumphant mood. He phoned Nemo and proudly told her the news. She tried to maintain a businesslike tone but couldn't disguise the excitement in her voice. Frankie didn't bother telling her that an old lady had phoned and just given him their address. Instead he emphasized the painstaking lengths he'd gone to to get this result and how priceless his expertise was.

"Don't worry. You'll be well rewarded for your efforts," Nemo replied. "But there is more to do yet. You need to move quickly to resolve this case."

"Of course," he said. "I'll take photos of the targets

for you. I'll make one hundred per cent sure we have the right people."

"I need more than that," she said. "I want you to put them under surveillance. I need to be sure that they haven't told anyone else about their situation."

"What situation?" Frankie asked.

"I can't divulge details," she replied.

"So how will I know if they're talking about it," he asked, confused.

"You'll know," she said emphatically. "And remember, Mr. Byrne, whatever you may hear you must pass onto me, and only me, and then you must forget you ever heard it. Do I make myself clear?"

"Yeah, sure – I know the score. I've dealt with cases like this before, you know," he replied indignantly.

"No, Mr. Byrne. I doubt that you have ever dealt with a case like *this* before," she said.

Frankie packed all his equipment into his car and drove out to the Bluebell Estate, which was dominated by the four ugly tower blocks. He parked close to the towers and, pulling the peak of his baseball cap low to shield his face, he crossed the concrete square that lay in the middle of them, surreptitiously noting all the CCTV cameras that were trained on every entrance. He assessed that Bluebell

Tower Two would be easy enough to access, but with all the security cameras, he couldn't risk breaking into the Frosts' flat. He'd have to come up with a convincing cover story to work his way in there and do what he had to do.

He needed to get a feel for the area and so he decided to pick his way through the estate.

What a dump, he thought as he passed a burned-out car and yet another smashed-up phonebox. The maze of identical slit-windowed houses gave the estate the look of a massive prison compound. This impression was reinforced by the pockets of people, young and old, who seemed to be aimlessly hanging around, killing time, as if they were inmates in an exercise yard.

As Frankie walked through one of the passageways, a gaggle of youths entered from the other end: swaggering young boys with their arms draped around an array of gum-chewing girls. Each female sported scraped-back hair tied into a tight ponytail, and make-up so thick that it managed to bury their youth and any natural beauty beneath it. The boys walked past, giving the big man an obligatory hostile look. Frankie reciprocated their stare and watched in amusement as they struggled to maintain their nonchalant pace out of the passageway.

Dodging piles of baking dog muck, Frankie made his way to the shopping precinct. Here he went from shop to shop, pretending to browse, while all the time listening in to people's conversations. He'd hoped to glean some useful information, but all he heard was talk of bad kids, bad husbands and bad debts.

He came to the bookies and decided it was worth a try. Gambling was one of the few vices that Frankie had managed to avoid. He knew only too well the consequences that visited people who'd fallen under its spell. He'd worked many cases for turf accountants, locating terrified gamblers who'd gone to ground after accumulating huge debts. Frankie knew that the bookies always got their pound of flesh in the end.

The bookies was packed with men shouting at TV screens which hung from the walls. Alternate blasts of hot then icy air billowed out of the dodgy air conditioning. Frankie watched the race's progress on the faces of the punters, as they transformed from hope and excitement to despair and anger. Betting slips were ripped up as they cursed the old nag they'd spent their last pounds on.

"Seeing as you take every penny we've got, the least you could do is get some decent air conditioning. It's bad enough sweating to death in my own flat, without having to come here to do it," shouted a disgruntled punter to the man behind the counter.

"Haven't they sorted out that heating yet, Roy?" The bookie tutted. "You should get on to them."

"What do you think I've been doing? Fifteen times I've

called them. It's been weeks. The whole building is like a bloody hothouse; hundreds of people suffering, and all they keep saying is that they're 'working on it'." Roy was getting increasingly irate. "They treat us worse than vermin."

Frankie chipped in. "You should go to the local paper. That'd get them moving."

"Yeah." Roy nodded. "That's not a bad idea."

"Which building is it anyway?" Frankie enquired casually.

"Tower Two. I tell you, the whole place needs demolishing. We'd be better off living in cardboard boxes," Roy ranted.

Frankie turned to leave.

"Aren't you going to have a flutter?" the bookie called to him.

"Nah, it's a mug's game," Frankie answered, deep in thought.

He went in the newsagent's next door and bought a paper, before returning to the foot of the tower blocks. He positioned himself out of sight of the CCTV cameras but still with a clear view of the entrance to Tower Two. Putting on his sunglasses, he opened his paper, keeping one eye on the entrance. For over an hour he watched people coming in and out of the building until, with great relief, he saw Celia emerge. She gambolled across the square, a bulky bag slung over her shoulders. Just then, a pleading voice rang out from the sky.

"Celia, you will phone me today, won't you? Don't let me worry, love."

Frankie looked up and saw a woman calling from the very highest row of balconies. She was still in her dressing gown and waving at Celia. But the girl didn't look up; she just kept walking across the square and out of sight.

Frankie decided it was time to make his move. He marched back to his car and, after looking around to check he wasn't being watched, he rifled through his bag of outfits until he found a boiler suit. Next, he peeled off the appropriate labels from his sheets of names and companies and proceeded to stick them onto a photo ID card. From the glove compartment he unwrapped three thumbnail-sized black discs, which he held delicately in his huge hands.

"In you go, my beauties," he said, carefully placing them in a metal toolbox. He stepped out of the car transformed into Paul Garner, Heating Engineer and, taking a moment, he mentally prepared himself for his performance.

Taking the lift to the twentieth floor was a deeply unpleasant experience. It seemed to take an eternity to ascend. The silver interior was covered in graffiti and smeared with what smelled like the remnants of a curry. Frankie struggled to hold his breath until the doors eventually juddered open at his destination.

He knocked at flat 2011. It took a couple of minutes before the door was opened a fraction. Janice's face peered out from behind the chain.

"Ms. Frost?" Frankie inquired.

"Who wants to know?" came the abrupt response.

"I'm Paul, the heating engineer," he said, showing his ID badge. "I've been sent out by building maintenance to have a look at your radiators."

Janice immediately let him in. "Thank God," she said. "Do you have any idea how unbearable it's been in here? We're having the hottest summer on record and our bloody heating has been on full blast day and night."

"I know, Madam," he answered. "But the company have got their act together now and hopefully it'll soon be sorted."

He gave Janice a quick look. This was definitely the woman in the grainy photo, but the years hadn't been kind to her. She looked worn out, shrivelled up – but there was still something about her, Frankie thought, something quite appealing behind her bloodshot eyes.

Janice felt his eyes pass over her and she suddenly became conscious of what a sight she must look.

"Sorry about this," she said, clutching her dressing gown to her neck. "I'm not feeling so well this morning. I'm running late for work." She bustled around the sitting room, grabbing the half empty bottle of gin from the coffee table and whisking it into the kitchen.

"I'll be out of your way soon. I just want to check the radiators," he said.

"I just need to get ready," she said, disappearing into her bedroom.

As soon as she was out of sight Frankie got to work, and within minutes he'd planted the three magnetic room bugs: one behind the back of the living room radiator, one behind the bathroom radiator and the final one under Celia's bedside table.

When Janice emerged he was on his knees with a wrench, pretending to be working on the radiator.

"Would you like a cup of tea?" she asked.

"That would be lovely. Milk and three sugars, please."

She busied herself in the kitchen and soon after presented him with a mug of tea.

"I don't know how you've stood it in here," he said, mopping his brow. "Must be terrible. Is it just you who lives here?"

"No. I live with my daughter."

"Is that her in the photos?" he asked, pointing to the wall full of pictures.

Janice nodded proudly.

"Lovely looking girl," Frankie said. "Looks about the same age as mine."

"Oh," said Janice, suddenly perking up, "have you got a daughter too?"

"Yeah, Megan. She's fourteen, but I don't know where my sweet little girl's gone; she's turned into a right stroppy madam."

Janice nodded in enthusiastic agreement. "I know what you mean. What happens to them?"

"I blame all those raging hormones – turns them into monsters for a few years. I think they should be put into hibernation until they're eighteen and have finished being screaming drama queens," Frankie said.

Janice found herself laughing.

"Don't get me wrong. I love her to bits and I only get to see her at weekends so I want every minute with her to be special," he said, straining with emotion.

"Don't you live with her mother then?" Janice wasn't usually one to ask or answer questions, but she was warming to this man.

"Nah. We split up. I found her cheating on me. I wanted Megan to live with me, but you know what the courts are like; they always give the kid to the mother, no matter what." His voice faltered.

Janice surprised herself, welling up with sympathy for this stranger. "I'm sorry," she said gently. "I'm sure that your daughter enjoys her time with you."

"Thanks," he said, looking embarrassed. "I'm sorry

about getting a bit emotional on you."

"Not at all. It's nice to meet a father who cares so much about their child." Janice smiled.

Frankie collected up his tools. "Well the bad news is there's no way I can fix your heating today. It's a much bigger job than they told me. It looks like the main boiler for the whole building will need replacing," he said apologetically.

"It's not your fault," Janice said sweetly. "It was nice to meet you anyway."

Frankie walked out, giving what he hoped was a winning smile. "It was a real pleasure to meet you too," he beamed, causing Janice's grey cheeks to flush.

Once Frankie was back in his car, he put in his earpieces and fiddled around with the multi-band receiver until he'd tuned into the correct frequency. Over the airwaves, the bugs transmitted the sound of Janice moving around the flat, followed by the sound of her singing "Somewhere, Beyond the Sea" in a surprisingly sweet voice.

It brought a smile to Frankie's face. *I love this Sinatra song*, he thought to himself. He started to sing along, his baritone voice performing a duet with the unsuspecting Janice.

Minutes later he heard the door being shut and the

airwaves fell silent. He knew that he probably had a long wait until he'd hear anything else. Making himself comfortable, he put his sunglasses over his eyes, and settled back in his seat. Within minutes the inside of the car was rattling with his snores.

21 *the bluebell inn*

It was 7.20 p.m. and Frankie was just opening a polystyrene box containing a congealed burger in a rock-hard bun, when, through his earpieces, came the sound of a key in a lock. "At last," he said.

There was the sound of the door opening and then the squeak of the shower control being turned, immediately followed by the thundering of water onto the bath. "Stinking chickens," he could hear Janice complain as she scrubbed herself clean.

After dressing, she left a message for Celia.

"Hi, Celia. You haven't phoned me since lunchtime. Are you coming home soon? Love you." Her voice was full of forced cheeriness.

There was a ping, indicating that her microwave dinner was ready, and then, Frankie assumed, she must have settled down in front of the TV, as the only sound coming through was shouting from some soap opera.

By the time he heard another key in the lock it was two hours later and Janice had succumbed to a couple of large gins, muttering something about "Dutch courage" as she gulped them down.

"Mum," he heard a girl's voice call out. He recognized Celia's voice from the diner.

Janice tried to make her interrogation breezy. "Hiya, love. Had a nice day? You're a bit late, aren't you? What have you been up to?"

Celia ignored her questions. "You seem a bit merry," she said suspiciously.

Janice tutted. "No, I'm not at all. I'm probably just a bit excited. I wanted to talk to you…about this place."

"This place? This flat?" Celia asked.

"Yeah. This flat, Bluebell Towers, the whole estate. It's not a great place, is it?"

"Ha! That's the understatement of the year."

"Well, I've realized I made a big mistake, dragging you here. This environment is no good for you. Now don't go panicking," she said quickly, looking at Celia's stormy face. "I'm not suggesting we pack up and leave right now. We can both plan this move; find a decent area, with nice neighbours and good schools. And, what if I promise to let you go back to school, Celia? Hey, isn't that what you want? I know you're angry with me, but I'm offering to make things up to you."

Celia was completely thrown. "I don't know what to say. This place *is* a dump and, yeah, I want to get my exams… but there's something here I wouldn't want to leave."

"It's that boy, isn't it?" Janice tried to sound sympathetic. "Well, you'll be able to stay in touch – phone, text – but to be honest, Celia, a few weeks away from this place and you'll probably have forgotten all about him."

Janice had blown it.

Celia bristled. "Yeah! You'd love that, wouldn't you? Take me away from the only friend that I've ever had. You know, for a second there, I actually thought that you were trying to do what was best for me. But I should have guessed that you were just trying to drag me back into your twisted little world."

"No, Celia," Janice said desperately. "This *is* what's best for you. Things are more dangerous than ever now."

"Oh my God, Mum!" Celia sounded despairing. "You're just madder than ever!" And with that, Frankie heard her stomp into her bedroom. Seconds later, raucous music blasted out from the CD player that sat directly over the bedroom bug.

In response, the sound of the TV soared as Janice

competed with the music's volume. The ear-splitting cacophony poured into Frankie's headphones. He tore them out of his ears.

Janice caved in first. The TV went dead and she shouted, "I'm going out. I can't stand this."

"Where are you going?" Celia shouted back.

"None of your business – see how you like it."

Celia snorted with contempt. "Well, it's not difficult to work out. It's not like you can go round to a mate's house, because you haven't got any mates. So sitting on your own in the Bluebell it is, then. Yeah, Mum, go and have another drink. See if it makes you feel any saner."

The front door slammed, the music stopped and all Frankie could hear was the sound of inconsolable weeping. Suddenly Frankie had a brainwave. What was the point of listening to Celia crying all night when he had the chance to make some real progress, face-to-face? He jumped out of the car, sprinted to the precinct and into the Bluebell pub.

Great, he thought, looking around the grotty interior. *She's not here yet. Let's just hope she turns up.*

He went to freshen up in the men's toilets. He wanted to look half-decent for the job in hand.

When Janice arrived at the pub, she was pleasantly surprised to spot Frankie in the corner. In desperate need of a friendly face, she was immediately drawn to him.

"Hello." She smiled, her eyes slightly glazed. "Fancy meeting you here."

Frankie rose to greet her. "Ms. Frost, isn't it? Lovely to see you again," he said with impeccable politeness.

"For goodness' sake, call me Janice – and you're Paul, aren't you? I remember," she said rather coyly.

"Can I get you a drink, Janice?" he asked.

"A gin and tonic would be lovely," she answered, trying to sound as ladylike as possible.

"Should I make it a double?" he tempted.

"I wouldn't usually, but go on then, you've twisted my arm," she trilled.

While he was at the bar, Janice took the opportunity to straighten her clothes and tidy her hair. She caught sight of her nicotine-stained fingers and bitten nails and decided to keep her hands under the table as much as possible.

"Do you live round here?" she asked, as he returned with the drinks.

"No. I'm just here to do this heating job. I've been at it all day. I really needed a drink," he replied.

"Yeah. Sometimes I feel like that," she said, staring at the glass longingly.

"Well, there's nothing wrong with the odd drink now and then, is there?" he said encouragingly.

"You're right," replied Janice, sinking the entire contents of the glass in one go.

"Wow! You must have had a tough day," Frankie said.

"I've had a tough life," Janice sniggered.

"Well, it must be hard bringing up a kid on your own. Do you have anyone to help you?"

"No. It's just me and Celia. It's only ever been the two of us."

"At least Megan's mum knows that I'll always come round if she needs help, but for you to have no one to turn to, well…it must be lonely."

"You have no idea how lonely. Celia's all I've got and now even she hates me." Tears burgeoned in her eyes. "All we do these days is argue; we used to be so close. She was always such a good girl, even though I've put her through so much. But now…well…sorry, you don't want to hear all my problems."

"No, go on, Janice. What's happened to change things between you?" Frankie looked attentively into her eyes.

"She doesn't trust me any more," Janice blurted out. "She won't let me protect her. Every day I go through hell until she comes home and I know things are okay."

"We all worry about our kids, especially when they're girls, but maybe you've got to give her some space, a bit of independence," he said.

"You don't understand." She shook her head. "Celia isn't the same as other kids. She needs to keep safe."

"Why? Is she ill?"

"I can't talk about it," she said, suddenly clamming up. "I can never talk about it. It's my responsibility, my burden."

"Well it might help to share that burden with someone. Sometimes things aren't quite as bad as they seem," he said softly.

Janice laughed bitterly. "You seem a lovely man, Paul, but you haven't got a clue. I haven't even told Celia. For years I've lied to her and she didn't put a foot wrong. I'm meant to be her mother, she trusted me completely, did whatever I said. But now she just thinks I'm mad." Janice stared at him with a crazed look in her eyes.

"Maybe it'd be best to tell her this secret if it concerns her. Maybe she has a right to know. Kids are a lot more resilient than we give them credit for," he said.

She leaned in towards him. "I can't tell her. It would make her life unbearable. So I carry it around in here." She thumped her chest. "And every day it eats away at me. I've had a permanent sick feeling in my stomach ever since I've had her, but now that she's running around doing God knows what, I'm completely helpless; holding my breath every day, waiting for it to happen – and when it does, I won't know how to stop it." Distress consumed her face.

"Whatever it is, I wish you'd let me help you, Janice," he said earnestly.

"I couldn't let you. It's dangerous," her hot breath whispered in his ear. "She's probably been looking for us all these years. Right now, there's probably someone out there trying to track us down."

Frankie shifted uncomfortably in his chair. "Who's 'she'?" he asked.

The faint voice in Janice's head that was telling her to shut up was drowned out by the effects of all the gin, which was lubricating her usually careful tongue.

"I was so stupid. I thought that if we kept on the move, kept our heads down and didn't tell a soul, I thought she might forget about Celia. But who was I kidding? How could she ever forget about Celia? And now, after all these years, there she was; everyone saying how wonderful she is. But I know the truth."

"God, Janice. This sounds like serious stuff. Why haven't you been to the police?" Frankie knew he was treading on dangerous ground, but he needed to probe further.

"I can't. They'd take my girl away from me. God knows what would happen to her."

Frankie reached out and rubbed her arm sympathetically. "Don't get upset."

"You're such a nice man, Paul, so easy to talk to. I don't know why I told you all that." She gave a silly grin. "It's weird, but I feel much better now."

"Anytime, Janice. Listen…I'll be working around here for a few days yet. If you ever feel like having another chat, here's my number." He wrote out his mobile number. "Now how about another drink? You could do with it."

22 the box room

Celia woke up with a stiff neck. She'd fallen asleep on her bed, fully clothed, exhausted from crying and worry. She checked her watch; it was nearly eleven p.m. Wandering into Janice's room, she saw that the bed was empty.

Celia scanned the flat. "Mum?" she called out. Janice was nowhere to be seen. "She's not even back yet," she said in disgust. Still half asleep, she ran her fingers through her bed-flattened hair; it sprang out as an idea sprang into her head.

I shouldn't be here when she gets back. She'll get the fright of her life. I'll show her that I can disappear if I want to… It's what she needs; a really big fright. Maybe she'll take me

seriously then – make an effort to get her act together.

She phoned Sol, pleased with her plan. His phone was off, but she was undeterred.

Half an hour later, Celia was nervously picking her way through the estate, only too aware that The Sovereign Crew could be round any corner. All was quiet outside Sol's, the whole house in darkness.

She called up to his window in a hushed shout: "Sol. Sol. Are you there? Wake up!"

Nothing stirred. She gathered up little bits of stone from the ground and threw them, one by one, up at the glass, hoping it wouldn't shatter.

A sleepy head poked out of the narrow window. "Celia?" He peered at her. "What are you doing here?"

"Can I come in?" she whispered.

"Hang on a minute."

Sol opened the front door with his finger to his lip, but Celia couldn't help smirking when she saw his Superman T-shirt and shorts. "Like the pyjamas."

"Shut up," he whispered. "Mum's asleep and Abs and Yac will be home soon. You'd better come up to my room."

They crept up the creaking stairs and into Sol's tiny bedroom. The recent liberal spraying of body scent for men just about masked the classic boy odours.

"I thought my room was small!" Celia said, standing centimetres from Sol in the narrow floor space.

"At least I *get* my own room. Abs and Yac have to share. You can imagine how impressed girls are with that." Sol suddenly became his brothers. "Yeah, darlin', you can come back to my place – as long as you don't mind my mum being in the next room and my brother farting in the next bed." Celia burst out laughing as Sol frantically shushed her. "If my mum found you in here she'd have me down the church to be exorcized."

"Don't worry, we can pretend we're revising." She grinned.

"Well, we can't stand here all night. If you want to sit down, you're going to have to go up there." Sol pointed up to his high bed, which housed a desk and wardrobe beneath it.

Celia climbed the short vertical ladder and shuffled along the mattress to make room for Sol. They sat crossed-legged as Celia picked at the plump blue duvet.

"Why are you here, Celia? What's happened at home?"

"Mum's gone out, and I want her to get back to the flat and have a heart attack when she sees I'm not there. I need to give her a fright, teach her a lesson. Tonight she started talking about us leaving here."

Sol looked alarmed. "You're not going to, are you?"

"No! I'm not letting her drag me anywhere. She's insane.

She's still saying those mad things. I can't stand it any more." Her face suddenly looked world-weary. "I don't know what I expected. Did I really think she'd get better just because I rumbled her?"

"Maybe it's time to get her help. It's too much for you to handle on your own," Sol said.

"And how do I do that without social workers getting involved? They wouldn't leave me with her – not when they find out what she's done. They'd take me away; I could end up anywhere."

"*Anywhere* anywhere?" Sol asked.

"Yeah, of course! They could put me in care anywhere in the country. They wouldn't want her near me."

"Then you can't!" Sol said urgently.

"What? Make up your mind, Sol. Now are you saying *don't* get her help?"

"Yeah. Don't get her help."

She searched his anxious eyes. "Okay," she said quietly.

Janice looked at her watch. "Oh my God! I had no idea it was that time. I'd better get back – check on Celia. Please forget what I've said. I've been talking rubbish all night. I think I might be a bit tipsy."

"Let me walk you back."

"You've no need to do that," Janice protested weakly.

"You shouldn't be walking around here on your own at this time of night," Frankie said chivalrously.

He put her arm through his to steady her and escorted Janice out of the pub. They looked an odd sight wandering through the estate, like a wrestler and his tiny wife.

At the entrance to Bluebell Tower Two, she strained her neck looking up at the big man. "Thanks for seeing me home," she slurred.

"What are friends for?" he replied.

Janice looked taken aback. Her face lit up. "Are we friends?" she asked shyly. "I've never had a friend before."

"Well, you have now," Frankie said gently, squeezing her rough red hands, before turning and walking into the night.

Five minutes later, Celia's phone started vibrating.

Celia listened to Janice's frantic message. "She's back at the flat, running round like a headless chicken. She hasn't got a clue where I am," Celia said with a satisfied smile.

"You should let her know you're okay. Say she phones the police?" Sol said.

"She won't do that. She's not going to want the police asking questions, is she?" Celia answered.

"I still think you should text her or something. You don't want her doing anything stupid."

"Okay," Celia sighed. "But I wanted to make her really sweat. She's getting off too lightly."

"Then why don't you stay here the night?"

Celia's eyes widened.

"I'd sleep on the floor," Sol added hurriedly.

"Could I?!"

"Yeah, why not?" he said shyly. "But Mum gets up for work at seven. You'd have to be gone by then."

Celia gave an enormous toothy smile. "Thanks." She texted Janice, *Staying wiv a friend. Back in morning*, and turned off her phone.

Sol climbed down from the bed.

"What are you doing?" Celia asked.

"What I said. I'm sleeping down here." He pulled an array of clothes out of the wardrobe.

"No! I'm not kicking you out of your own bed," Celia said.

He ignored her and lay down in the sliver of space, draping the clothes over his prostrate body.

Celia leaned over the side of the bed, looking down on her friend. "Sol," she whispered. "I mean it. I'll go home unless you let me sleep on the floor."

He lay perfectly still, eyes closed, ignoring her.

"Sol," she said in a sing-song voice, "are you asleep?"

Still, he didn't move.

She leaned further over the side, pillow in hand, and

when she had him in range, she whacked him with it.

He gasped, his whole body jumping as though she'd given him an electric shock. Celia shook with the effort of holding in laughter. Sol grabbed the pillow and turned it on her, getting in two swift, clean, body shots, which nearly toppled her off the bed.

It was Celia who heard the noise first.

"Quiet!" she hissed. "What's that?" It sounded like a herd of elephants coming up the stairs.

"Oh my God!" Sol froze mid-swipe. "It's my brothers."

Celia hit the light switch, hugging herself in an attempt to control the rising laughter.

"Can you hear something?" Abs said to Yacob as they reached the landing.

"Yeah, it's coming from Sol's room. Bit late for him, isn't it?"

"Hey," Abs whispered. "I think he's crying."

They put their respective ears to the bedroom door and heard the distinct sound of sobbing. They looked at each other, concerned.

Abs nudged his brother. "Go in there and see what's up."

"No, you go in. It could be something embarrassing."

"We'll both go in then."

Abs tapped on the door.

"Sol," he said gently, "are you all right? Can we come in?"

Sol and Celia were on the verge of hyperventilating, producing periodic gasps as they tried to stifle their laughter. Sol scrambled up the ladder. "Hide," he mouthed to Celia.

Celia dived under the duvet, her cloud of orange hair poking out.

"Don't come in," Sol said through gritted teeth. "I'm fine." He pulled Celia by the ankles so that her hair disappeared from view. He jumped in the opposite end and smoothed the duvet over the suspicious mound.

"You don't sound like you're fine," Yacob said, opening the door a fraction, light from the landing penetrating the room. The brothers' faces appeared around the door. Sol popped his head up, desperate to stop them coming in.

"What's the matter with you two?" he said groggily. "Why have you woken me up?"

"We thought you were crying," Abs said, puzzled.

"Crying? I've been asleep."

"Listen, buddy, there's no shame in having a little cry every now and then. If something's bothering you, you can tell us." Abs started to edge further into the room.

Sol could see the duvet moving with Celia's quivering. He put his hand out like a policeman stopping traffic.

"Honestly, I'm fine. I must have been having a nightmare, that's all. You two get to bed – you need your beauty sleep."

"Okay, but you know, Sol, any problems, anyone giving you a hard time, and me and Yac will sort them out."

"Yeah, yeah. I know. Thanks, guys," he said, watching his brothers' heads disappear and the door shut once more.

Celia threw the duvet off, gasping. "Oh my God! I thought I was going to die of laughter under there. They are so sweet, aren't they?"

"They have their moments. Listen, I'm going back on the floor," Sol whispered.

"Don't be stupid. We're both up here now, so let's just stay like this; heads and tails. I promise to keep my hands off you."

"Okay," Sol's voice squeaked.

Ten excruciating minutes passed as they lay there in the dark, listening to each other's breathing, terrified to move a muscle in case they touched, acutely aware that there was only a layer of body heat between them.

Sol couldn't stand it any more. He sat bolt upright in the bed. "Actually, Celia," he whispered, "I think I will sleep on the floor after all."

"Okay then." She nodded with relief. "If you're sure."

23 *the alleyway*

Celia couldn't resist the lure of the Giran household. She'd planned to go straight home from the flooded quarry this evening, but when they reached Sol's house, Mrs. Giran had invited her to come in. Two hours later she was still there, watching TV with Sol and devouring delicious home-made biscuits.

"Your mum's the best!" Celia sighed, sipping her sweet, treacly, Ethiopian coffee.

"Yeah, well, for some strange reason she thinks you're great, but she might change her mind if she knew you spent Wednesday night in my bedroom," he whispered, wagging his finger at her.

"Shut up!" Celia blushed.

"You should phone *your* mum, you know. She keeps ringing. You should answer her."

"Why should I? I've already phoned her once today. She's got to stop stalking me. I tell you what, though," Celia said excitedly, "something's going on. I think she may have found herself a man."

"Are you sure?"

"Well no, but for the last few days she's been getting these phone calls. Every time it rings she dives into her bedroom to answer it. Next minute I hear her giggling like a schoolgirl, and when she comes out she's all pink, with a stupid smile on her face."

"Well, haven't you asked her?"

"Of course I have. She just said why should she tell me, when I won't tell her anything?"

"Suppose that's fair enough."

"Anyway, I'd love it if it *was* a boyfriend. That's what she needs; someone else in her life. Maybe then she'd stop obsessing about me."

Mrs. Giran appeared in the room carrying a fresh supply of coffee and biscuits, just as Celia's phone rang again. Celia tried to ignore it.

"Aren't you going to answer your phone, Celia?" Mrs. Giran asked.

She picked it up reluctantly. "Hi, Mum… The chicken's

burned? What are you talking about? What chicken? …Oh, did you? I mustn't have heard my phone… Okay. I'm coming home now anyway… Just around… Out and about… Listen, don't worry, I'll see you in a minute."

"That was your mother?" Mrs. Giran asked.

"Yeah – she wants me home."

"Well, maybe next visit you'll bring her with you. I'd love to meet her. It's hard for us women bringing up our children alone. I want to tell her what a wonderful job she's done with you."

Celia flashed an angelic smile and then turned to Sol, pulling a cartoon face of horror. The thought of Sol's mum meeting Janice sent shivers down her spine. The shame of Mrs. Giran meeting her deranged mother – no way was that going to happen.

"You know that you're always welcome here, Celia. There's a lot of *bad* things out there and it makes me happy that my boy has a nice friend like you to keep him away from trouble." Mrs. Giran beamed, as she ruffled Sol's hair.

"Mum, get off!" Sol said, squirming.

"Walk Celia home, Sol, but make sure you come straight back. Goodnight, darling girl." Mrs. Giran threw her arms around Celia, pressing her into soft, ample flesh.

Celia was overwhelmed by the embrace and hugged her back. She realized that things were far from perfect in this family. On top of living with the agony of trying to find her husband, Mrs. Giran had two wayward sons to contend with and a third who, though she was blissfully unaware of it, had been bunking off school. However, despite all these stresses, there was no hint of the suffocating tension that Janice created in their own home. Sol didn't have to endure any wild-eyed interrogation every time he walked in the door. He didn't have to cope with a mad, out-of-control mother.

Is this what it's like to have a normal mum? Is this what I've missed out on all my life? Celia was suddenly in danger of crying. She quickly released Mrs. Giran, letting go of the comfort and safety that enveloped her in this woman's arms.

"You okay?" Sol asked, puzzled.

"I'm fine. Let's go," Celia blustered, hiding her face.

They headed towards the dark towers. The evening air was still warm from the day's sun. A perfect full moon sat so clear in the sky that it looked possible to reach up and grab it.

"I'm starving. Do you fancy going to the chippy?" Sol said.

Celia was incredulous. "Don't you ever stop eating?"

"I'm a growing boy." He shrugged. "Come on, I'll race you. Last one there buys!" Sol started running before he'd finished his sentence, leaving Celia standing, but her long-legged strides soon closed the gap. They weaved in and out of the blocks of houses, skidding around corners, yelling through the echoing passageways, swerving past the burned-out wheelie bins that were strewn around like some modern art installation. They didn't take any notice as they ran past the figure, who looked up on seeing them, then quickly reached for his mobile.

A minute later they became aware of someone sprinting up behind them. A voice shouted, "Hey, you two! Stop, please stop. I need your help!"

Celia and Sol slowed down and cautiously looked behind. The youth was panting, beckoning them towards him. Sol and Celia maintained their distance.

"What's up?" Sol called to him.

"It's my mate," the boy spluttered. "He's been beaten up, he's hurt bad. Please…help me. I'm on my own with him. I don't want to leave him."

"Have you called an ambulance?" Celia asked.

"Yeah. They said they'd be ten minutes. I don't want to be on my own with him for ten minutes. Please…I don't know what to do."

Celia and Sol looked at each other. The boy's panic was palpable. They couldn't walk away.

"Okay. Where is he?" Sol asked.

"Thanks, mate! Thanks! It's this way." The hooded boy ran ahead of them, leading them to the entrance of a long, dingy alleyway.

"It's a dead end." Celia's anxiety was growing.

"Yeah, I know. He's down the bottom. Come on! He was bleeding bad," the twitchy teenager said, corralling them down the unlit alley.

They reached the end of the alleyway, but all that could be seen were piles of black bags full of stinking rubbish, which had been dumped among other debris.

"What's going on? There's no one here," Celia said tensely.

"God! I don't know, honest," their guide said innocently. "He was here. He must have crawled away or something."

"This doesn't feel right, Celia. Let's get out of here. Now!" Sol took her hand, but as they turned to go, they saw figures enter the alleyway.

"I don't believe it!" the boy announced in mock-shock. "Here he is now. Praise be to God – it's a miracle!"

Sol immediately looked around for an escape route but high walls surrounded them on three sides; the only way out was to go past the approaching rabble.

"Don't worry. Just play it cool. They'll let us pass," Sol said nervously.

But Celia could see the huge, mangy Rottweiler approaching, its owner tugging on its chain. "They won't," she whispered with dread. "They're here for me."

The group now stood in a line in front of them, barring any exit.

"What you doing down an alley in the dark? You and her up to dirty things?" Razor said sleazily. "You don't look capable of it."

The gang of shadow-faced followers cackled and jeered, lager spilling from their clutched cans. The dog started to get agitated, picking up on the growing tension in the air.

"Look," Sol said, trying to sound relaxed. "We don't want any trouble. Just let us pass." He stepped forward but the gang responded by moving in.

"You ain't going nowhere," said the leader. "We have business with your girlfriend. She's caused me a lot of bother. The pigs have been hassling me, taking up my valuable time. But they ain't got nothing on me. It's police harassment, that's what I told them."

"You should sue 'em, Razor," laughed one of the gang.

"Look at you," Razor sneered at Sol. "You ain't even got the balls to be part of a crew, have you?"

"I just mind my own business," Sol replied.

Razor gave a look of disdain before jerking his head and spitting in Sol's face.

"Stop it!" shouted Celia, her face screwed up in anger. "Leave him alone."

"You're right," Razor said shrugging. "It's not him we've come for, it's you."

Sol moved in front of Celia, trying to shield her, even though she stood head and shoulders above him.

"Hold him," Razor ordered his rabble. They pounced on Sol, pulling him away from Celia and pinning him to the ground.

Razor dragged the dog towards Celia as she backed against the wall. "Rocky hasn't eaten for a few days. I like to keep him hungry, it keeps him nice and mean."

The dog looked disinterested, his anvil head bowed, his black eyes dead. Razor delivered a sharp kick to the animal's belly. Rocky let out a sickening yelp.

"Come on, boy, have a good sniff. You lookin' at your dinner, but maybe you need the smell of blood to get your juices flowing," he said darkly.

Celia flashed a look of terror at Sol, who stared up helplessly from the ground.

"What you going to do with her?" asked Shane.

Razor handed him the dog's chain before grabbing hold of Celia's mop of hair and turning her to face the wall. He kicked her behind the knees and her legs immediately buckled. As she crumpled he took hold of her and pushed her body against the wall, scraping it down the rough bricks like cheese down a grater. Celia felt the heat of the friction. She fell in a heap on the ground. Her flayed skin smarted as blood sprang from her bare knees and elbows.

"Now Rocky might think you're a bit more tasty. He likes raw meat," Razor hissed. "Hey, Shane! I hope you're getting all this."

The scrawny lad fumbled around in his pockets for his mobile. "Yeah, no problem, Razor," he sniffed.

"See that bitch over there," Razor said, strutting for the video, "she's about to become dog meat."

The baying gang bounced around like they were on hot coals, grunting and howling as they whipped themselves up into a bloodlust.

Celia crouched in a ball against the wall as Razor pulled the dog in closer.

"What you think, Rocky?" he said. "How about a bite to eat?"

The whole gang joined in, trying to wind up the animal. They threw their cans at him, clapping in his face, whooping and taunting. "Kill! Kill! Kill!" they chanted, jabbing their fingers towards Celia.

Rocky began to growl and snap.

"That's more like it," said Razor approvingly. He let out the chain. Rocky was so close she could see the dripping pus from the infection that had spread over his entire mauled ear. His hot, stinking breath sailed up her nostrils as he bared his yellow pointed teeth. Celia buried her head in her knees, her hands over her head, rigid with fear, waiting for his jaws to clamp down and rip into her. But things weren't happening quickly enough for Razor, who yanked the chain viciously, snapping the dog's neck back.

"Get on with it!" he roared, kicking Rocky's festering ear.

The dog howled, throwing himself about, jerking Razor around like a stunt kite in the wind. The chain was torn out of his grasp. The gang backed away as the unfettered dog jumped up at Razor, felling him to the ground and sinking his teeth into his thigh. Razor let out a scream as panic swept through his followers.

A couple of them ran at the animal, attempting to kick him off their leader, but Rocky deepened his bite, his teeth hitting bone.

"Stab him!" wailed Razor.

Shane brandished his knife at the dog, jabbing it towards him. The dog unlocked his jaws and turned on him. Shane took one look at Rocky's blood-soaked mouth and backed off down the alleyway. The rest of the gang followed, dragging the writhing Razor behind them.

Celia rose shakily to her feet, leaning against the wall for support. Sol edged towards her, not taking his eyes off the dog, who was charging around in front of them, shaking his head violently and snapping at the air as his chain whipped the ground. But then Rocky paused, fixing wild eyes on Sol. Blood-stained slobber hung between his bared teeth. Every wasted muscle in his body quivered, poised to attack.

Sol frantically looked around for some protection. In one corner he saw a broken shopping trolley and on the other side, among the sacks of stinking rubbish, he spotted a snapped broom handle. Sol inched sideways and grabbed for the handle – but as he felt it in his grasp, Rocky ran at him, launching into the air with open jaws. Sol swung the handle with all his strength. It delivered a blow to the dog's chest that sent it hurtling to the ground.

Sol repositioned himself, standing with legs apart, hands gripping the ends of the broom handle like a Samurai warrior. He watched as Rocky rolled back onto his feet and started patrolling in front of them, snarling in between deafening barks. Celia crept towards Sol, dragging the mangled shopping trolley.

"What's that for?" Sol asked.

"We can trap him under it. It's like a cage," Celia answered quietly. Sol flashed her a look of incredulity. "Have you got a better idea?" she hissed. "Get behind it. We need to get close enough to trap him."

They slowly moved behind the three-wheeled trolley. Celia strained to keep it upright as it tilted forwards.

"Now what?" Sol asked.

"Get ready with your stick," Celia warned, and she started shouting at the crazed dog: "Come on! Here boy!"

Rocky bolted towards them, but as they were about to tip the trolley onto him he swerved to the side, where Celia stood, unprotected.

"Duck!" screamed Sol as he swung the handle, narrowly missing Celia's head but making contact with Rocky's front legs. The dog fell backwards but instantly sprang up, more aggressive than ever.

"Quick! Pull the trolley round to face him," Celia rasped.

They dragged it around as Rocky leaped towards them again but Celia held her nerve, waiting for the perfect moment before she screamed, "Now!"

They grabbed hold of the bottom of the trolley and flipped it upside down. It landed right on target, stopping the animal in his tracks.

They stood back, watching as the trapped dog rammed his body against the cage, pushing his nose through the grids, his teeth chomping down on the metal. When this didn't work he started to paw at the concrete ground, his overgrown nails scratching the surface in a futile attempt to tunnel out.

"What should we do?" Celia asked, trembling.

"Get out of here, quick. I don't know how long that trolley can hold him and we don't want to be around if any of those bastards come back."

She winced as she stepped forward. Blood oozed out of the flayed skin on her elbows and knees.

"Come on, Celia. We need to get you home and clean you up." He reached out to her.

"It's okay, I can manage," she said, rejecting his hand and hobbling along the alleyway. "You've done enough for me already. I feel so bad that you got dragged into that."

"Don't be stupid, Celia. It's not your fault," he said.

"You get home. I can make my own way back."

"No way! I want to check you're okay."

"I'll be fine," she said firmly. "I promise I'll ring you once I'm back. Please, Sol, go home."

He knew it was no use arguing with her. "Okay," he said reluctantly. "But you'd better phone me, or I'll come round whether you want me to meet your mum or not."

24 *kiss it better*

Janice had been entertaining Frankie all evening, even if she wasn't aware of it. She'd returned from work around six, by which time Frankie was already ensconced in his car, ready to listen in to her every sound. The evening had started off well. Janice seemed in a buoyant mood, which he liked to think was due to his little phone calls. There was the sound of the kettle being boiled, clattering in the kitchen, and singing along to the radio.

She'd phoned Celia and left a message: "Hiya, love. Make sure you're home for seven. I'm making us a lovely chicken dinner. You know I can't stand the sight of the things after spending all day mopping up their guts, but it's your favourite and nothing's too much trouble for my girl."

However, as the evening wore on and Celia didn't arrive home, Janice had graduated from cups of tea to glasses of booze. She'd left several more messages, each one more rambling and uptight than the last. She warned Celia that she was late, demanding to know where she was, pleading with her to phone back. Later on there was the sound of overzealous chopping, halted by a screech. "Oww! I'm bleeding over the bloody dinner. Where are the bloody plasters?"

Frankie considered whether it was a good time to ring Janice. She was agitated and a little drunk; an ideal state to extract information from her. Anyway, even if she wasn't forthcoming with information, Frankie still enjoyed their little chats. It felt good to speak to someone who seemed so happy to hear from him, even if he knew it was all a charade. But as he rehearsed what he would say to her, the sound of gentle snoring started filtering through his earpieces.

Janice's snoring continued for over an hour until it was eventually replaced by coughs and splutters, followed by a shriek. There was frantic activity in the flat: the sound of the oven door being flung open, taps turned on, trays being slung out onto the balcony – then tears and an angry call to Celia, who did pick up this time.

"Celia, where are you? The chicken's burned to a cinder... The chicken I've been cooking for our dinner! I've left you loads of messages telling you to get home... Don't give me that. You've just been ignoring my calls. I've nearly sliced my finger off cooking this dinner and now it's ruined... You're damn right you're coming home now. Where have you been anyway? ...What do you mean 'just around'? I want to know where... Who are you with? What have you been up to?"

The call ended without any goodbyes and Frankie could hear Janice pacing up and down the flat, calming herself.

"At least you know she's all right," she was mumbling. "She's on her way home, so don't jump down her throat as soon as she comes in, Janice. Let's have a nice, relaxing night. No more arguments, no more shouting. Everything's fine."

However, as an age seemed to tick by without any sign of Celia's return, even Frankie began to get worried.

Celia had forced herself up every step to the twentieth floor, the grated skin on her knees and elbows oozing with each movement of her joints. By the time she appeared in the doorway to their flat, blood was trickling down her limbs.

"Celia!"

"Mum," Celia whimpered, grabbing hold of Janice's hands.

Janice looked down. Celia's blood-stained hands were wrapped around hers. "Let go of my hands!" she screamed.

"What?! Why?!"

"Just do it, just do it. Let go now!" Janice's face was rigid.

The startled girl obeyed. Janice inspected her shaking hands. The plaster on her cut finger was still in place but now smeared with Celia's blood.

"What's the matter?" Celia asked, flabbergasted.

Janice scurried to the bathroom. Celia followed her, watching as Janice manically washed her hands over and over again, dousing them with a concoction of disinfectants, checking every centimetre of skin before repeating the whole process. "It's fine, it's fine," Janice was muttering to herself, grappling to pull on a pair of latex gloves.

"You look terrified," Celia said, alarmed. "Why are you terrified?"

"What are you talking about? You know your old mum, always a bag of nerves," Janice jabbered. "It's you I'm worried about."

Celia watched as Janice discreetly clasped her hands together in an attempt to quell their tremor. Her eyes narrowed. She searched Janice's agitated face. "You cut your finger, didn't you? You said so, on the phone."

"Yes. But it's nothing to worry about, just a little cut," she answered dismissively. "Now come on, love, tell me what happened to you."

Celia's mind was too distracted to go into detail. "A gang attacked us. They set their dog on us."

"'Us'? Who was with you?"

"A friend."

"Was it that boy? The one from the drawing in the book? Did he touch you? Did anyone touch you?"

"What do you mean, 'touch me'?" Celia asked, needing to hear her say it.

"When you were bleeding, did anyone touch you?"

"What would be the problem if they did? Why are you always so bothered about people touching me? Don't let people help you without gloves – isn't that one of your rules? You've always been obsessed with keeping people away from me, away from my blood."

"I'm not obsessed with it," she tutted. "It's…it's just not hygienic, is it?"

"Even someone as neurotic as you, Mum, doesn't react like that just because it's not hygienic." Celia suddenly fell silent. She stood perfectly still, a hundred thoughts colliding behind her darting eyes.

"What are you doing, Celia? I need an answer. Did

anyone touch you?" Janice couldn't mask her rising panic.

Celia spoke slowly, her brain unscrambling her thoughts. "I know that the blood clotting disorder was a lie. But what if all your crazy behaviour isn't crazy at all? What if you know something about my blood, something that makes it dangerous, and all these years you've been trying to make sure people keep away from me?"

"You're in shock. You're talking nonsense," Janice said aggressively.

"Am I? You were terrified – terrified of my blood touching that cut on your finger."

"No I wasn't!" Janice retorted.

"Are you sure of that?" Celia asked.

"Yes!"

"In that case you won't mind doing something for me." Her voice fluttered with nerves.

"What?" Janice asked tensely.

Celia lifted her arm to Janice's mouth, fresh blood seeping from the skin. "Kiss it better, Mum."

Janice pulled away, sealing her lips tight.

"What's the matter?"

Janice forced out a hollow laugh. "Don't you think you're a bit big for that kind of thing?"

"But you've never done it, have you? Mums are meant to do things like that. If you loved me, you'd kiss my poorly elbow better," she said, tears of anxiety pooling in her eyes.

Janice backed out of the bathroom, keeping her eyes fixed on Celia. Stumbling through the doorway, she landed in a heap on the living room floor. "Celia...please... Stop it!" she begged.

Celia towered over the cowering woman. "*Why* do you want me to stop?" she asked desperately. "I need to know the truth, Mum. Please don't make me do this." Celia leaned in closer, the burgeoning blood from her quivering arm ready to drip onto Janice's pursed lips.

"No, Celia, no," Janice whimpered, bending her head away.

"Then tell me! Why are you terrified of my blood?"

Janice bowed her head in surrender. "Because it can kill," she muttered.

Celia must have misheard. Janice couldn't have said that. "What did you say?"

"I said...your blood can kill."

"You're lying!" Celia said, reeling.

"I wish I was. I can't do this any more, Celia. I'm so tired." Janice's head flopped into her hands. "I promise to tell you everything, everything. But I need to know if anyone came into contact with your blood."

"No," Celia said in a daze.

"Are you sure?" Janice asked anxiously.

"Yes."

Janice struggled to her feet and gently led the stunned girl back into the bathroom. "Let me cover up your cuts," she said, cleaning the blood away and smoothing plasters over the scraped skin. Janice took a pair of gloves from her supplies and put them on Celia's limp hands.

The woman's face crumpled in despair. "I can't go on like this. Everything's out of control. I shouldn't have let it get to this."

"What's wrong with me?" Celia stared desolately at her gloved hands.

"You have a virus. You can infect people with your blood."

"But you must have taken me to hospital. What did they say? Why haven't I been getting treatment for it?"

"Hospital was the last place I could take you. I've never let doctors near you. If they started testing you, they'd take you off me – I wouldn't know who'd get hold of you. You wouldn't have been safe."

"But then how do you know I've got it? Was I born with it? Is it a genetic thing; did you give it to me?"

"Even if it was genetic I couldn't have given it to you."

"Why not?"

"Because, Celia, I'm not your mother."

Celia's face was paralysed in a bewildered grimace. Janice reached for her but she pulled away, bolting into the living room. Her eyes scanned all the photos on the wall. She'd known that there were no baby pictures. Janice had told her that all her baby mementos had been lost in one of their many moves. But hadn't Janice always been more than happy to recount Celia's birth: the quick, straightforward labour, how Celia popped out bearing a shock of orange hair? That, despite the stress of finding out about Celia's blood clotting disorder, she knew that, together, the two of them could deal with it.

"Am I adopted?" Celia asked, staring at the photos.

"Celia...I'm your mother in every other sense of the word," Janice said pleadingly.

"Just answer the question." Celia turned to face her. "Did you adopt me?"

"No." Janice looked her straight in the eye. "I had to take you!"

"What are you talking about?" Celia threw her arms out. "Where did you take me from? Did you kidnap me?! Oh my God! You did, didn't you? You took me from my real parents!" She lunged at Janice, seizing her brittle arms, aggression suddenly welling up in her. "Have they been looking for me all these years? Do they think I'm dead? You've put me through this crappy life with you, telling me a pack of lies instead of getting me help, when all the time I could have been with my real parents. They would have let doctors sort me out, found a cure for my blood. What kind of twisted freak are you?" Celia's voice was piercing, hysteria taking control.

Janice grappled her way loose and, without warning, slapped Celia hard across the cheek. Celia's arms dropped down in shock, the imprint of Janice's palm visible on her burning cheek.

"I didn't take you from your parents. I took you from a clinic. You were being used like a lab rat. I saved you! They were going to murder you!" Janice's voice was steady and strong.

Celia slumped onto the sofa, her mind in overload. "Please stop these lies," she wailed, putting her hands over her ears.

"Celia, I had to lie about the blood clotting. I had to think of an illness that would make people careful around you and make sure you never took any risks. I thought it was better for everyone to think that you were only a danger to yourself. I couldn't let them know that your blood could kill them."

"But why didn't you tell me?"

"How would you have coped? Even when you discovered I'd been lying about the blood clotting, I reckoned it was better that you thought I was mad than have to live with the truth. But I was wrong, because once you believed you had nothing to fear, you've been more dangerous than ever."

"So all these years, you've let me wander around putting people in danger."

"What was I meant to do? I saved you. I couldn't keep you a prisoner. I had to give you some freedom, some kind of life. I've tried my best to keep you safe – every day feeling sick until you were safely back home; every day living in terror that you might infect someone."

"But who did this to me? What is this virus in me?" Celia whispered in self-disgust.

25 *the cleaner*

Janice's eyes brimmed with anguish as she sat down next to Celia. "I only ever wanted to keep you safe, protect you from the truth, but I can't do that any more. You're going to have to be strong, Celia. Listen and be strong.

"I was twenty-two and I'd been drifting around since I left care. All I'd managed to achieve was a four-month stretch in a young offender institution because I kept shoplifting. I was a mess. No one to look out for me, no place I belonged. I kept moving around the country, doing any rubbish job I could. When I'd saved up some money, I'd just get on a bus to another place, hoping it would be better than the last.

"Then one time, just for the hell of it, I got off at this tiny village in the countryside. I got talking to a girl in a cafe. She'd been working as a cleaner at a clinic on the moors, miles from anywhere. She told me that it was a specialist place for sick babies. She was leaving because it was so depressing and the cleaning was too much for one person. I told her I wouldn't mind working there – after all, I wasn't one for mixing, I didn't mind hard work, and I'd spent my entire life in depressing places, so I was used to it. She put in a word for me and the next minute I had the job. Cash in hand, no questions asked. I didn't even give them my real name – I never did; always paranoid that people would check up on me, find out about my record.

"I rented a room in the village and every day I'd get the bus out to work. It passed right by the driveway, but there was no sign outside, nothing to tell people what lay up that long, steep path. Security was tight at the clinic, CCTV all around the outside and codes to get into the rooms, which they changed every day. I was impressed. It made sense – they needed to be careful when they were looking after sick babies. From the outside, the place was an ugly-looking prefab building, windowless except for skylights in the roof, but inside it was spotless, with state-of-the-art equipment. There was a room for you babies, an office, and a small operating theatre with a little bedroom next door. Then there was a lab where they'd take blood samples and God knows what to test. I wasn't allowed in there. The doctor insisted on cleaning it herself.

"I only ever saw three staff. They didn't tell me their names and I didn't ask. I was told to address her as 'Doctor' and the other two women as 'Nurse'. As soon as I arrived they had me in all this protective clothing, covered from head to toe. They said it was to help prevent any infection being brought in that could harm the babies. The whole atmosphere in there was draining and there was a constant noise from the generator which made my head throb. No one bothered to talk to me. The staff were forever checking you babies, writing up charts, adjusting all this equipment that surrounded each cot. It was all way above my head. But I tell you, I'd never worked so hard in my life – scrubbing, disinfecting, sterilizing the rooms. And no sooner had I finished than I'd have to start all over again. When I got back to the village each evening I just used to collapse, I was so knackered.

"I soon realized that the girl had been right, the place was depressing. When I first arrived, there were eight babies. I didn't know anything about babies – I guessed some were as young as a few weeks, others a few months older – but they all looked so weak, like they were struggling to stay alive. Sometimes that room would be filled with their pathetic cries; it cut right through me.

"Each one of you was hooked up to a drip. It was horrible

seeing all your little arms covered in pinpricks, but I just kept telling myself that you were all lucky to be getting such special care. But it didn't take me long to notice that none of you were ever picked up unless you were being examined. No one cuddled or even talked to you. Day after day, the babies just lay in their perspex cots, covered by these plastic tents, sealed in like they were buried alive. But you – you, Celia – you weren't having any of it!

"You were older than the rest. I'd say about a year. You were always trying to climb out of your cot, jumping up and down on the mattress, trying to pull your drips out. You'd bang your little fists against the plastic tent, squealing to get out. Once or twice I saw the nurse give you an injection; it must have been a sedative, because straight away you'd be out for the count. It wasn't fair. I used to watch you and long to give you a cuddle. You made me laugh; this strange, spindly-looking thing with tufts of tangerine hair. You had massive round eyes and a big mouth. I used to wonder how you'd ever grow into your features.

"I'd spend as long as possible cleaning around your cot, just so I could talk to you. You'd give the most enormous gummy smile and gabble a load of gibberish at me. I loved being around you. I couldn't believe how bright and smiley you were and when the staff weren't looking I'd pull funny faces to make you laugh and have a quick game of peek-a-boo – anything to make you happy. But one time, one of those nurses spotted me and I got a lecture. She said that I was 'endangering your health'; that you babies were too sick to cope with any stimulation. But then I started asking questions and she didn't like it. I wanted to know why you kids never had any visitors and what were your names; why there were only barcodes on the charts at the end of your cots, as if you were something in a shop? Secretly, I'd started calling you Celia. It just felt right to name you after the only person who'd ever shown me love. Anyway, that nurse told me it was all because of patient confidentiality and although someone like me couldn't be expected to understand, I should just accept that everything being done was in the best interests of the babies. Then she warned me; she said that if I felt it necessary to keep asking questions then maybe this wasn't the right job for me. So I stopped asking, but kept watching and listening. I was good at being invisible; the kind of person others would forget was even in the room. That suited me fine.

"But as the weeks passed, those babies began to look sicker rather than better, until even the crying stopped and they would just lie there, dead-eyed. I watched as their skin turned grey, their cheeks sank and their eyes hollowed. Despite all the liquid being pumped into them, they were all losing weight. Soon most looked like shrivelled old men. I'd come to work and one by one they'd be gone, until eventually only two of you were left. It was so upsetting, I had to ask what had happened. I was told that the parents had been with the undertakers and collected the bodies. The nurse said that the high death rate was normal with such sick children, that their chances of survival had always been low. But this only made me more upset. I convinced myself that you were going to end up like the other babies.

"But it was the doctor who reassured me. I was fascinated by her. I never saw her go home – I'm not even sure she had a home, I think she slept in the clinic at night. She didn't have time for small talk either. She worked so hard, always shifting between the lab and the babies' room; monitoring, examining, putting up new drips, taking blood samples. Most of the time she looked exhausted, as though she'd been awake all night. I was in awe of her, to tell you the truth. I'd never met anyone so clever, so dedicated.

"I didn't even think that she'd noticed me, but one day she saw me chatting to you. When I realized she was there, I thought I was going to get another telling-off, but I didn't. She just said to me, 'It's best not to get attached to them, you know. It's easier that way.'

"I forgot myself, I was so annoyed. I snapped at her, 'Easier for who? Even if they do die, isn't it better that they were shown a bit of love?'

"'It's Clare, isn't it?' she said.

"'Yes,' I lied.

"'Well, Clare,' she said. 'You must just trust me. I know it's distressing when they die, but the challenge is to keep focused, keep strong. When I feel down, I look at this little one.' She pointed at you. 'I have great hopes for her. She's a survivor.' I tell you what, she said it with such feeling that I believed her.

"Then, early one morning, I looked out my window and saw there was a storm brewing. I thought about not going in. I felt knackered and I didn't fancy catching the bus into the wilds and trudging up that endless driveway. But then I thought about you and knew that I had to see you. I couldn't let you go a whole day and night without anyone talking to you. So I got wrapped up and went for the bus.

"As soon as I walked in I knew there was something wrong. There was a terrible tension about the place. Something had happened overnight. The other baby was gone and you'd been moved out of the room. When I asked the doctor what was going on, she seemed anxious, flustered. She just said that I should go home; that I wasn't needed today. She went into the office and came back with a wad of money. She thrust it into my hand. It was loads more than I was owed, but she didn't care – she just wanted me out of there. She told me that I'd be contacted when I was needed again.

"I didn't know what to think – all I knew was that there was no way I was leaving without seeing that you were okay. So I hung around, made myself inconspicuous. Her and the two nurses were too busy to notice. She kept going in and out of the operating room. I watched carefully and memorized the new security code. As soon as the corridor was empty I let myself in.

"I can't tell you how relieved I was when I saw you there in your cot, as bright and beaming as usual. Nothing seemed to be wrong. As soon as you saw me you held out your skinny arms and jabbered away through the plastic tent. I said to you, 'Why are you in here? What have you been up to, you cheeky girl?' You just blew a raspberry at me, and dribbled. 'I can't stay today,' I said. 'They've told me to go. But maybe they'll get me back when they sort things out. Don't worry, I'll see you soon, I promise.'

"You looked so sad, as if you understood every word. I knew it was against the rules, but I wanted to cuddle you so much. Just as I was about to unzip the tent, the door started to open. I panicked; I wasn't meant to be in there. I didn't even have protective gear on – the doctor would be furious. My first instinct was to hide. I went and crouched under the operating table. It had a green sheet draped over it, which I pulled towards the ground to hide me. I could hear you squealing with delight, thinking I was playing some game. My heart was pounding as I pictured you pointing to me, giving me away. But the next thing I heard was a man's voice.

"'So this is the one? How could you let this happen?' His harsh voice silenced your squeals.

"'I didn't *let it* happen,' came the doctor's voice. 'There were always risks involved with using live, volatile viruses. I was convinced that I had it right this time. I made the most minute modification to the virus's genetic sequence. I couldn't have predicted that it would have this effect.'

"'Didn't you inject the same virus into both babies?' he said.

"'Yes,' she replied. 'The other baby died within forty-eight hours of receiving the injection. The post-mortem revealed an incredibly virulent new strain of the virus. Instead of attacking only the cancerous cells as I'd hoped, this strain invaded all the healthy cells as well, destroying them and multiplying at great speed, leading to rapid death.'

"'So why does this child look the picture of health?'

"'This is the fascinating aspect of it, sir. The virus isn't behaving the same way in her. It's possible that she has her own immunity to it.'

"'She may be immune, but could this child still spread the virus?'

"'In its present state, yes. It's blood-borne, so any blood-to-blood contact with her could transmit it.'

"'And could it keep spreading?'

"'It's possible that any new hosts could spread it. However,' she added quickly, 'it's vital I have more time. I need to see if this virus develops in her. She's my longest survivor. My most responsive subject. The multiple cancers I introduced in all the other babies just kept spreading, no matter how I modified the virus, but in her, the tumours aren't growing as quickly.'

"'Aren't growing as quickly?' The man raised his voice. 'We've poured millions into your research and your biggest achievement is that! We've had treatments for years that can slow the growth of tumours. You convinced us that by these experiments, using human subjects like this,' he said with distaste, 'you could create a virus that would eradicate cancer for ever!' He breathed deeply, lowering his voice. 'I'm so deeply disappointed, doctor. I was expecting great things from your project.'

"'How can you say that when I've already achieved so much? And with this baby, I was making significant progress. I just need more time with her.'

"'This child could put the population at risk from a fatal virus for which you have no antidote, no cure – so don't you dare ask me for more time. Luckily for you, the solution to your mess is quite simple. Destroy her before she can infect anyone.'

"'But I need her!' The doctor sounded outraged. 'I need to study her.'

"'The decision has been made. You've had long enough. My associates and I have taken an enormous risk in backing you and you have not delivered our cure. We are classing your project as a failure.'

"'You can't do this,' she pleaded. 'Setbacks are bound to happen, but we learn from them and make progress. If you close me down now, all those babies would have died for nothing.'

"'Maybe, but that's entirely your fault, isn't it? You've got until tonight. Get rid of this child, dispose of the virus and clear this place out. I don't want a trace left of what went on here. Do you understand?'

"'Yes,' she said bitterly. He left the room but she remained. She spoke to you. She sounded so broken. 'I had such hopes for you. I'm sorry, I'm so sorry.'

"You clapped your hands and giggled like you were trying to cheer up this sad lady. I was petrified that she was going to kill you there and then. My mind was racing, trying to work out what to do, how I could stop her, but then I heard her walk out of the room. As the door closed behind her, I didn't have time to think. I just knew I had to get you out of there.

"When you saw me crawl out from under the table, you shrieked with excitement, but I was desperate for you to be quiet. I kept hushing you as I opened up the tent. You were bouncing up and down, holding out your arms to me.

Even though I couldn't help thinking about that virus in your blood, I picked you up and you clung onto me like a monkey. I remember stroking your cotton-wool tufts of hair, all the time quietening you. There was a box of disposable gowns under your cot. I grabbed a load and completely covered you in them.

"'No more noise, Celia. Don't make a sound,' I whispered into the bundle. I put my ear to the door; the corridor seemed silent. I edged it open, holding my breath. The coast was clear. I had to stop myself from running as I headed for the entrance, where my bag and coat hung. As I reached it, a voice sprang on me from behind.

"'I thought I told you to go home,' she said, staring at the bundle of gowns in my arms. I was willing you not to move.

"'Yes, Doctor. I'm on my way out. I was just disposing of these used gowns.' I was convinced that she would see right through me. I must have looked so terrified, but she had other things on her mind. You stayed perfectly still.

"'Well, for God's sake dispose of them properly. Don't be walking around spreading infection.'

"I nodded and to my relief she walked off down the corridor, bypassing the operating room. I put you, still wrapped up in all the gowns, inside my coat, leaving a sliver of a gap for you to breathe. And with shaking hands I buttoned the bulging coat up and walked out into the wild storm that was raging. As I crossed the threshold the outside light flashed on and I knew that the security camera would be filming me.

"I started to panic as I pictured the doctor entering the room and discovering you were gone. I cradled my arms around the bump and started to run. The storm was in full flow now. The rain was blinding my view, the wind pushed at us like it was trying to blow us back to the clinic. Thunder rumbled in the black sky as I left the driveway and cut across the moor. I ploughed through icy streams and stumbled over rocks. I could hear my panting breath and the moaning wind and the bleating of sheep from the darkness. I swear that if there is a hell then it feels like the moor on that day.

"I never once looked back, terrified that they'd be behind me. I only went down to rejoin the road after I'd been running for what seemed like an eternity. I sheltered behind a massive rock, exhausted. I remember opening the buttons of my coat and seeing your face peeping out like a dormouse out of its straw. I expected you to be screaming, being jolted around like that, half suffocated, but instead you just gave me the most enormous smile, as if you were having the best fun in the world.

"The moor road was deserted, so as soon as I saw a car I jumped out in front of it. The poor bloke got such a shock and then he didn't know what to say when I got in and he saw you in my coat, wrapped in a nest of plastic gowns.

"If I was going to get the police then that was the time to do it, but instead it just came out. 'We got caught in the storm. I was trying to keep my daughter dry.'

"'Where are you heading to?' he asked.

"'Where are you going?'

"'Well, I'm going home to Glasgow, but you won't want to go all the way up there.'

"I nodded like a mad woman. 'Yes! Yes! That's exactly where we want to go.'"

Janice fell silent, trembling from having relived that day. She searched Celia's blank face.

At last Celia spoke, her voice strained. "Why didn't you go to the police?"

"Because I was terrified that they wouldn't believe me. I didn't know who I was up against. The doctor, that man, they must have been powerful people. They could have come up with any story; made it look like I'd kidnapped you. Who are the police going to believe: a respected doctor or a messed-up care kid with a criminal record? I couldn't risk her getting you back. She would have killed you for sure. I didn't know what to do. I just kept running with you. I didn't know whether you'd get ill, die like that other baby. But you didn't and after the first few months, when no one found us, I couldn't give you up. You felt like mine."

"But what about my mum and dad? Didn't they come looking for me?"

"Celia, no one came to visit you at that clinic. After I rescued you, there was nothing on the news about a missing child. No parents appeared, pleading for your return. I don't know where that doctor got you from. I don't even know how long you'd been in that clinic."

"She's that professor, isn't she? Professor Hudson," Celia whispered. "The one on the news. The one who's developed the Saviour Virus. The other week, when you were shaking, I thought it was the drink – but it wasn't, was it? It was seeing *her*."

Janice nodded. "That was the first time I'd seen or heard about her since the day I took you. It made me sick; there she was, bold as brass, talking about her Saviour Virus. Her, a professor now, everyone singing her praises. I thought she'd been made to stop the experiments – I thought that man was shutting her down – but now I wonder how many more babies died to get her virus right."

"But she knows I'm out here somewhere, a danger to everyone. She must have been looking for me all these years."

"Her and God knows who else. Why do you think we

kept moving? It wasn't just when people started getting suspicious about the blood clotting story. Why do you think I've never had a legit job, never let anyone get close to us? I've been scared of my own shadow for the last thirteen years; panicking if someone seems too interested in us, if someone walks behind me for too long. Anyone could be after us and we wouldn't have a clue until it was too late."

"How could you have lived like this?"

"I'll tell you how," Janice said, her voice unwavering. "Because life with you has been terrifying but wonderful. Loving you, keeping you safe, has made my life worth living, made me a better person. But I've had no one to talk to. I had to work out for myself what was the best thing to do. I'm sorry if I've messed up."

Celia massaged her temples with her fingertips, her face pained. "All these things you've told me... What you did! What that professor did! The *virus* in me! I...I can't take it in." She stood up woozily.

"Celia, come and sit down," Janice said softly. "We'll work out what to do."

"No...I'm sorry. I can't stay. I need some time on my own. I feel like my head's going to explode," Celia whimpered. And she walked out of the flat in a daze.

26 *whatever it takes*

Frankie Byrne sat in his car, stunned by the conversation that had just poured into his ears. He wasn't a man who was easily shocked – after all, he made his living getting his hands dirty in matters any decent person would shudder at. But this! These devastating secrets spoken out loud for the first time. Babies used as lab rats; a deadly virus contained in that girl's blood, only ever a skin's breadth away from spreading. And Nemo! Where did she fit into all this?

The sound of a distant car horn brought him round. He ran his meat-cleaver hands down his face and shook out his arms as if he were ridding himself of pins and needles.

"Stop thinking," he reprimanded himself, "and do what you're getting paid for." He phoned his client.

She answered immediately. From the background noise, he guessed that she was at some kind of dinner party.

"I need to talk to you right now," he said.

"Excuse me a minute. I've just got to take this call. Do continue without me," he heard her say pleasantly to the other guests.

A minute later Frankie had her full attention as he repeated everything he'd just heard. Not once did she interrupt him. Even when he'd finished, the line remained silent.

"Are you still there?" he asked.

"Yes. Now listen very carefully, Mr. Byrne," she said. "You must get that girl right now, by whatever means necessary. But you mustn't make a scene. No one must see and whatever you do, she's not to be harmed. There's a place I want you to take her to. I'll send your phone the location. We're not to meet in person. You drop her off, make sure she can't escape, then leave. Keep in contact and let me know when you've got her. Do you understand?"

"Listen, lady! I don't want to know who you are," Frankie replied, "but I'm a private detective not a kidnapper."

"I beg to differ, Mr. Byrne," she said disdainfully. "I did my homework before I chose you for this job. I know that you'll do whatever it takes to get your fee."

"But this is different; we're talking about an innocent kid here."

"No, we're talking about a walking time bomb!" she retorted. "Would you rather the girl was left mingling with the public every day, only an accident away from unleashing this virus? Is that what you want? Would that be the right thing to do? I'm the only person who can deal with this properly. By bringing her to me, you'll be doing the right thing for once in your life."

There was a heavy pause until Frankie eventually spoke. "What are you going to do with her?"

"Take her back to where she belongs," came the enigmatic answer. "Now for God's sake, get her before it's too late."

As Frankie sprinted towards the Bluebell Towers, Celia was making her way unsteadily down the stairs. She called Sol's number. His voice jumped on her with relief.

"Celia! What have you been doing? You said you'd call me."

"Are you feeling okay?" Celia asked, her voice vague, spaced out.

"Yeah, *I'm* fine. It's you I'm worried about. What's going on? I'm coming over to see you."

"No, you can't. I don't want you to. I need to be alone,

have some time to think what to do."

"What are you on about? What's happened?" Sol said anxiously.

"Sol – everything's changed." Celia's voice cracked. "You've got to keep away from me; everyone's got to keep away from me."

"Celia, you're not making any sense. I'm coming over," he said, finishing the call before she could protest.

Celia turned off her phone and quickened her step down the stairs.

Frankie slowed to walking pace as he entered the courtyard of the tower blocks, aware of the CCTV cameras. His eyes scoured the area, but there was no sign of her. He'd been quick, maybe she hadn't left the building yet. He entered the starkly lit lobby of Tower Two and looked up at the numbers above the two lifts. One displayed a *10*, but the other was showing it was on the twentieth floor – Celia's floor.

Could she still be up there? Frankie wondered. *Maybe Janice persuaded her to come back.*

He hesitated, debating what would be his best course of action. He looked like he had a nervous twitch, his head jerking back and forth between the lift displays and the outside courtyard. He deliberated for a few seconds more;

if he'd missed her, he didn't have any leads on where she might be heading, so what could he lose by going up to the flat and checking out if she was still there? Yes, decision made! He pressed the button to call the lift. It seemed to reach him so quickly, he wondered if it was in free fall.

The doors pinged open and he entered the empty box, pressing the button for the top floor. A stinking yellow liquid sloshed around his feet. The doors began to judder shut. He momentarily looked up from the foul substance, only to see a figure crossing the lobby and passing out into the courtyard, the flash of orange hair unmistakable.

Frankie reacted immediately, thrusting his foot into the wafer-thin opening, but the doors continued to close, regardless of the obstruction. He dragged his foot out before it was completely crushed. He hit the button to open the doors but they ignored the command and sealed tight shut. He punched *1, 2, 3, 4,* desperate to stop the lift's ascent, but all to no avail. The lift creaked and squealed its way slowly and painfully, like an arthritic old man, on its unstoppable mission to reach the highest floor.

"Who the hell takes the stairs from the twentieth floor?!" he fumed, kicking the wall of his stinking cage.

27 *here to help*

Sol's bike weaved through the passageways towards Bluebell Towers. As he took a sharp corner he slammed on his brakes, skidding to a stop. In the distance, walking towards the main road, he spotted Celia. He shouted out to her, "Celia, wait up!"

He wasn't sure whether she heard him or not, but she didn't turn around or even hesitate as she continued onwards. She disappeared around a corner and Sol went racing after her, but as the main road came into view he saw where she was heading. The last bus into the city sat at the stop opposite, its engine ticking over. The bus driver folded up his newspaper and the doors hissed open to let

Celia on. She made her way past the smattering of other late night passengers and sat on the back seat. Sol shot out across the road and banged on the window, shouting. "Celia – where are you going? Why won't you talk to me?"

Wordlessly, she pressed the palms of her gloved hands against the window and looked at him with such sorrowful eyes that he felt an overwhelming sense of dread. The bus crunched into gear and moved off. Sol shouted hopelessly after it.

Meanwhile, a furious Frankie Byrne had extricated himself from the lift and was sprinting back towards his car as fast as his heavy frame would carry him. He didn't have a clue where to look next. He briefly listened in to Janice to see if he could pick up any leads, but only sobbing filled the airwaves. He had no better option than driving around the estate, keeping his eyes peeled.

He knew that every minute that passed decreased his chances of finding her. His car crawled around the estate, passing bored gangs and loud drunks. He reached the junction which led onto the main road. He glanced both ways before pulling out, slamming on the brakes as a boy riding an unlit bike came tearing out of nowhere. The boy's skinny legs were pumping the pedals like a maniac, his teeth were gritted, and he was concentrating so hard that he didn't even notice the car that had nearly ploughed into him. Frankie's hand hovered over the horn, but he stopped as the boy's face was momentarily illuminated as he sped under a street light.

"I know that face. It's her friend, the boy in the cafe. Now where's he going in such a hurry?" A hopeful glint appeared in Frankie's eyes as he watched Sol's progress down the road.

Frankie followed at a discreet distance, letting other cars pass. The boy's pace was relentlessly fast as he powered along the tarmac. Cars beeped angrily as their headlights fell on the reckless cyclist shrouded in darkness.

Frankie calculated that they'd gone about five kilometres and was convinced that the boy must be heading all the way into the city, but then, without warning, Sol swerved off the road and bumped his way across one of the surrounding fields. Frankie pulled over and jumped out of the car. The boy was heading straight for a wood. Frankie must have passed it on his journey to and from the city; but he hadn't paid any attention to the sprawling area. He couldn't afford to lose sight of the boy if there was a chance he would lead him to Celia. He opened the glove compartment and prised away its false back to reveal the small chamber behind. He pulled on a pair of leather gloves and wrapped his hand around the cold metal of the gun concealed in the chamber. Then, from out of the boot, he grabbed a weighty rucksack and slung it over his shoulders, before yomping after the disappearing boy.

Sol abandoned his bike at the treeline and picked his way through the woods. The moonlight struggled to penetrate the tree canopy, but the darkness wasn't an obstacle to Sol. He knew this place too well and within minutes he'd reached the discreet hole under the wire fencing. He slithered under as effortlessly as a snake. Even though he'd lost sight of the bus within minutes of pursuing it, Sol was convinced that Celia would be heading for the flooded quarry. He felt it in his bones.

Frankie Byrne was surprisingly light-footed when necessary and he stalked his prey through the woods like a nimble ballerina. Only the hooting of an owl disturbed the eerie quiet. His night-vision goggles were trained on the green figure cutting in and out of the trees ahead of him. He ducked behind a thick tree trunk and watched as the lithe boy slid under the fence and continued deeper into the woods. As soon as Frankie dared, he got out a pair of pliers from his rucksack and snipped the wire, before pulling it apart to form a gap that he could squeeze his ample belly through.

Sol may have been in front but it was Frankie who saw

Celia first. As he skirted around Sol's path, he glimpsed her through the trees; a desolate figure standing at the top of the slab steps. She was looking out over the lake, her head bowed, her arms wrapped around herself. He had to act quickly; he had to stop the boy before he saw her. Frankie couldn't afford to have any witnesses.

Sol was fast approaching the lakeside – any second now Celia would be in view – but Frankie was behind him so quickly it was as if he'd been teleported. Sol heard a sudden rush of breaking twigs on the ground, but before he even had time to turn around he felt a hammer-like blow on the back of his skull and then…nothing.

Celia heard a thud as Sol's body hit the ground. She turned around, calling out anxiously into the dark forest. "Who's there? Sol, is that you?"

Frankie immediately walked out of the shadows to reveal himself and shield Sol's form from view. "Hi, Celia." He approached her with his palms raised as if he were surrendering.

"Who are you? How do you know my name? What are you doing here?" The questions came tumbling out in alarm.

"Don't worry. I'm here to help you." Frankie spoke as gently as a purring tiger. "I'm Detective Inspector Paul

Garner." He pulled out a police badge from a pocket and flashed it at her.

She peered at him in confusion. "I know you from somewhere. I've seen you before. You…you were that bloke in the city, the volunteer in that fire act."

Frankie gave a convincingly playful laugh. "Yeah, how stupid did I look?"

"But why are…" Celia struggled to finish, her mind already overloaded.

"We've been following you, Celia. We had to make sure we had the right person. We've been looking for you for years. We know about the virus, we know about everything. I can help you."

"If you really knew about the virus then you'd know that no one can help me," she replied bitterly.

"You're wrong, Celia. I don't know what you've been told but an antidote has been developed. It was ready years ago. If Janice had only gone to the authorities, you wouldn't have had to go through all this. But all that matters is that we've found you. Just come with me and we'll get rid of this thing."

Celia shook her head. "No! It can't be true."

"Of course it is. Now, come with me." He smiled, holding his hands out to her. She stepped hesitantly towards him, their fingertips touching, when, out of the darkness, a moan rose up.

Her hands shot away from his. "What was that? There's someone there!"

"It's just an animal," he replied quickly. "This place must be teeming with them. Come on, it's creepy here. Let's go."

"That's no animal." She ducked past him and saw Sol's inert body on the forest floor. "Sol!" she screamed. "What have you done to him?"

Frankie had positioned himself in front of her, blocking her way. "He'll be fine," he said coldly. "Now come with me."

Celia's eyes darted around, looking for an escape route. She faltered backwards onto the top slab. There was no way past his brick-wall body and only the lake lay far below her.

They shifted and swayed, as he mirrored her every move, like two mismatched sumo wrestlers in deadlock. Celia tried to wrong-foot him, jerking right, then left, but this only amused him.

She stepped back. Her heels hung over the edge of the slab, a sheer drop below.

"Come on, little girl," he scoffed, moving in on her. "You're not in the playground now. There's nowhere to run."

But he was suddenly silenced as, without warning, Celia turned her back on him and threw herself into the lake.

She shattered the surface of the still waters, causing pandemonium among the sleeping wildlife. Birds flew up in fright; foxes called out from the woods, sounding like distressed babies; and flustered mallards skimmed across the water, offering a chorus of laughter in response to Celia's inelegant entry.

"Oh for God's sake!" shouted Frankie, throwing his arms up in frustration.

Celia kicked her way to the surface and gasped as she trod water. Her clothes clung to her; her trainers felt like bricks weighing down her feet.

"Stop mucking about. I don't have time for this," Frankie sighed, pulling out his gun and pointing it at her bobbing head. "Get out now or I'll shoot."

Logic may have dictated that she should do as he said, but her instincts were telling her not to. If that man, whoever he was, captured her, she had no chance of helping Sol. She had to believe that she could save her friend. She had to believe that both of them could make it out of this alive.

She was a sitting duck; she had to get moving. Screwing up her eyes, she waited for the bullets to fly as her arms and legs splashed against the water.

Frankie couldn't believe that she was defying him. "What's wrong with you, Celia? Do you want to die? Get here now!" he roared, but still she continued.

After a minute she unscrewed her eyes and dared to look back at the figure on the slabs. The gun was hanging down at his side. Frankie knew he wouldn't shoot, but this teenager either had a death wish or had just called his bluff. Either way, he knew he had to try a different approach.

"Don't be stupid, Celia. What's the point of all this? Unless you're Spiderman, I can't see you getting out of this lake any other way but past me," he said, waving his gun around at the surrounding barricade of cliffs. "You'll have to come out sometime and, when you do, I'll be here, waiting for you." He walked down the steps to the bottom slabs and made himself comfortable, as if spectating a show.

He continued to call out to Celia as she struggled further out. "Why are you making things hard for yourself? I'm not going to hurt you. Look, I'll put the gun down. I was just trying to scare you. It's not even loaded." He laid the gun down and shrugged his shoulders. "Someone just wants a word with you – someone who can help you. I promise."

Celia didn't respond; she was concentrating hard on keeping her head above the water and moving at the same time. She hadn't managed to get far. Her artless stroke produced more splashing than motion.

Frankie continued to work his way under her skin. "Look at you, Celia; this is painful to watch. You swim like a toddler. You're going to get into trouble out there. Think about it. It could be a hundred metres deep and you're right in the middle. You could get cramp any minute, seize up and then…well, it would distress me to watch you drown."

His words sailed over and tried to capsize her. They burrowed into her mind, causing it to dwell on the fathomless depths below her dangling legs. Her limbs flailed about; water lapped into her mouth as quickly as she could spit it out. The reflection of the full moon illuminated the lake with a ghostly glow. Suddenly it seemed as vast as an ocean and there she was, an insignificant dot, bobbing in the middle of it. She tried to concentrate on the mechanics of swimming, but the more she thought about it, the more it seemed impossible. Frankie kept up his psychological assault.

"Celia, you're sinking. You're not going to make it. Quickly! Swim back to me."

Don't let him get to you. Come on, Celia, block him out, she ordered herself.

Seconds later, shaky, half-sung words from The Undertones' teenage anthem began to rise from the lake.

Frankie roared with laughter. "You crazy kid! What are you doing?"

But Celia wasn't listening. She continued singing "Teenage Kicks", focusing only on her favourite song.

Her arms and legs responding to the beat, her body started to move across the lake and towards the reeds. She was pleased with herself, but there was no reason to celebrate yet. She knew a far bigger challenge lay ahead.

28 *if my life depended upon it...*

Celia skirted around the tall, brittle reeds and out of sight of her assailant. She trod water, catching her breath, as her eyes searched the rock face in front of her. It only took a minute to locate the cluster of overhanging plants cascading out of the rock at her eye level. She thrust a hand through them and felt the freezing space concealed behind.

This is it, she thought with trepidation. She brushed the camouflage aside to reveal the sliver of a tunnel. Her stomach churned as she peered into the endless darkness. It looked even narrower than she remembered. How could she possibly put her body in there?

Frankie was looking over at the reeds. He'd lost sight

of her but was unperturbed. "Come on, Celia, give me another song. I enjoyed that one," he taunted. "Or are we playing hide-and-seek now? Well, I'll tell you what, why don't I count to twenty and if you don't show yourself, I'll come in there and drag you out? One, two, three, four, five…"

As his counting boomed out, Celia's body prepared itself for action, like an athlete under starter's orders. With white-knuckled hands, she gripped the mouth of the tunnel. Bobbing down into the water, she then thrust up sharply, heaving her torso inside the slit. She lay there, face down. The slimy stone pressed hard against her exposed skin, the icy air chilled her wet body. Her feet scrabbled in the water as she attempted to push the rest of her body up. At last, her whole body disappeared into the tunnel. The plants fell back over the entrance, entombing Celia in pitch-black.

Frankie had heard the frenzy of splashes coming from behind the reeds. "You'd better not be drowning on me!" The silence that followed concerned him even more and he cursed as he hurriedly stripped down to his underpants and vest. An almighty yelp echoed around the lake as he lowered himself into the bracing waters.

Celia lay on her stomach in the tunnel, paralysed by fear. She'd entered her own private hell. Her mind fixated on the tons of solid rock encasing her. *It's going to collapse.*

I'm going to be crushed to death. Her chest tightened; she felt like there were hands squeezing her throat. She sensed the walls of the tunnel closing in. Her head knocked against the roof as she lifted it to gulp in air.

A voice in her head screamed for her to back out now. *It doesn't matter if he captures you, at least you'll be alive. At least you won't have to crawl through this.* But another voice rose above it, shouting it down. *You've got to get through this tunnel. This isn't just about you. You've got to save Sol. What good will you be to him if you get caught? You can't just leave him. Now get moving!*

Defying every instinct in her body, her shaking frame began to slide deeper into the tunnel.

Frankie swam through the water like a hippo. He powered into the bed of reeds, using his arm to swipe through them like a scythe. But Celia wasn't to be found. He looked around the still surface and started to panic. Taking great gulps of air, he dived down, only able to see as far as the moonlight penetrated the dark waters. He dived again and again feeling around. But it was futile. He should have gone in to get her sooner. He could have prevented this. *It may be hours before her body surfaces, if it ever does*, he thought grimly.

He trod water, panting noisily. He'd pushed himself too far. He felt his heart about to burst. He was convinced that he would be joining Celia in her watery grave.

Celia hadn't progressed more than a couple of metres when she came to a sudden halt. Something was stopping her. She could hear the metal of her belt buckle scratching against the rock beneath her waist. But the more she tried to move forward, the firmer the buckle became snared.

Frankie's panting had eased and his ears tuned in to a scratching sound, which seemed to be coming from a nearby cluster of plants hanging off the rock face. He swam up to them and put his ear against it. *There's definitely something in there*, he thought, perplexed. As he grabbed the plants, they peeled away from the cliff, exposing the narrow entrance to a tunnel. He peered into it, but his eyes were met by darkness. He held onto the entrance with one hand and thrust the other deep into the slit. All he could feel was icy air, but now the scratching sound was louder, more frantic.

He rammed his shoulder hard against the entrance in his efforts to reach further into the tunnel. Celia let out a squeal as his fingertips found the sole of her trainer. He put his head into the mouth of the icy tunnel, his triumphant voice deafening Celia. "That's a great hiding place, Celia, but I've found you. I win, fair and square."

He grabbed for her foot again, trying to get a proper hold on it. She had to get moving; she had to get the buckle free before his brute force dragged her out of there. She shook her foot as his fingers grasped at it. She held her stomach in and edged an arm under her body. Her fingers were able to feel the buckle, snagged on a jagged rock, but she couldn't dislodge it.

She felt his fingers closing firmly around her trainer. In desperation she rocked her whole body from side to side. Her hip bones ground painfully into the rock but she felt the buckle release. Yet before she even had a chance to crawl forward, Frankie strengthened his grip on her foot and began to drag her back. She dug her fingers into the contours of the rock, fighting against his pull. Grunting, she repeatedly kicked her foot against the side of the tunnel, battering and scraping Frankie's hand on the rock, until he eventually released her with a pained growl.

As soon as she felt her foot was free she scrambled onwards, her fear of the tomb-like space supplanted by blind panic. She slid out of the tunnel with a gasp, like a baby taking its first breath.

Frankie's curses were replaced by a more conciliatory manner. "Hey, Celia, it must have taken some guts to crawl through there. Now let's not kid ourselves; we both know that there's no way I can fit through to come and get you. But wherever you've just crawled through to, I'm betting you're trapped, which means you don't have many options. You either crawl back out now or stay there and face a very slow, very painful death. If you haven't got any water you're looking at three days; water but no food, you could survive up to three weeks, but you'll go mad with the light deprivation and die of hypothermia first. No one knows you're here, Celia. So let's be sensible about this. Come back out and we'll sort something out."

Celia didn't answer, she hardly dared move, but she had to feel her way along the cave walls to the foot of the shaft. She felt for the foot holes. Frankie strained to decipher the scrambling noises filtering through the tunnel; suddenly he realized the pursuit wasn't over yet.

"Oh, I see! Have you got another way out? Well don't worry, Celia; either way I'll get you."

Frankie's voice made Celia want to scream, but he didn't linger to torment her. He had to get to shore as quickly as possible. He pushed himself off from the rock, causing a tidal wave as he swam back towards the slabs.

Her climb up the shaft was agonizingly slow. If she was too hasty and lost her footing Celia knew that she'd end up at the bottom of the shaft, with not a soul to come to her rescue. At last she felt the makeshift cover above her. She pushed it clear and clawed her way out, collapsing on the forest floor, every fibre in her traumatized body begging to rest. But she knew it would be fatal to stay there, so hauling herself off the ground, she staggered to the trees that lined the cliff top. From here she had a clear view of her pursuer as he dragged his dripping bulk out of the lake. He threw on clothes that leeched onto the contours of his wet body and then climbed the steps before disappearing into the trees, heading in her direction. She could easily make it out of the woods and away to safety before he had time to get anywhere near her. But Celia wasn't even tempted to run; the only thought in her head was to save Sol.

She crept through the thick undergrowth, listening and watching; all her senses heightened like those of a hunted animal, freezing at the sound of every twig breaking, flinching at the rustle of the trees, praying that the night air wouldn't carry the stench of her fear to him. But with the fear came adrenalin and the last drops were secreting into her blood stream.

A few minutes later she'd made it back to where Sol's body remained crumpled on the ground, like a little boy in a deep sleep.

"Please be okay," she whispered. But as she bent to touch him, something grabbed her from behind, lifting her off her feet. She let out a half formed scream that was silenced by a huge gloved hand enveloping her face. Her arms were pinned to her sides, her head restrained. She kicked and kicked but made no impression on the immovable mound that held her.

Tape was slapped across her mouth and she was flung across shoulders like a captured animal. A hand closed around her wrists and another locked around her ankles.

Her head dangled down, eyes looking at the ground nearly two metres below.

Frankie turned his mouth to her ear. "I knew you'd come back for him. You should have got away while you had the chance."

His tone was neither mocking nor threatening, it seemed heavy with genuine regret — and this made Celia all the more terrified.

29 *a seed of hope*

Like on a bone-shaking fairground ride, Celia's body was jolted up and down with every stride Frankie took on their path out of the woods. Once they neared the road, he waited until there were no headlights approaching and then jogged to the car with his catch. He lowered her onto the back seat, which he'd covered with a plastic sheet. She flopped down, grateful for the soft landing. He reached over to the front seat and produced a tracksuit top, which he offered to Celia.

"Here," he said, "you're shivering."

She snatched it from him and put it on, rolling up the sleeves, begrudgingly grateful for the warmth of his tent-sized top. But before she could even swing a futile punch at him, Frankie had bound her ankles and wrists with thick gaffer tape, careful to wrap it over the fabric of the top and her socks; the last thing he wanted was for her to spill any of that blood.

"Now lie down and keep out of sight or I swear I'll put you in the boot," Frankie said to the trussed-up girl.

As the engine started she heard the click of the central locking and knew that all her exits were sealed. Celia lay there, helpless and exhausted, but her mind was in overdrive, conjuring up images of Sol's body on the forest floor, thinking of all the terrifying things that could possibly lie ahead of her. Frankie pressed the accelerator to the floor and the car screeched off along the tarmac. He was anxious to deliver this parcel as quickly as possible and forget about this whole terrible business.

He tried to concentrate on following the directions to their destination but the muffled sobs coming from the back seat were eating into him. He tilted the rear-view mirror and looked at the distraught girl; tears streamed down her face.

Frankie couldn't keep his mouth shut. He needed to make himself feel better. "Listen, Celia, I didn't want to have to get you this way. If you'd just cooperated, all this wouldn't have been necessary. Anyway, I know this looks bad but you shouldn't worry, you're not going to come to any harm. I've been told that you're going back where you belong."

Celia tried to control her sobs so she could hear his words.

"Now, I've been thinking about it, and what if that means your real parents? Maybe they've been looking for you all these years. Maybe you're going back to them. Hey, wouldn't that be great?" he said. He saw the confusion in Celia's eyes.

He's lying, she thought. However, despite her doubts, Frankie had planted a seed of hope and, in the bleakness of that journey, she allowed it to grow.

The stress of listening to her sobs was now replaced by the unbearable weight of silent hope and Frankie was buckling under the tension. He turned on the radio. The mellow tones of the graveyard shift DJ spoke to them. "*We're approaching midnight on this beautiful moonlit evening and I have just the song to take us into tomorrow.*"

Dean Martin's velvety voice filled the car with the joyous sound of "That's Amore".

"Hey, I love this one," Frankie chirped up, as if he were a friendly taxi driver. "I bet Janice loves it too," he added spontaneously, immediately smarting with guilt.

* * *

Sol slowly lifted his lead-weight head off the ground. He groaned as he became conscious enough to register the splitting ache and the ground shifting beneath him. Cradling his throbbing head, he felt the thick, sticky blood plastered to his hair. Sol couldn't work out what had happened. He searched for his mobile. It was still in his pocket. The screen lit up the darkness but there was no signal. He stumbled through the trees like a drunk feeling his way home. He made his way into the open and phoned Celia, but the number was dead.

"What's going on?" he moaned to himself. He knew who to call in a crisis and as Abs answered, Sol could hear the din of the Bluebell pub in the background. Sol slurred out his plea for help.

"Sit tight," Abs responded. "We're coming to get you."

Sol had made it to the roadside as his brothers drove up. The car headlights illuminated him as they checked him over.

"Well, I don't think you need stitches," Yacob said, inspecting his head. "But you're going to need some heavy-duty headache pills and an ice pack."

"What happened?" Abs asked the groaning boy.

"I don't know. I was looking for Celia in the woods. I heard something behind me and the next second it felt like my skull had been cracked open and I was out cold."

"Did they rob you?" Yacob asked.

"No. Nothing was taken. I wasn't touched. Why would someone do this?"

"Maybe it wasn't 'someone'. Maybe something just fell on you from one of the trees. Why were you looking here for Celia anyway?" Abs said.

"I saw her get on the bus. I thought she must be heading here but I didn't see her and her phone is dead."

"But why would she go to some woods? If she was on the bus, wouldn't she have been heading for the city?" Yacob asked, puzzled.

Sol ignored the question. Even in his dazed state, he wanted to protect their sanctuary. "I know something's wrong," he slurred. "After she went back to her flat, she was weird, really freaked out."

"What are you rambling on about?" Yacob said. "Have you two had a lovers' tiff? Maybe it was her who hit you on the head then."

Abs high-fived Yacob, impressed by his joke. Then he said sagely, "Seriously, you should give her some space, instead of chasing after her. You've a lot to learn about girls, Sol. She's probably meeting a mate in town. She might stay out all night, try and get into some clubs, but she'll come back in the morning and everything will be fine."

"No. We should call the police," Sol said.

At this, the brothers flashed a look of alarm at each other.

"No way! We don't need them getting involved. Anyway, what would you tell them? Something hit you on the head in the woods and you're worried about your girlfriend because she got on a bus," Yacob mocked. "What do you expect them to do about it apart from laugh at you, and maybe caution you for trespassing? And think of Mum. There's no way you want her to find out. It will worry her to think that her only good child is sneaking out at night to wander around some creepy forest."

"Okay then," Sol said reluctantly. "But I have to talk to Celia's mum. I need to know what's going on. I should tell her that I saw Celia getting on the bus. She'll be really worried about her."

"You're in no state to do anything apart from go home to bed," Abs said.

"But she needs to know," Sol whimpered.

"Then tell her in the morning. We need to sort you out. We'll smuggle you into the house. I'll just tell Emama that you were knackered and went straight to bed. Tomorrow we'll think of some story to explain that bump, and you should just keep your mouth shut," Yacob advised.

"But what if she doesn't come back?"

"Stop being such a drama queen. She'll be back to kiss and make up."

"I've told you already," Sol said wearily, "we're just friends."

"Yeah, right." The brothers winked at each other as they helped Sol into the car. Sol was in no state to keep protesting.

30 *the destination*

They'd been travelling for over an hour when Frankie
turned off the unlit road that cut through the moorland.
As the car crawled on and on up the driveway, he peered
into the darkness, unsure if he'd got the right place.
Driving over the brow of the hill, the full beam of the
headlights fell on a building standing in isolation on the
black moor.

Frankie turned around and spoke to the prostrate girl.
"Celia, are you awake?"

Celia had been fighting sleep the whole journey,
determined to stay alert, but she'd lost her battle against the
lulling motion of the car and the soporific hum of the engine.

Sleep had transported her to the flooded quarry. She was standing at the lakeside, bathed in brilliant sunshine. She turned on hearing footsteps. For a few moments the sun blinded her. Her eyes struggled to adjust, but as her sight cleared, a vision approached: a man and a woman, their arms outstretched, joy etched on their faces. She instinctively recognized herself in them: the long limbs of the pale-skinned woman with the mile-wide smile, the mop of unruly tangerine hair on the round-eyed man. Their agonizing years of waiting over as they whispered to her, "Celia, we've come to take you home."

Celia's eyes flickered madly behind her closed lids, moans contained by her gag as a single teardrop toppled from her eye.

Frankie shook her. "Wake up, we're here."

She sat bolt upright, disorientated, the blanket of dreams ripped from her as she realized she was back in her waking nightmare.

He locked her in the car and, taking a torch, went to investigate the building. From the outside, the shabby prefab appeared disused but, despite the battering of the elements and the ivy that covered its walls, the building appeared intact. He tried the door. It was locked. The door and its frame seemed surprisingly solid.

The night air was chilly now in the cloudless sky. He gave an involuntary shudder. This place really was in the middle of nowhere, no sign of life, no lights for miles. He phoned the client.

"I'm here. What do you want me to do?"

"Secure her just outside the building and then go," she answered.

Frankie hesitated. "I'm not sure that I should leave her alone out here. Maybe I should wait until you arrive."

"Absolutely not," she answered, irritated. "Leave her and go. I'll be in touch with you soon."

"You're not going to hurt her, are you?" he asked uneasily. His answer was a dead line.

He stood and looked over at his teenage captive, who defiantly returned his stare through the car window. A few seconds later he shook off the stranger that was his conscience, and went to the boot of the car, pulling out some rope. Then he lifted her out of the car and bound her to the trunk of a nearby tree, before leaning in towards her, fingers grasping at her top. Celia shook her head violently, her cries of panic muffled by the tape over her mouth, but he proceeded to rearrange the tracksuit top that was hanging from her, zipping it right up to her neck.

She was confused and repulsed by his seemingly caring act.

"I don't want you to get cold," he said. "I've got to go now, but someone will be along soon, someone who can help you."

He dared to search her petrified features as he placed the torch upright on the floor. "I'll leave the torch for you," he said. He turned and walked away, mumbling into the ground, "This is for the best."

As Frankie drove off, he opened the window. He was choking with doubt and guilt. He couldn't possibly have spotted the silent black Mercedes hidden from view that fired up its engine as soon as he drove out of sight.

On hearing the car, Celia thought that the man must have turned around; maybe he'd had a change of heart, maybe he was going to let her go.

She was dazzled by the car's headlights. The driver got out and walked towards her. Celia was unable to make out the approaching figure until it stood only centimetres away.

The impeccably groomed woman couldn't take her eyes off Celia. She gazed at the girl as if she were an exotic animal. "Just look at you, my survivor," she whispered in awe.

A cloud of sumptuous perfume enveloped Celia as the woman gently caressed her cold cheek. Celia didn't even see the needle as she felt the lightning-quick sting in the side of her neck.

* * *

By the time Frankie reached the motorway he practically had the road to himself. He sped along, trying to rid his head of Celia's frightened face. Instead he filled it with thoughts of going home and sleeping in his own bed. He was aching to get away from everything to do with this case, but he knew that he had suitcases full of his belongings back at the hotel in the city. He made a decision. He didn't care how late it was, he'd go to the hotel, collect his stuff and drive straight home, even if it took him until dawn.

But his comforting plan was shattered by the ringing of his phone.

"Mr. Byrne, I have the girl but I need you to do one last job for me."

"What is it?" he asked coldly.

"You need to get rid of Janice Frost," she said in a businesslike tone.

Frankie found himself grappling for words.

"Do you understand, Mr. Byrne? You have to get rid of her and you have to do it tonight."

"I can't do that!" Frankie retorted, finding his voice.

"You have no choice unless you want to be locked up for a very long time."

"What are you talking about?" he snapped.

"Illegal bugging, hacking into confidential files and now kidnapping a girl – and God knows what the police will unearth once they start investigating you and your practices."

"You're bluffing. You wouldn't go to the police, you'd be exposing yourself."

"You're right. *I* won't go to the police, but Janice Frost will, unless you stop her. Think about it: once Celia has been missing for a day or two the woman will have nothing to lose by going to the police and telling them everything in the hope of finding her."

"But that's your problem. Janice Frost knows nothing about me or my involvement."

"I'll make sure that my problem becomes your problem. She's the only person who could lead the police to me and I swear that if she does, I'll lead them straight to you."

"But the girl knows everything too."

"Forget about the girl. That's all under control. Now, are you going to do the job?"

"I can't kill someone."

"Really, Mr. Byrne?" she said. "Just think about all those people you've tracked down and dragged back into the hands of loan sharks and gangsters. Do you lose any sleep about what happened to them? Isn't this just a more honest approach, instead of always being the middle man?"

Frankie couldn't respond.

"It'll be easy to make it look like an accident, even suicide. After all, hasn't her daughter just run away, not able to stand her crazy mother any more? No one will be suspicious, or even care. The police won't waste their time on the death of another tragic nobody from some dead-end estate."

"There must be another way," Frankie said, his sweaty palms sliding on the steering wheel.

"No. This is the only way. Dead people can't talk and once it's done we'll both be safe. No one will be able to touch us. You can go home, forget all this ever happened and let my generous fee ease your conscience. Mr. Byrne, if you don't do it, you have everything to lose and nothing to gain. You know I'm right, don't you?

"Yes." It was the hardest word Frankie had ever had to say.

31 *a friend in need*

Janice stumbled around the flat, desperately searching for where the ringing was coming from. She flung the sofa cushions on the floor, fell to her knees and crawled on all fours to the coffee table, knocking her drink over in the process. She had to answer it before it rang off. It must be Celia. Who else would be ringing her at two thirty in the morning?

Now it was coming from above her. She lurched to the window sill and picked it up. "Celia!" she rasped down the phone.

"No, Janice, it's me, Paul."

Her eyes narrowed in concentration. "Paul," she

eventually responded.

"Listen, Janice, I hope that I haven't woken you. I'm sorry for calling you at this ridiculous hour but I just couldn't stop myself."

Janice plonked herself down on the sofa, one hand holding her head upright to keep the room still. "Oh," was all she could muster, reasoning that the less she spoke, the more sober she would sound.

"Please don't think that I'm a weirdo or anything, but I just had this terrible feeling that you were in some sort of trouble tonight. I couldn't shake it off. I just had to phone to make sure that you were all right. I know that I must sound like such a nutter but—"

"No...no," Janice interrupted, overwhelmed by the connection this man must have with her.

"I am in trouble," she blurted out, sobs gathering in her throat. "Celia's gone! I don't know what to do."

"Have you called the police?" he asked, holding his breath for the answer.

"No. I was going to wait until the morning, see if she turned up."

"Yeah, that sounds sensible. You shouldn't bother them just yet. Listen, what about if I come over right now and help you sort this out?" Frankie said heroically.

"Would you?" She sounded like a little lost girl. "I'd really appreciate that."

"Of course, Janice." He spoke tenderly. "I'll be there in half an hour."

Janice was regretting having tried to drink herself calm. While she dragged herself to the kitchen to make a strong coffee and splash cold water over her face, Frankie pulled over at a twenty-four-hour convenience store and bought a large bottle of gin and a small bottle of tonic water, before continuing his journey.

The gentle tap on the door came just after three a.m. Frankie's mouth smiled but his eyes remained cold as he presented her with the bottles.

"I've bought a little pick-you-up," he said, the irony lost on Janice, who took them with a lopsided smile. Her futile attempts to sober up had made little impression on her brain. However, she did notice that he was wearing leather gloves.

"Cold?" she enquired, baffled.

"Oh, these?" he said casually. "Burned my hands on a job today. Doctor said I need to keep them covered up to help them heal."

"Oh, you poor thing," she pouted, gently patting his gloved hands. "Come on in. Excuse the mess. I'm afraid I'm in a bit of a state."

Frankie went in and took charge, sitting her on the

sofa while he poured her a very stiff drink.

"You not having one?" she asked.

"Driving, aren't I?" he said, sitting so close to her that their jean-clad knees touched. "Come on, get that down you. It'll make you feel better," he said, as if it were medicine. She drank it down as he smiled approvingly. "Now Janice, tell me what's happened."

Janice fumbled for words; the nearness of his body was distracting her. She could feel herself gravitating towards him. "Celia ran off tonight, she's not come back, she's not let me know if she's okay."

"Well, it won't be the first time a teenager has got into a strop and run off for a few hours," he said reassuringly.

"But this isn't just some teenage tantrum. If you knew, you'd understand why I'm so worried." As she spoke, the panic resurfaced. She leaned away from him, guilty for letting her attention wander. "God knows what she's thinking, what she might do."

"Come on. Calm yourself down," he said pouring her another drink.

"No, I shouldn't. I've got to keep my wits about me," she said, springing up too quickly. Her legs buckled, as if on an ice rink. Frankie helped her up. Janice bowed her head in shame. "What must you think of me?" she slurred. "A pathetic, drunken woman."

"I don't think that at all, Janice. You're just a good mother who's worried about her child."

Janice smiled meekly. "And you're a wonderful man," she said, prodding his chest with a finger. "You come here, in the middle of the night, to help me, to listen to me. All my life I've never had anyone I could talk to, no one to rely on…but then, you came along."

Frankie couldn't meet her doe-eyed gaze, her pupils dilated by alcohol and the chemicals of attraction. He had to get this over with before he lost his nerve. "You need some fresh air." His voice as unsteady as she was. He took her gently by the arm and guided her onto the balcony. He surveyed the hundreds of other balconies clinging to the surrounding tower blocks. All were empty and shrouded in darkness. Everyone tucked up in bed, oblivious to the evil act about to be perpetrated in their midst.

32 *where you belong*

The woman was in the middle of preparing the glass slides when her mobile rang. She broke off from the delicate task in order to take the call that she'd been anxiously waiting for.

"It's done. Janice Frost is dead," the voice said.

"Were there any complications?" the woman asked.

"No. You were right. It was easy. It looks like an accident. No one will suspect."

"Good, good," she said with relief.

"How's the girl?" he asked.

"Forget about her. You've done your job and you'll get your money, but I'm warning you, for your own protection as well as mine, you must destroy every bit of information that relates to this case. You are never to contact me again. This mobile will be destroyed. This case never happened."

"Hang on a second—" he said, but she hung up. She had work to do and nothing more to say to him.

The drone of the generator registered in Celia's ears even before her eyes opened. She was greeted by the sight of the woman stood behind a table, staring intently down the lens of a bulky microscope, which had a monitor attached to it. Celia fought to sharpen her dulled senses. She noted the door in the wall behind the table. If she ran now, she could get out before the woman even had a chance to react. Bracing herself, Celia attempted to spring up from the seat. For a horrifying second she thought she must be paralysed, her body unable to obey her brain, but looking down, she saw that she was in a wheelchair, her four limbs strapped to its frame with thick tape. The tracksuit top had been removed and a small, blood-stained plaster sat in the crook of her left arm.

Celia couldn't quell her mounting panic. The noise of her ragged breathing alerted the woman, who raised her head. The concentration on the woman's face was instantly replaced by an expression usually reserved for a loved one.

"Celia!" she said, walking towards her. "How lovely to see you're awake."

Celia shattered the air with cries. "Help," she bellowed, rocking the squeaking wheelchair as she fought to break her hands and legs free. "Someone help me, please. Help! Help!"

The woman crouched next to the wheelchair, patting Celia's restrained hand as if calming an infant throwing a tantrum. "Shush now, Celia," she purred. "No one can hear you. You could scream all night and no one would come."

Celia had seen how isolated the building was. She knew from her captor's calmness that she was telling the truth.

The woman smiled apologetically at the terrified girl. "I hope that you're not uncomfortable. I know it seems uncivilized, restraining you like this, but it will allow us to talk without any silly distractions."

Celia craned her neck, trying to take in her surroundings. She could taste the dust in the air, see that the neglected room must have been stripped a long time ago, leaving only work surfaces and chipped sinks clinging to the windowless walls. Above her, dotted among the harsh ceiling lights, were skylights that framed the starry night, allowing a snapshot of beauty into the bleak interior.

The woman watched for any flicker of recognition in Celia as she absorbed the room. "Do you know who I am?"

"Yes." Celia looked her straight in the eyes. "You're the woman who experimented on me, who gave me this virus. You were going to kill me."

The woman appeared momentarily shaken. Words evaded her for a second, before she regained her composure.

"I'm Professor Hudson," she retorted proudly, meeting Celia's saucer eyes. "I'm the woman who's devoted her whole life to trying to develop a cure for cancer, trying to prevent millions of people from dying."

"And what about me? What about this virus you gave me? You've got to get rid of it."

The woman started laughing. A sound of genuine joy filled the room. "I would never get rid of your virus, Celia."

Celia was appalled. "What's so funny?"

"My beautiful girl, I've been busy while you slept, examining blood samples I took from you. And do you know what I saw?" Hudson's eyes danced.

"What?"

"I saw this!" Hudson rushed back to the table like an excited child. She turned the monitor towards Celia, revealing a screen filled with iridescent spheres covered with spikes, wobbling in perpetual motion. "Isn't it the most beautiful thing you've ever seen?" Hudson whispered reverently, transfixed by the image.

"What is it?" Celia asked, bemused.

"It's my Saviour Virus. It's in you, in your blood," she replied.

"What are you talking about? I thought the virus you put in me kills."

"That virus has behaved differently in you. It's evolved into everything I've ever worked towards," she gushed.

"But how's that possible?" Celia struggled to comprehend.

"We scientists like to think we can find an explanation for everything, but so much is still a mystery about how viruses behave and mutate in their hosts. That's what makes them so incredible to work with. But you always responded better than all the other babies. I knew I was close with you." Her voice suddenly hardened. "I told him I needed to study you, see if the virus developed, but he wouldn't listen."

"But you've already got the Saviour Virus. I saw you on the news, talking about it."

Hudson shook her head bitterly. "That's not my Saviour Virus. Even as I was giving that interview, I knew things had started to go wrong in the trials, but I didn't want to admit it. I was desperately hoping I could fix things, but I haven't succeeded – the cancers are growing back in the trial patients. So you see, Celia, the only true Saviour Virus is in you."

Celia grappled with the enormity of what she was hearing.

"Have you any idea how wonderful this feels?" Hudson said giddily. "The first couple of years after you were taken were torturous for me. The stress of thinking that you were out there, carrying a fatal virus for which I had no cure. Every day I dreaded the news of an outbreak."

"Am I meant to feel sorry for you?" Celia spat.

"No, Celia, I don't expect your sympathy. But I took a terrifying risk. I couldn't let my backers know you'd been abducted from the clinic. They would never have let me try again. I told them that I'd destroyed you as they'd instructed and, eventually, they gave me a second chance. My backers are business people, interested in the billions a cure could make them, not in the lives it could save, so when they realized that no other scientist was any closer to finding a cure, it confirmed to them what I'd always known; human experimentation was the only logical way forward. They gave me better facilities, more funding, and I was able to continue my research."

"So you kept experimenting on babies?" Celia said, sickened.

"It was the only way," Hudson retorted defiantly. "And my gamble paid off. When you were taken from the clinic, your body was riddled with cancers I'd introduced into you. No amount of conventional treatment could have prolonged your life for more than a couple of years so, after this time, logic dictated that you must be dead and the population safe from the virus. But I just couldn't let you go. I kept thinking how responsive you'd been to my experiments. I knew that the virus was behaving differently in you from the outset. I became fixated with the idea that you were still alive. I started following up leads which I thought might be you, but they all came to nothing. And, after all these years, I was on the verge of giving up my search, accepting it as a vain dream. But when my computer flagged up the A & E report from the hospital in Wales, I just couldn't resist, even though I expected it to be another wild goose chase. Celia, you can't imagine my joy when I got a positive ID from your hair follicles. I believed that the only explanation for your survival was that my virus had worked in you, and I was right!" she proclaimed triumphantly, her face aglow.

"But why have you brought me here? You're meant to take me back where I belong. That man who kidnapped me, he said you would."

Professor Hudson threw her arms out. "And I have. This is where you belong, here, with me. This was your room. You shared it with the other babies. For a long time I hardly ever left this place. I worked day and night, but then I was forced to shut it down. This clinic hasn't been in use for thirteen years, but it's stood up to the elements well. The generator is still working; we have our own water supply from the moor; the structure seems sound." She spoke like an excited estate agent. "It shouldn't take long to set up my lab again, get all the necessary equipment installed. We won't be disturbed out here, Celia."

"I don't belong here!" Celia bawled. "I belong with my parents!"

"But, Celia," the scientist replied, "you have no real parents."

33 *a small price to pay*

"Of course I have parents," Celia spluttered. "Everyone has parents."

"But your biological parents don't even know of your existence. You were just an unwanted embryo that they'd created. Their other embryos were selected to be implanted in your mother's womb. They were the ones that became the longed-for children. You were simply surplus to requirements. Like thousands of other frozen embryos in clinics all over the country, you were just waiting to be destroyed. It's only because of me that you were given life at all."

Celia shook her head, confused, distressed. "I don't understand."

"For my research purposes, I took dozens of unwanted embryos which were then implanted in surrogate mothers. Those women gave birth believing that they were providing babies for childless couples, but in fact I used those babies for a far greater purpose. Without them, the Saviour Virus would never have been developed."

Professor Hudson was in her stride now, captivated by her own words. "It was astounding being able to study how the virus behaved in them. And with each death, I was able to perform meticulous post-mortems, working out how to refine it before trying again on another subject. Eventually, as I kept modifying the virus, it became more effective, the babies were surviving the cancers for longer. Some lasted weeks, others months, but you, Celia, you did more than survive."

"So you bred us to experiment on. You riddled us with cancer." Celia's face was twisted with fury. "You watched and made notes as all those babies suffered and died for your research... You're a monster!" she roared.

The professor snapped back indignantly, "Think of all the millions of people that I could save. Can't you understand that the lives of those unwanted babies are a small price to pay?"

"You can't use human beings like that!"

"Do you have any idea of the courage it took to take that step? Don't you think other scientists would secretly applaud me for doing it, while they're too cowardly, wasting their time using rodents and monkeys. But the irony is that if my methods were ever exposed, those same scientists would have to be seen to condemn me. And the ignorant, idiotic public, who've been crying out for a cure, will be the ones to be outraged; demanding to have me locked up. But you'd better believe that those same people will be the first to queue up to be treated with my virus. In the end, they won't care how the results were achieved, as long as they have their cure. They're all hypocrites! I'm the only one with any integrity. So you see, Celia, I'm no monster. I did what had to be done. I need you, of all people, to understand that."

"I understand the difference between right and wrong and what you've done is wrong!" Celia raged.

"You're being naive. Wouldn't it be simple if everything was really as you see it? Black and white, right and wrong. But I'm afraid life is more complicated than that. Those messy grey areas keep getting in the way."

"But you have children of your own – twins. I saw a photo of them when you were on the news. Don't you look at them and feel sick about what you've done; don't you look at me and think about every baby you ever experimented on?"

For the first time the professor turned her eyes from Celia, her voice unsteady. "If I'd allowed my emotions to cloud my judgement then I would never have achieved my goal. What I have done is for the greater good of humanity."

"And what about me? What's going to happen to me?" Celia said quietly.

"I need to study you, Celia. Discover how and why the Saviour Virus works in you. Every part of you will tell me more. Your body holds the key to the most important cure in the world."

"So you're going to keep me locked up here, pick me apart while I'm still alive. And what then? What happens when you've finished with me? Will you bury me on the moor too? Is that where you put all the other babies you killed?"

Distress darkened the woman's face; unwanted tears welled up in her eyes. "This place is full of ghosts," she whispered. "But with you I can exorcize them. You're proof that their sacrifice was worthwhile. Having the Saviour Virus will justify what I did. I promise you won't be in any pain. You'll be sedated. You won't be aware of anything."

Celia desperately tried to stay clear-headed.

"You can't do this to me," she blurted out. "My mum knows about you. When I don't come home, she'll call the police, tell them everything. They'll come looking for you, they'll find out what you've done. You've got to let me go."

Hudson smiled. "I will always be grateful to Janice Frost. If she hadn't kidnapped you, I would have destroyed you, destroyed my virus."

"She didn't kidnap me, she rescued me! She's spent her life protecting me." Celia suddenly felt overwhelmed by shame, thinking of all the loathing and contempt she'd shown Janice.

"Janice won't be phoning the police, Celia. She's dead," the professor announced bluntly.

Celia stared at her, open-mouthed.

"The man who brought you to me then went back to your flat and killed her." She watched as a look of horrified disbelief invaded Celia's face. "I had no choice," she continued. "I couldn't risk her exposing me. I can't go to prison. With you, Celia, I have my Saviour Virus. I want to go down in history as the scientist who developed a cure for cancer, not be remembered for my methods, not be shunned by the medical community and the world for my bravery."

"My mum is dead," Celia repeated to herself.

"So you must understand, Celia, no one is coming to rescue you. And when you don't reappear, the police will assume that you're just another runaway teenager who escaped from a crazed parent. You have no one left in the world who cares about you, no one who will bother looking for you."

Celia stared into the distance as if catatonic.

"Celia." The professor bent down and stroked Celia's hair. "Together we can wipe out the most terrible disease in the world. What greater achievement is there?"

Celia sat motionless, unable to process what she'd been told, as the scientist walked to the table and picked up a syringe filled with a clear liquid. Dexterously she screwed a needle into the end, before partially depressing the plunger, sending a jet of liquid shooting into the air.

The professor returned to the wheelchair, holding the syringe. She spoke soothingly. "You'll slip into the most beautiful, peaceful sleep."

Celia couldn't speak. A thick quiet hung in the room, only disturbed by the noise of the generator. Her mind was numb, her body a lead weight, drained of the will to fight. The scientist recognized submission in the girl and had to stifle the euphoric sense of victory growing in her.

"I knew that I could make you understand. I knew that you could accept what has to happen." She smiled serenely. "You're a hero, Celia. Because of you, millions will be saved."

34 the balcony

"I love it out here," Janice said tipsily, leaning on the rickety table that lived on the balcony. "I spend hours out here, smoking, having a think. I feel…untouchable, like me and Celia are safe from the world up here in the clouds." Her face suddenly fell. "But now it's all come crashing down."

"Think positive, Janice. Celia will be back before you know it," Frankie replied.

But she wasn't listening. Janice was caught up in her own reverie. "Do you see those beautiful birds in their golden cages?" she said, pointing randomly at the balconies opposite. "I try not to look at them, because they make me feel sad. If you watch them, you see how they frantically flutter around in their tiny prisons, damaging their feathers against the bars. They don't sing like normal birds, you know. I can hear the difference. I can hear the distress in their song. They look out and see other birds able to soar in the sky, and what must they be feeling? Their hearts must be breaking."

Frankie remained a brooding bystander.

"Then I feel even more depressed, because you know what?" There was no need for Frankie to respond. "I know that I've done the same thing to my Celia. I may have saved her, but for what? So she has to spend the rest of her life trapped in a cage I've built for her, watching everybody else have their freedom. What kind of life have I given her?" she asked with self-loathing.

"Whatever you did, I'm sure it was for the best," Frankie said soothingly.

"It was because I'm terrified for her, you see…and for what could happen."

Frankie remained silent.

"Do you want to know what could happen? Because I will tell you, Paul. I need to tell someone," Janice said anxiously.

Frankie shrugged. "That's between you and Celia."

Janice let out a punch of a laugh, slapping him on the shoulder. "That's one of the things I like about you, Paul.

You're a listener, not a questioner. You're one in a million. You're a good, honest soul. Not like me, oh no. I'm a liar!" She pointed a finger at herself. "I've lied and deceived the only person in the world I love and she's been such a wonderful girl to me; I just don't know what to do now she knows the truth."

She slumped over the railings, but quickly raised her head as the ground swam below her. Frankie stood back, watching her unravel.

"How am I going to find her, Paul? She could be anywhere."

"Shame *you're* not a bird. Then you could fly off and look for her." His syrup-coated tones slipped the image into her addled mind.

She lit up, the crazy idea seizing her. "Yeah, you're right," she said excitedly. "Help me up."

Frankie's heart started to pound as she put her small, rough hand in his and clambered onto the rickety table. She giggled uncontrollably as she attempted to get up on her feet, her legs like jelly.

Frankie shushed her. "Quiet, Janice, you'll wake people up," he whispered, terrified that they would be spotted, searching for lights going on in other flats.

She gave him a theatrical wink and put a finger to her lips with a stage whisper. "Shush!"

He held onto her bony hips to steady her and, once she

was standing upright, he let go and stepped back into the shadows. She towered above the railings, her arms outstretched like a bird preparing for flight. She filled her nicotine-stained lungs with the night air and raised her head to the majestic moon.

Frankie's stomach churned but, as he watched, he couldn't help noticing how she seemed transformed up there on the table, her bag-of-bones body now held with balletic poise, her features softened by the silver light of the moon. Without being conscious of it, a smile spread across his face, pleased to see her so liberated.

"I'm feeling seasick," she cackled, the table quivering like a tightrope with her slightest movement. Frankie's heart was in his mouth. He knew that all it would take was one jolt and he'd send her plummeting to her death. His trembling hand crept towards the table top, his mouth so dry he was unable to swallow his self-disgust.

"Just one small step and I'll be lifted on the wind, soaring above the ground, able to find my Celia," she announced giddily, the table wobbling.

It'll be over in seconds, Frankie convinced himself. *With all that booze down her, she won't feel a thing and I'd be gone, unnoticed into the night. Nemo's right: it'll just be a tragic accident of a drunken, broken woman.* His hand hovered under the table. *Do it! Get it over with!* he ordered his resisting limb.

When he looked up, she'd turned her head over her shoulder and was squinting at him. "Paul, are you okay?" she slurred. "You don't look well at all. Help me down and I'll make you a nice cup of tea."

As she reached her arms towards him, the table wobbled violently, rocking back and catapulting her forward.

Janice screamed as her body flew head first over the balcony. Immediately the distant ground was rushing up to meet her. There was nothing she could do, no time to even think, until she felt the jolt... She swung there, twenty floors above the ground, like a squawking chicken being held upside down. All the blood rushed to her head and the swaying ground became a blur. She didn't know what had happened, only that any second her fall could continue. Frankie's body was wedged against the railings, his face puce, his hands locked around her ankles. His hands began to slip as she flailed around, terrified. He had to get a better grip.

"Hold still!" he ordered through gritted teeth. It was a terrible risk, but he knew that he had to momentarily let go with one of his hands if he was going to have any chance of keeping hold of her.

Janice felt him release one of her ankles and screamed. "Don't let go!"

She felt the impact of his vicelike grip clamping onto her leg. Grunting and groaning, Frankie levered her up and slid her back over the railings, where she landed on top of him.

Janice looked down on the man she was sprawled over, her face still rigid with shock, but her eyes dizzy with gratitude. "I…I…" she managed, before her cheeks puffed out, her stomach heaved, and a stream of vomit spewed out all over Frankie Byrne.

"I'm sooo sorry!" Janice cringed as she saw his stinking top.

"It's the least I deserve," he muttered, carefully extricating himself from his sick-covered shirt, revealing a greying vest. "I couldn't do it," he whispered, relieved. "When the moment came, I just couldn't do it. I didn't even think about it; I saw your feet lift off that table and my instincts took over. You see, that proves it; I'm not a killer – despite everything, I'm not a killer!" he said triumphantly.

Janice was bemused. "What are you talking about? Of course you're not a killer; you're a hero, Paul. You're *my* hero!" She beamed and threw her arms around his thick neck. He prised her off and sat her back on the balcony floor.

"Will you listen to me, Janice?" he said gravely.

"Yes," she answered, unnerved by his manner.

He looked her unflinchingly in the eyes. "I came here tonight to kill you."

Janice gave a nervous laugh. "That's not very funny, Paul."

"My name is Frankie…Frankie Byrne. I'm a private investigator. My job was to find you and Celia. But believe me, I had no idea what I was getting myself into. I wouldn't have taken the case if I'd known it was going to end like this."

Janice suddenly felt as if he'd plunged her head into a bucket of ice water. Of all the emotions bombarding her, she couldn't help feeling crushing humiliation at being deceived into thinking this man may have cared about her. How desperately she'd wanted to believe it, how pathetic she felt. "Who are you working for?" She dreaded the answer.

"I don't know for sure. We've never met; the client wanted to be anonymous. But they said that they were the only person who could deal with Celia, with the virus."

"You know about the virus?"

"I know everything," he replied.

"Who told you?" she demanded.

"You did."

"That's a lie. I haven't told you anything!" she shouted.

"I bugged your flat, Janice," he said, ashamed. "I've been listening in to everything that has happened here."

Her flesh felt like an army of ants was crawling over it. She scrambled away from him, huddling in the corner of the balcony, her sharpening mind started to piece it together. "You know where Celia is, don't you?" Her voice quaked.

"Yes. I took her to this place in the middle of nowhere. The client has confirmed that she's with Celia."

"She?!" Janice shouted. "The client is a woman? It must be Hudson."

"I can't know for sure; maybe other people are looking for Celia – people who can help her."

Janice pounced on him, raining down blows on his barrel chest with her inadequate fists. "Of course it's her! That woman will kill her. You've sent Celia to her death!" she cried, hysteria tightening around her windpipe.

Frankie restrained her by the wrists and held her at arm's length. "Shush, Janice. Listen."

They both fell silent as they heard the knocking at the door.

"Are you expecting anyone?" Frankie asked suspiciously.

"Celia!" Janice rushed to the door and flung it open, revealing a weary-looking boy.

Despite the headache tablets and ice pack, Sol's head still throbbed. He'd tried to do as his brothers had instructed, but he couldn't lie in bed any longer when he knew that Celia was in some kind of trouble. He had to tell Janice. He had to check if Celia was back.

Janice gazed at the boy.

"Miss Frost, I'm sorry for coming round at this time. You don't know me, but I'm Celia's friend, Sol. Has she come home yet? I'm really worried about her."

"I do know you," Janice replied, as if speaking her thoughts out loud. "You're the boy in the drawing. You're the boy who makes Celia smile."

The baffled boy just nodded politely, aware of Janice's mental health problems. He was ushered into the flat, where the atmosphere felt like a war zone. He watched, uncomfortably, as Janice circled the vaguely familiar man in a vest.

"You're right to be worried about her, Sol," Janice said, not taking her dagger-eyes off Frankie. "This man has put Celia's life in danger." She thrust her finger angrily at the accused.

"Calm down, Janice. I can sort this out." Frankie's mind was racing. "The client will be expecting to hear from me, to confirm that I've done the job. I don't want her to get twitchy. I'll call her, try and find out if Celia's okay. Now, you two, don't even breathe. I need complete silence."

Janice and Sol stood petrified as Frankie called Nemo and launched into his chilling dialogue.

"It's done. Janice Frost is dead..."

By the time the brief call had abruptly ended, Sol was staring, slack-jawed, at the worried-looking man.

"Tell me about Celia! Is she all right?" Janice barked.

"I…I don't know. She didn't say," Frankie said guiltily.

"She could be dead. Hudson might have killed her already," Janice screeched, searching for her phone. "Tell me where you took her. I'll get the police over there."

"No," Frankie said firmly. "Let me phone the police. I know all the details. It'll be quicker."

Janice hovered around him.

"Give me some space, Janice! I need to concentrate. I don't want to forget anything important." He strode into the kitchen to make the call, emerging a couple of minutes later. "The police are on their way to get her. Get your bag, we should drive over there."

"Hang on!" Sol piped up. "If you're going to get Celia then I want to come too."

"What do you think this is?" Frankie growled. "A school trip? I'll take Janice, I owe her that, but I don't need a kid tagging along too."

"Sol, you should wait in the flat. Someone should stay here in case they send police round to get more information," Janice said.

Frankie quickly interjected. "On second thoughts, maybe we should take him. He might come in handy."

"Thank you," Sol said, surprised but flattered that the big man should consider him an asset. "Now let's stop wasting time and go and get her," Frankie ordered.

Janice felt a pang of gratitude. Frankie could have got

away if he'd chosen to. Instead, by phoning the police, she knew that he'd resigned himself to prison. "You're doing the right thing," she said.

Frankie looked down at his shoes. She could have sworn that he was blushing.

35 *the night drive*

Ever since they'd reached the moor, all Frankie could see out of the corner of his eye was Janice, rocking like a distressed child.

"Bloody hell, Janice!" Frankie said, through gritted teeth. "Have a cigarette to calm yourself down. That rocking is driving me insane. Its pitch-black out there, I'm going 110 mph and I'm trying not to crash into these stupid sheep that keep coming out of nowhere, so for God's sake, stop it!"

Janice's voice trembled. "But I know where we're heading. She's taken her back to that place. She's got her at the clinic."

"Why haven't the police phoned to let us know what's going on? Maybe you should phone them back, Frankie?" Sol said.

"No. We're best to leave them alone and let them get on with the job," Frankie said with authority. "Anyway, we're almost there."

They drove on, in oppressive silence, the car rocketing along the moor road; Frankie hunched over the steering wheel, his brow furrowed, Sol sat in the back, his stomach in knots, and Janice dragging on a cigarette held between her shaking fingers.

36 *no heroics*

Frankie took the corner so fast that the car swerved off the driveway and onto the moor, leaving skid marks in the peaty earth. He fought with the steering wheel to get the car back on track and came to a halt halfway up the drive; the clinic hidden over the brow of a hill.

"We'll park here," he said to his passengers. "We don't want her to hear the car and give her time to do something stupid. We need to surprise her. Catch her unaware. Come on, we'll run the rest of the way."

"But the police must already be there," Janice said.

Frankie didn't reply. He pulled himself out of the car and started pounding up the driveway. Sol shot out of the passenger door and sprinted after him.

Sol reached the building first, Frankie panting behind him and Janice out of sight, still struggling up the incline.

"Why aren't the police here?" Sol said, seeing the lone car parked next to the prefab building.

"Because I didn't call them," Frankie said breathlessly.

"What?!"

"If I got the police involved, I'd end up spending the next fifteen years in prison, and I'm not ready to do that. They'd only mess this up anyway, put Celia in more danger. It's better that I sort this out. I know what I'm doing. Trust me."

But trusting him was the last thing Sol felt like doing.

Celia felt the professor's fingers tapping on her arm. She looked down as the blue vein rose towards the surface, offering itself to the needle. Celia was suddenly struck by the healthy glow of her skin. She was so used to it being deathly pale that she'd forgotten how it had been transformed by the sun over the past weeks, while she ran wild in the flooded quarry. Her mind turned to Sol. How different she felt since meeting him. How brilliant life was with him. And what about Janice? She'd sacrificed everything for a child who'd been a stranger to her, who she owed nothing to. Celia wouldn't let herself believe that

Janice was dead. She needed to let her know how much she loved her; how she now understood all that Janice had done for her. She couldn't give up on Janice, on Sol. She had to find them, make sure they were all right.

Celia raised her eyes and saw the bowed head of the professor with the needle, poised to insert it into her vein. Rage gripped her body, sparking it into life once more. How dare this woman expect her to sacrifice herself, expect her to accept this as her fate? She was not an escaped lab rat! She was Celia Frost, daughter of Janice Frost, best friend of Solomon Giran!

The roar of her battle cry tore through the walls of the building as Celia butted her head into the professor's. Hudson staggered backwards, the syringe flying out from between her fingers. She fell to the floor, her leg twisted under her body.

Celia's cry sent Frankie and Sol sprinting to the clinic door. Frankie kicked at it, but it held firm. He rammed his shoulder against it again and again, but it was unyielding. "It's reinforced," he panted to Sol. "There's no way I can break it down. We need to find another door, a window, anything to let us in there."

Sol ran frantically around the building, clawing at the ivy to see if it was concealing any windows. Janice staggered over the brow of the hill, bent double, her nicotine-filled lungs fit to burst.

"We can't get in!" Sol shouted to her. "There's no windows."

"On the roof," Janice wheezed, getting out her phone. "Get on the roof…there's skylights."

Sol called to Frankie. "We need to get on the roof. Give me a hand."

"I should be doing this," Frankie said guiltily.

"You can't. It's too high for you to reach and I can't take your weight to push you up there. It's got to be me."

"Okay," Frankie said, bending down to let the boy climb onto his shoulders. "But no heroics, do you hear? Just get in there and open the door for me."

"Fine," Sol said, wobbling as he stood upright on the big man's shoulders and pulled himself onto the flat roof.

The dazed professor was clutching her forehead, her face twisted with anger and pain. "No, Celia," she scolded. "This isn't the way to behave. You have a duty to all those suffering people."

Her eyes scoured the room, looking for the syringe. Celia jolted the wheelchair, struggling futilely to break her bonds, knowing that she'd only managed to delay her fate.

But they were both stopped in their tracks by the sound of footsteps thudding across the roof. They looked up in bewilderment as the soles of two trainers started pounding against a skylight above them.

Sol grunted as he sat on the roof, slamming his feet down on the glass until the pane cracked, then shattered, glass spraying the floor below. He kicked out the jagged shards left around the edges and jumped down into the room like a cat from a tree. The aghast professor began to scramble across the floor towards the syringe.

Celia screamed at her friend. "Sol, the syringe! Get the syringe!"

Sol dived across the floor like a goalie trying to save a penalty; his fingertips made contact with the syringe, sending it spinning out of Hudson's reach. He tumbled after it, grasping it as the woman hauled herself to her feet and limped towards him.

"Stay where you are," Sol said, his heart beating out of his chest.

She held her hand out, speaking to him like a reprimanding headmistress. "Give that to me. I'll put it away safely. We both know that you wouldn't use it. It would send me into a coma. I wouldn't wake up. It would be like murder and you, young man, don't look like a murderer to me."

Sol looked at Celia. She saw the panic in his eyes. She knew that she had to intervene.

"Hey, professor," she snarled. "You're right. He doesn't

look like a murderer, but looks can be deceptive, can't they? Just look at you!"

Hudson glared at her.

"He may have a baby face, but this boy would stick that needle in you and wouldn't care less. Isn't that right, Sol?"

Sol nodded his head, swallowing hard.

"Sol the Psycho, that's what they call him on the estate. And it's not just the kids that are scared of him. I've seen adults terrified as well. He's unpredictable you see: one minute calm, angelic; the next, out of control, raging, tearing the place up. They've had him in and out of secure units. They don't know what to do with him."

Hudson scrutinized the nervous boy in front of her as he wiped the cold sweat out of his eyes.

"It's not his fault, the violence," Celia said sombrely. "When he was little, his mum used to disappear for nights on end, leave him locked up in the bathroom."

"I don't believe you," the professor said arrogantly. She moved closer to him, bawling, "Give me that now!"

Sol tightened his grip on the syringe, stepping back from her.

"You can believe what you want," Celia continued earnestly. "It doesn't change the truth. Just look at him; making his way out here, to the middle of nowhere, jumping through windows – it's all nothing to him. He does crazy things all the time, especially for me. For some reason, he really likes me. He'd do anything for me. He's very protective – a bit *too* protective. He broke a boy's leg once for swearing at me, so I don't think he'll be too happy to know that you were going to put that needle in me."

Sol seemed to suddenly transform. His eyes turned wild. He began swaying from side to side, throwing the syringe from one hand to the other. Hudson watched him with growing alarm as he started jabbering at her.

"I'm a good boy. I try and be a good boy. But if people are bad to Celia then I have to hurt them. Do you understand? I don't want to, but I have to." He jabbed the needle towards Hudson, who let out a gasp.

"It's okay, Sol. Stay calm!" Celia said.

Sol took deep breaths, waving the syringe at Hudson. "Should I hurt her for you, Celia?" He stared manically at Hudson.

"Sol," Celia said sweetly, "she'll be good. There's no need to hurt her."

"But I don't like it when people are bad to you. I don't think I can stop myself." He looked pleadingly at Celia.

"Don't let him!" Hudson panicked.

"No, Sol!" Celia said firmly. "I'll be upset with you if you hurt her. Now, just tell her what you want her to do and she'll do it."

He started bouncing up at Hudson, chanting, "Open

the door! Open the door! Open the door!" Hudson hurriedly obeyed.

As soon as the front door was unlocked, Janice flew into the building, Frankie behind her. Professor Hudson flinched with shock at the sight of them.

"Where's Celia? Is she okay?" Janice asked Sol.

"She's through there." Sol pointed down the corridor. "She seems fine. Tied up, but fine."

Janice walked past the professor, giving her a look that could have turned her to stone, but Hudson grabbed hold of Janice's arm, drawing her in, whispering in her ear.

"You'll never be able to protect Celia now. Everyone will want the Saviour Virus and they need her to get it."

Janice prised her fingers off, confused and furious. "Get your hands off me! I'm going to see my daughter."

Sol, still clutching the syringe, ushered the professor towards Frankie.

"You'd better give me that," Frankie said, pointing nervously at the syringe.

"God, yes! *Please* take it off me," Sol said with relief.

Frankie grinned at Sol, slapping him on the back. "I knew you'd come in handy."

Frankie led the professor down the corridor and into the nearest room, where a metal stand bolted to the middle of the floor was the only remaining evidence that an operating table had once occupied this space. "After you,

Nemo," he said. "And I don't want to hear a word out of you. Don't go trying to freak out Janice with any more of your poisoned remarks."

"You're a great disappointment, Mr. Byrne," she said scornfully. "You're obviously not the man I thought you were."

"I'll take that as a compliment," he replied. "Now you just make yourself at home, you could be here some time."

37 something to deal with

As Janice ran into the room she was gripped by the sights and sounds of thirteen years ago. Her skin erupted in goose bumps as she heard the pitiful cries of the babies, saw them enclosed in their cots with their pinpricked arms and hollow eyes, staring blankly at the ceiling. The memories seemed to paralyse Janice, until Celia's cries broke through them.

"Mum! Mum!"

"Celia! Are you okay?" Janice gathered herself.

"She said you were dead."

"Well, running up that driveway did nearly kill me, but I'm definitely not dead," she joked, determined not to let

Celia pick up on her distress. "How about you, love? She didn't hurt you, did she?"

"No. I'm fine. I just want to get out of here."

Janice looked around at the smashed glass covering the floor.

"That was my friend, Sol. I couldn't believe it! He jumped through the skylight! He was brilliant," Celia said with pride.

"He seems like a great boy." Janice smiled, picking up a shard of pointed glass. "Now hold very still, Celia. I'm going to cut through the tape with this. I don't want to catch you."

"Mum, you don't need to worry about my blood any more. Hudson took a sample, examined it. She said that the virus in me doesn't kill – it cures! It's mind-blowing, Mum. She said it's the Saviour Virus and I'm the only one with it. She wanted to pick me apart to see why it works in me. She said I had a duty to sacrifice myself, to save millions of people." Celia hesitated, looking anxiously at Janice. "I don't, do I, Mum? I don't have to let them pick me apart?"

"Now, you listen to me, young lady," Janice said, incandescent with rage. "That…that…WOMAN is warped and twisted. She's tried to mess with your mind. No one would expect you to sacrifice yourself. No one will be allowed to touch you. Let them get their cure another way. Do you hear me, Celia? You're my beautiful girl, not some lab rat to be experimented on. All that's important is that you're safe and well. We're going to forget you've even got this Saviour Virus and we're going to start living at last, okay."

Celia nodded, flooded with relief and remorse, no longer able to hold back the tears.

Janice peeled off the tape from Celia's wrists and ankles, massaging the deep welts left in her skin. "Don't cry. You're safe now, baby. I promise I won't let anyone touch you."

"I've been such a cow to you, Mum. All you've done for me...but I didn't know, I didn't understand," Celia garbled through sobs.

"Shush, love. You don't need to say anything. It's okay."

"But I need to tell you, Mum. When she said you were dead, I thought that I'd never get a chance to say sorry, tell you how much I love you, to thank you for saving me from this place, from her. You looked after me all these years, living with all that unbearable stress. You gave up the chance of a normal life, a better life, risking everything for me, and I've given you such a hard time. I wanted to make you suffer and you just took it, always putting me first."

"You daft girl, don't you understand? I wouldn't have wanted any other kind of life if it meant not having you!" Janice laughed, tears rolling down her face. "We've both had a rough time. You've been through so much, Celia, and I kept messing up. I wasn't sure how to protect you, so I ended up suffocating you your whole life. No wonder you hated me, when you thought I was some mad woman who'd made everything up. Now, come on. We can't just sit here all day blubbing. We need to get you up and get your circulation going."

Janice kissed Celia's wet cheeks, helping her up. Celia quivered as she rose unsteadily from the wheelchair.

Celia hobbled around, supported by Janice, her whole body feeling like it had been run over by a bus. As they circled the room, Celia could sense Janice's unease. "Is being back here freaking you out?" she asked.

Janice nodded. "It's not my favourite place on earth."

"Then you should think about it like this, Mum. Terrible things happened here, but this is where we met, so I reckon something great happened here too."

Janice smiled. "Yeah, you're right. It's obvious you didn't get your brains from me, saying clever, deep stuff like that." Suddenly Janice's own words made her smart, reminding her of a question she dreaded, but knew she had a duty to ask.

"By the way, Celia." She tried to sound casual. "Did she tell you anything about your parents? Anything that would help us trace them?" Janice held her breath.

"Only that they don't even know I exist. I'm not

interested in finding them anyway," Celia said dismissively. "You're my mum. You're the best mum. Why would I want anyone else?"

"Okay, love," Janice said, throwing her arms around Celia and practically squeezing the life out of her. "We can always talk about this some other time."

"There's no need. I'm not going to change my mind *and* I am going to make it up to you," Celia announced. "I'm going to be the best daughter ever. I'll do anything you say – first time, no arguments."

Janice laughed, stroking her child's hair. "We'll see how long that lasts."

"How did you get here anyway? How did you know where I was?" Celia asked.

"Frankie Byrne, the man who brought you here, he drove me and Sol to get you."

"Why would he do that?" Celia was puzzled.

"I think he was trying to do the right thing, as far as a man like Frankie *can* do the right thing. In fact..." She called out to Sol who'd been loitering in the corridor. "Sol, can you come in and take over from me?" She draped Celia's arm round her friend. "Keep walking her around and don't listen to her if she begs to sit down. We can't have her seizing up. I'll be back in a minute. I just have something to deal with."

38 *a threat or a promise?*

Janice stepped out of the old clinic and filled her lungs with the crisp, moor air. She studied the wild, sweeping landscape, just beginning to stir in the dawning light.

"Beautiful, isn't it?" Frankie appeared next to her.

"It's different from how I remember. I'd always pictured it as a bleak, godforsaken place, but you're right, it really is quite beautiful."

"Well, you can relax now, Janice. Everything's under control. I've tied up Nemo, put tape over her big mouth so she can't spout any more rubbish. And Celia's fine, isn't she? So all in all, job done!" he said with a satisfied smile.

"You're a real hero, aren't you, Frankie?" Her words dripped with sarcasm.

Frankie looked hurt. "What do you mean?"

"I came out to find you, but, to be honest, I didn't expect you to still be here. The police are on their way you know. I phoned them when we got here and I realized that you'd been lying to us."

Frankie couldn't look at her.

"You put Celia's life at risk just to save your own skin," she said in disgust.

"Please hear me out, Janice," he said, desperate to defend himself. "I admit there was some self-interest – I didn't want to end up in prison. But you've got to believe me, I knew I stood a better chance of saving her by keeping the police out of it."

"Oh, yeah," Janice said, bristling. "And what made you think that?"

"Because I know the police. They would have messed this up. They would have arrived here and Nemo could have hidden Celia, spun them some story and got rid of them. By the time they'd made all their enquiries, done all their paperwork, and come back here, it would have been too late. So you see, Janice, it was better that I handled it."

Janice gave an exasperated sigh. "You always make everything sound so convincing. You're lucky that Celia's okay, otherwise your life wouldn't be worth living."

"I would have handed myself in if anything had happened to Celia. I wouldn't have been able to live with myself."

"That's easy to say now, isn't it?"

He stared into her eyes with an unflinching intensity. "I can't pretend that I'm a good man, Janice, but maybe, if I'd had you in my life, I could have been a better one."

Janice glared at him. "You can stop with all the corny lines. You don't have to keep up the act any more."

"Would you believe me if I said I'm not?"

"Oh, for God's sake! Just get out of here!" she said, trying to hide her blushing face.

"What do you mean?"

"I mean, get going before the police arrive."

His face lit up. He grabbed her hand but she pulled away, like a petulant child. "You're a wonderful woman, Janice. And I'm telling you, if you and Celia ever need help, I'll come and find you."

"Is that a threat or a promise?" she sniped.

She watched as he ran down the driveway towards his car, stopping to blow her a kiss before disappearing out of sight. Janice shook her head disapprovingly, but was unable to stop a trace of a smile forming on her lips.

39 *letting go*

Sol laughed as he watched his brothers vying for control of the barbecue. Celia beckoned him over to the far corner of the sun-bleached yard.

"I feel bad not being able to tell your mum what really happened," she said uneasily.

"Listen, it's not like we're lying to her. The police told you, me and Janice that we weren't allowed to discuss it with anyone yet, and that includes my mum. We have to do what they say. We don't want Hudson getting off with it because we opened our mouths and ruined their investigation."

"Yeah, I suppose you're right. Anyway…" Celia bit her

lip. "I wanted to talk to you about something."

"Go on," Sol replied, studying her pensive face.

"I've been thinking a lot about things and I don't reckon that I should ignore this virus in me. I know my mum wants me to forget about it, but I can't. The whole thing is too big, too important. Mum seems to think I can just live a normal life with it, but I need to know for sure. And it's not just about me, is it? Can you imagine if the Saviour Virus really can cure cancer? What would you do, Sol? Could you keep it to yourself when there's a chance that you could help so many people?"

Sol was hesitant. "Well…no…I suppose not. But you know that Janice is terrified of what they could do to you. Just look at what Hudson was prepared to do."

"But other doctors aren't twisted like her. There are rules, laws. I'd be protected from people like Hudson."

Sol looked uneasy. "Don't go doing anything stupid, Celia."

"I'm not going to. I know that doctors want to talk to me and I just want to hear what they have to say. Maybe I can give a few blood samples, let them take scans of my body. If I can help them, then I should!"

"But there's no way Janice will let you even talk to them," Sol said.

"I'll just have to work on her; there's no rush. But I need you to back me up. Will you, Sol?"

Sol remained silent.

"Please, Sol! I don't think I'll have the guts to do the right thing if I haven't got your support."

Sol nodded resignedly. "Okay, I'll help you to persuade Janice on one condition; if those doctors start talking about operations and cutting you open, then you'll tell them where to go?"

"Of course! I promise," Celia declared solemnly.

Abs called over to them, mopping his brow as the heat of the sizzling barbecue rose up in his face. "Hey, Celia, are you ready for another perfectly cooked burger?"

"Sounds good," Celia answered. "And may I just say, Abs, you look lovely in that apron. Pink is definitely your colour."

A disgruntled Yacob chipped in. "I'd look even better in it, if he'd stop hogging the barbecue and let me have a turn."

"Back off, brother." Abs waved a spatula at him. "You stick to frying the onions and leave the hard stuff to an expert. Now could someone *please* get Emama and Janice out of that house? They've been in there for ages, cackling away like two old witches."

"I heard that!" Mrs. Giran boomed, emerging from the kitchen with Janice, arms linked like two old school friends. "My boys do a lovely barbecue, Janice, but if you want to taste some proper food you should come around

339

next week and I'll cook you a traditional Ethiopian meal. What do you think? Do you have time?"

"Yes. I'd love to," Janice said, delighted.

"What have you two been talking about all this time?" Sol asked.

"If you must know, we've been swapping notes on how to survive living with teenagers and overgrown boys," Mrs. Giran answered.

"You'd be sorry if we left. You love having us at home." Abs preened.

"Ha! I'm waiting for a couple of nice girls to come and take you two off my hands." Mrs. Giran winked at Janice.

"Yeah, well, if you didn't interrogate every girl we brought home then we might have more success," Yacob complained.

"I'm only trying to get to know them; someone has to. Remember that girl who sat here in the shortest skirt I've ever seen and no underwear!" Mrs. Giran wagged her finger.

Yacob put his head in his heads. "She had a thong on, Mum."

"I don't care what you call it. It didn't cover the appropriate places. I was so embarrassed for the poor girl that I offered her a pair of mine."

"Yeah, and surprisingly after that she dumped me," Yacob said indignantly.

"You had a lucky escape. He should be thanking me, shouldn't he, Janice?" Mrs. Giran said.

Janice sat under the umbrella, unable to speak for laughing.

Sol whispered to Celia, "Do you fancy getting out of here before we have to listen to any more embarrassing stories?"

Celia nodded. "Okay. My mum's having a great time. She won't miss me if I go."

"You don't mind if me and Celia head off for a bit, do you?" Sol asked with a winning smile.

"Where do you two go every day?" Mrs. Giran asked.

"Nowhere special. Just around." Sol shrugged. "Go on, Mum, can we? We'll make sure we're not home too late, honest."

"It's okay with me if it's okay with Celia's mum," Mrs. Giran said, noticing the smile fall from Janice's face. Celia noticed it too.

"Mum?" Celia took Janice's hand and gave it a reassuring squeeze.

Janice hesitated, battling against years of ingrained fear.

"Mum, I'll be fine. Let me go," Celia said gently.

Janice nodded, tears pricking her eyes. "Of course you'll be fine. Go! Have fun!"

Celia's face lit up. She planted a smacker of a kiss on her mother's cheek before running to the front door with Sol.

Sol picked up his pace as the bike reached the main road. "By the way," he shouted to his passenger, "'Psycho Sol'?! Baby-faced nutter with an obsession with YOU?! Thanks a lot!"

Celia burst out laughing. "Come on, you've got to admit, I was pretty good."

"No, *I* was pretty good. You just sat there spouting rubbish. It was me who had to give the Oscar-winning performance."

"You must be joking. She could have killed us both in the time it took you to get warmed up."

He glanced over his shoulder at her, raising his eyebrow. "One needs time to get into character, darling."

She gave him a shove. "Seriously, Sol, you do realize that's the second time you've saved my life."

"Can I help it if I'm such a hero?" He laughed.

"But you know what this means." Celia paused, adopting a melodramatic tone. "This means that we're now bound together until the day I repay the debt by saving *your* life!" She suddenly became very conscious of her hands holding onto his waist. Nerves started to creep up on her as she waited to see how he'd respond.

Sol looked over his shoulder, his face bashful as if he were summoning all his courage. "Well then, I hope that day never comes," he said, hurriedly looked forward again.

Celia grinned at the back of his head. "Me too," she whispered.

"Did you say something?" Sol shouted back.

"No! Just get a move on. Pedal faster," she blustered, blushing.

"Celia," he puffed, "I have *got* to teach you how to ride a bike."

Letting go of Sol's waist, she raised both arms up in the air, her mouth in a mile-wide smile.

"I...can't...wait!" she shouted to the skies.

acknowledgements

My heartfelt thanks to Sara Grant, Sara O'Connor and everyone involved in SCBWI British Isles Undiscovered Voices 2010, which opened up opportunities I could only have dreamed of.

A massive debt of gratitude goes to the wonderful Jo Unwin, my agent at Conville and Walsh. Thank you to Megan Larkin; also to my editor, Rebecca Hill, and Sarah Stewart – their commitment and skill has enabled the delivery of *Celia Frost* without the need for forceps – it's been a pleasure working with them; to the publicity and marketing team and all at Usborne for the brilliant job they have done.

Thanks to my mum for buying me and my siblings all those Ladybird books when we were little; to my friend, Julie Burke for her support and allowing me to drag her to literary events in the hope of improving our minds and procuring free alcohol; to the loves of my life – Stan, Archie and Sadie. What would I do without them? (Get more work done but have less fun.) Finally, thanks to another love of my life, my husband David. His blind faith in me and incredible practical support (e.g. correcting typos at two in the morning) has made this happen. Thank you all!

about the author

Paula Rawsthorne's talent for writing has already seen her become an award-winner. One of her first stories won the BBC's 2004 Get Writing competition and was read by Bill Nighy on Radio 4, and *The Truth About Celia Frost*, her first novel, led to Paula becoming one of the winners of the Undiscovered Voices 2010 competition.

Paula lives in Nottingham with her husband and three children, where her writing is fuelled by a diet of coffee and cakes.

www.cceliafrost.co.uk

L.A.WEATHERLY

ANGEL

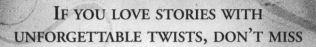

Just one *kiss* will take your breath away...

DEAD
BEAUTIFUL

YVONNE WOON

DEAD BEAUTIFUL

DESIRE. DANGER. DESTINY.
Little did I know that this is what I would find
at Gottfried Academy.

Coming from sunny California, the mist-shrouded Academy
was a shock, with its strange customs, ancient curriculum and
study of Latin – the language of the dead. Then I discovered
that the school has more than one dark secret…

I also discovered Dante. Intelligent, elusive and devastatingly
gorgeous, most people can't decide whether they love, hate or
fear him. All I know is that when we are together, I've never
felt more alive – or more afraid.

DOES FINDING YOUR SOULMATE MEAN LOSING YOURSELF?

"Riveting and different…a real page-turner." SLJ

www.deadbeautiful.co.uk

Beautiful...
Passionate...
Brave...
Discover more incredible novels at
www.fiction.usborne.com